"I love you," Meg said in Grace's ear, so quietly Grace wasn't sure what she heard. But Meg pulled back and looked at her so intently that Grace knew she wasn't mistaken. "So much," Meg said simply.

There was no way of knowing who moved first, no way to determine which one of them had inclined slightly forward. Like the hands of a clock, there was no way to see their progress, only that the time had changed. But somehow Grace found her lips on Meg's, and Meg's on her own, both suddenly and slowly, strangely and naturally. For one long, lingering beat, neither of them moved, paralyzed by the fact of their lips together. Then they kissed, a hungry, innocent, knowing pact that made Grace lightheaded and clammy, that made the soles of her feet tingle and the bottom of her stomach drop out. They were tipping backward and Grace heard the whistling of December's breath against the windowpane, eager to find its way inside. But nothing could reach them, no other light or sound, no protest, no doubt, no caution.

Diane Salvatore

BENEDICTION

Diane Salvatore

BENEDICTION

NAIAD
1991

Printed in the United States of America on acid-free paper
First Edition

Edited by Christine Cassidy and
    Katherine V. Forrest
Cover design by Catherine Hopkins
Typeset by Sandi Stancil

Library of Congress Cataloging-in-Publication Data

Salvatore, Diane.
Benediction / by Diane Salvatore.
    p.   cm.
    ISBN 0-941483-90-8 : $9.95
    I. Title.
PS3569.A46234B4   1991
813'.54–dc20   90-21995
                                                          CIP

— 1 —

The spiritual life is the most important life you girls, as Christians, lead," Sister Mary Alice said to the sophomores gathered that spring morning.

The retreat weekend was finally underway, and Grace was fidgety with excitement. It was her first entire weekend away from home, and she was going to be spending it with friends in the tiny cottage with stained-glass windows and community bathrooms. Such excitement, so unspiritual in nature, was sure to be inappropriate, so as much as she was able, she kept it to herself.

"We all lead many lives, girls," Sister said. "Many lives wrapped up into one life," she added cautiously, lest some girl with a slovenly memory report home to her parents that a nun was espousing the theory of reincarnation. "We lead an emotional life, in which we make friendships like the very ones you have made among your classmates. We lead an intellectual life, a life that has been and will continue to be nurtured and encouraged here at Immaculate Blessing Academy for Girls. And for those of you who go on to be wives and mothers, you will also lead a sexual life."

The room exploded with laughter, but Sister Mary Alice had only to hold up one cool palm and turn her head away just slightly to reduce the group of thirty or so fifteen-year-olds to solemn silence. "But of all the lives you lead, your spiritual life — the life that puts you in touch with the everyday miracles of God — will be your most rewarding."

"Maybe for her," Anne hissed, surreptitiously leaning closer to Grace as they sat cross-legged on the sunny room's clean beige carpet. "As for me, I'm looking forward to the sexual life."

Grace giggled appreciatively, though she did not share Anne's sentiment. Anne Natale was her best friend, and Grace knew that unilateral agreement on such sensitive topics was therefore required. Yet for Grace, something trembled inside when Sister Mary Alice talked about the spiritual life and God's everyday miracles. The nun, with her look of perfect calmness and control, made Grace believe that the sexual life could be had by anyone, while one had to be chosen for the spiritual life. What was more, Sister

2

Mary Alice had been chosen, and Grace admired her ferociously.

She was a young nun — barely in her mid-twenties, Grace guessed — and disconcertingly attractive. The students preferred their nuns with chin hairs and jiggly underarms in order to explain away their rejection of the physical world and all its pleasures. Sister Mary Alice, on the other hand, had auburn hair worn stylish and short, and she had small, sharp Irish features and green eyes that any of the girls would have killed to have. She wore a lay person's clothes as did most of the younger, post-Vatican II nuns at Immaculate Blessing, that made evident her trim, enviable figure. For all these reasons, she was a mixed blessing. It was a special honor to be able to say she was your retreat leader — to be associated with her in any way, in fact — but it also troubled the girls that a woman so clearly desirable to men would choose the convent.

On this April morning, however, the spiritual life was the only game in town. Sister Mary Alice turned to two seniors dressed in jeans and soft pastel blouses — permissible attire for the weekend only. During the week, when the students commuted to school from their Queens homes by subway and bus, they wore uniform skirts — different plaid patterns marking the caste of their year. The two senior girls were wearing, however, their white blazers with the Immaculate Blessing emblem on the pocket, blazers that only seniors had the privilege to own. Grace thought it a wise and calculated move on their parts to maintain that single hallmark of uniformed authority. It was enough to keep everyone awed.

"You all know Joan and Linda, I trust," Sister Mary Alice said. It was an understatement. Joan Sweeny was famous as the editor of *Voices,* the school's prestigious literary magazine, and Linda Amato was the star center of the champion basketball team. The two most popular girls in the school, they were best friends to boot, and their friendship was nearly legendary and completely envied. All the girls would have given anything for the cachet of having either one of them as even a casual associate. "They will be my auxiliaries during this weekend, and you should feel that you can turn to them with any details you need help with." Sister smiled approvingly at them till they both blushed. Joan delivered a cool and mannered, "Welcome," and Linda gave an embarrassed smile and wave. The sophomores couldn't imagine diplomats on a first-class flight feeling any more pampered.

Anne appeared in Grace's doorway just as Grace had finished unpacking. "Jesus, I think your room is actually worse than mine," Anne said. All the girls had been assigned to single rooms for the weekend, and at lights-out at 10:00 p.m. there was to be absolutely no movement between rooms. This was to guard against impromptu late-night pajama parties during which the topic of discussion inevitably would be sex and boys, and to encourage meditative and solitary thinking about weightier subjects such as God and the fate of their souls.

"You've got one of these lousy beds, too," Anne

said, shaking her head. It was true; the bed was gruesome. It was unnaturally high off the ground so that the average girl had to jump to get atop it, and its mattress was narrow and hard. "Look at these walls — rigor mortis white," Anne went on. "Tastefully decorated with one wooden crucifix, guaranteed to depress the hell out of you or your money back."

"Shhhh," Grace reprimanded, unsuccessfully suppressing a laugh. "Someone will hear you."

"Christ," Anne said, rolling her eyes.

"Beside him. And stop cursing. It gives me the creeps. In a place like this." She snapped her tiny blue suitcase shut and slid it under the bed. Later, she thought, when she was alone, she'd take it out and keep it in full view. It was her grandmother's suitcase, and her mother had packed for her. It was the only thing in the room that wasn't white or mahogany, and Grace found its familiarity reassuring.

"Everything here gives me the creeps," Anne said, hoisting herself up on the bed. "Place is like a freaking prison, and we're all in cells. No television the whole weekend — can you bear it?"

"I know, but I like Sister Mary Alice, and we got a decent group. At least we didn't get all the brown-noses from Jamaica Estates or the Ozone Park thugs. And I like the idea of keeping a journal." Grace still had at least one undisclosed secret from Anne: that she hoped someday to be, among other glamorous fantasies, a writer.

"Yeah," Anne said, her face softening. She was swinging her heels hard against the metal frame of the bed and twirling a long tendril of her dark hair round and round one finger. "I miss Rick already, though. I hope he doesn't go to the dance without me."

"He won't. He loves you, he told you so."

"Yeah," she said, looking up and smiling. There was real pain on her face, though, and Grace wasn't sure of its source.

"Come on, kids, first meeting's in the community room," Linda breezed by to say. "Now," she added, winking, and then was gone.

Grace turned to Anne. "She's so cool, don't you think?"

"Yeah. I wish I were tall enough to play basketball."

The sophomores had spent the better part of the afternoon in the community room, doing various exercises aimed at raising their spiritual consciousness. Sister Mary Alice read from Psalms, and the students were required to share their feelings about what they'd heard. Then Father O'Dougherty, in his wrinkled vestments and tired monotone, arrived to remind them to lead exemplary lives as Christian women. His sermon was that much more unbearable because they had hoped to hear the new, young priest who was rumored to quote the likes of Ntozake Shange. Quiet time followed, during which the girls were supposed to free-associate in their journals. Grace peered over Anne's knee and saw Rick's name on her pages. When Grace looked up, Joan was scowling at her. Grace blushed hotly and decided on the spot that it was Joan's perfectly straight, shoulder-length blonde hair that gave her that air of moral superiority.

Grace began scribbling the first thing that came to mind: "I wish Sister Mary Alice were my big sister. Then we could do things together outside the convent, maybe even go to the beach or to the movies. I don't have any sisters. I used to have a cousin who was a nun, but she died in the convent of a brain hemorrhage at thirty. That was back in the fifties, and I've heard that the nuns then were told to offer all their suffering up to God and not complain. Lots of nuns had ulcers or were epileptic and no one ever knew. I hope Sister Mary Alice is not secretly dying of something she can't tell anyone about."

For Grace, however, the highlight of the day came when Sister Mary Alice and Linda took guitars out of the storage closet and led everyone in church songs. Sister handled the instrument fondly and easily but Linda regarded her own fingers suspiciously, never looking away once, occasionally nibbling at her bottom lip, particularly if a bar chord was involved. The sound of all their voices together, sweet and lush and ardent, stirred Grace in a way she couldn't name. When they wrapped up with "I Believe," a tingle played up and down her spine. By the time they reached the last verse, most everyone was fighting tears.

Dinner was a buffet, in a large, darkly paneled room. On tables at the front were huge aluminum trays of spaghetti in sauce, heating over Bunsen burners. Two of the gray-haired women who usually worked the cafeteria at school stood grimly behind the tables, spooning out tangled masses as each girl walked by with her shiny white plate in front of her,

Oliver Twist-style. Everyone uncertainly took a seat at long tables for ten, and Anne and Grace quickly put their plates down next to each other.

Sister Mary Alice, Linda and Joan had eaten earlier so that they could circulate among the students, stimulating conversation in the right direction. "The Lord ate meals among his friends and intended both to be shared," Sister had explained. Grace wondered if Sister and the seniors had eaten together, and if so, had Sister tried to chat about Linda's one-handed lay-up shot or Linda about the pros and cons of celibacy. Both prospects seemed absurd, and Grace couldn't stifle a sudden laugh. A tiny piece of chewed spaghetti shot out some six inches in front of her plate, just as Joan was taking the seat at the head of the table. Joan fixed on Grace the same glare from the afternoon. Grace's face went so hot, she thought her head would swell. Then Joan used the ultimate reproach: she ignored her.

A pleasant but subdued hum settled over the room as the girls strained to make the kind of conversation appropriate for meals with elderly relatives. The power of Joan's coolly modulated voice, however, did not escape Grace, even in her exile. Several of the sophomores at the table, previously girls of wit and intelligence in their own right, had let their forks dangle as they listened in awed silence to Joan's recollections of her own first retreat at Immaculate Blessing. "I was shy," she was saying, "but I realized that shyness is self-involvement and therefore not very Christian." A polite murmur of consent floated over the table. "It also wasn't much fun," she said to a burst of admiring guffaws.

"Could you gag?" Anne asked through a mouthful

of spaghetti, seconds after Joan headed for another table. Each sophomore unofficially aligned herself with one of the two seniors. Anne had chosen Linda for her wholesomeness, while Grace secretly aspired to Joan's more cerebral air. "I wish Linda would have come over instead," Anne said, craning her neck. But Linda was at the other end of the room, working the tables in the back.

"Well, maybe Sister will come over," Grace said. "Can you imagine her eating spaghetti?"

"Maybe she grabs each one at the end," Anne said, demonstrating, "and sucks it up through her teeth." A long strand of spaghetti raced up from her plate and disappeared between her lips, but not before the tail end whipped some sauce onto her chin and nose.

"Enjoying your dinner, Anne?" Sister asked, suddenly seated at the head of the table.

"Yes, spaghetti is one of my favorites," Anne said, wiping her face and not skipping a beat. It was a talent Grace envied. Grace's own face, barely cooled from Joan's rebuke, heated up all over again.

"And you, Grace?"

"Oh, absolutely," she said, nodding vigorously. Totally at a loss, she blurted, "We were just wondering if you, I mean, the nuns, ate spaghetti a lot, or if this was just for us?" Anne kicked her so hard under the table Grace lost her breath.

Sister Mary Alice laughed, and Grace relaxed enough to give Anne a filthy look. The rest of the table had fallen mute, envious of the extended dialogue. Grace imagined that she and Sister Mary Alice were dining at an elegant restaurant. It was Grace's treat (since the nuns, due to their vow of poverty, were so poor), and Grace had just made a subtle, intellectual joke.

"Well, we don't exactly make meals of Communion hosts seven days a week," she said, resting her chin in her hand. All the sophomores at the table held their collective breath for a second, stunned by the faintly irreverent tone of her remark. After a moment, they decided it was okay to laugh. Grace knew she had been gently mocked, but it seemed a small price to pay for prompting a coveted moment of candor from the nun.

"She is definitely okay," Anne said solemnly when Sister was several tables away. "I wonder why she became a nun."

The question riveted and terrified Grace. She concentrated instead on the shrinking pile of her spaghetti. She tried Anne's suction trick, but lost her nerve before gathering the necessary velocity, and nipped the strand in half. The lower half fell dejectedly back to her plate.

"Huh? Why do you think?" Anne insisted. She pushed Grace's elbow off the table. "Wake up."

"You'll laugh, or think I'm weird or something."

"No, I won't," Anne said. It was every teenager's lie. Grace had said it herself with the same amount of transparent insincerity. Still, she suddenly felt she had to talk to someone or explode.

"I think I sort of know what she feels. It's kind of peaceful, when I see them, the nuns, I mean, in the halls together. I mean," Grace went on, her face steaming with embarrassment, "it must be like they're all really good friends, something like you and me, you know? Like they all know the same secrets, and are sworn to them for life. It's almost — romantic."

Anne looked stricken. "You don't mean *romantic* romantic. You mean the other kind of romantic, like when people talk about exotic vacations."

"Of course," Grace said quickly, not at all sure what she meant, but certain she had said too much either way. "Speaking of the other kind of romantic," she said, desperate to change the subject, "you had something to tell me about Rick."

Anne shot a derisive look down the length of the table, populated by girls who were not part of their clique. "Not here. I'll tell you later. Let me into your room fifteen minutes after lights-out tonight and I'll tell you everything."

"Are you crazy? You know there's not supposed to be any visiting between rooms after ten o'clock."

"Who's going to tell?" she asked, her eyes full of dare. Grace saw that she had no choice.

At exactly 10:15, Grace went to her door and knelt down to peek under the crack into the hallway. She couldn't see much, though, because the hall, like all the rooms, had been plunged into complete blackness. "Pssst," came a sound close to her face. "Open up, it's me." Grace reached up and carefully turned the door knob. Then she slowly started to inch the door open, praying for it not to squeak.

"Jesus, what do you think I am, a muskrat? Open it like a normal person so I can get in."

Grace let the door yawn open all at once, grabbed the neck of Anne's pajama top, and dragged her in. Anne slid noiselessly on her knees across the polished wood floor into the room. "Are you out of

11

your mind?" Grace hissed when the door was safely shut. "Shouting in the hall like that! Are you deliberately trying to get us both expelled or did you just leave your brain on ice?"

"Cool your pits, Grace. No one heard us. Besides, I don't think we're the only ones who thought of this." Her voice in the dark was thick with mischief.

"What are you talking about? Wait, I can't see a thing in here. Don't say another word yet." Grace groped her way over to the dresser, expertly slid open the top drawer without a sound, and took out the pen-sized flashlight she'd brought along. "There," she said, flicking it on, "that's much better. At least now I can see your face, sort of."

"Pretty swift thinking," Anne said. Her hair was pulled back into a ponytail, and her face, scrubbed of makeup, was freckled and rosy. "Hey, you look pretty funny in pajamas," Anne said, giggling. "Or maybe it's just *those* pajamas."

"Knock it off," Grace whispered, feigning disinterest. Grace's pajamas, a Christmas gift from her mother, featured yellow ducks in pink bonnets. Grace had liked them well enough until this moment. "What are you talking about — not the only ones who've thought of this?" Grace interrogated, holding the penlight to Anne's mouth like a microphone. She watched as it cast distorting shadows over Anne's face. Another of Grace's fantasies was to become a television news reporter, thrusting fat black mikes under people's noses at incredibly painful moments in their lives.

Anne grinned slowly. "Why should I tell you? Maybe you'll have to tell me a secret first." She folded her arms across her chest — a chest, Grace did

12

not fail to notice, more ample than her own. Though Grace had gotten her period a whole two and a half years ago, she was still waiting for breasts that would distinguish her from a boy when viewed from the side.

"Anne, this is not the time for games," Grace hissed, trying her best to approximate Sister Mary Alice's cool, authoritative tone.

"No? What were you planning on having us do in this armpit of a room? Perform a seance?"

"Don't say stuff like that, please," Grace said. "It really makes my skin crawl. My mother said that in the house where she grew up, after her grandmother died, the rocking chair would rock by itself and there'd be fingerprints on the mirror in the morning. Her grandmother died in that house. They had the wake right in the living room."

"No, I don't believe it," Anne said, slack-jawed.

Goosebumps sprang up along Grace's own arms. She had Anne's complete attention. "Now tell me what you saw."

"Well, nothing much," Anne whispered, her tone ripe with scandal, "except Linda just slipped into Joan's room." Both girls were silent for a moment; the thought of the seniors defying Sister's rules was too much to digest.

"How do you know?" Grace asked, stern and suspicious, imagining her interview subject reduced to tears and the truth as the cameras rolled.

"How do you think, dummy? When I stuck my head out to check if the hall was all clear before I came down here, I distinctly saw Linda march down the hall, open Joan's door and glide right in."

Grace sat back, impressed by the import of Anne's

news. "How could you tell who it was in the pitch black?"

"It's not as black as it looks when your eyeball is pressed to the floor, Grace. I had my whole head out the door, and there was some light from the window."

"Oh great, so if you saw her, she had to have seen you. She's probably in there right now discussing with Joan how and when to turn us in. You've got to get out of here — now!" Grace started shoving Anne back toward the door.

"You know, you're going to have a nervous breakdown by the time you're twenty-one if you keep this up," Anne said, shaking her head sadly. "I've been in here ten minutes already and no one has come down. She didn't see me at all."

Grace considered this and decided Anne had a point. She took a different tactic. "Well, how do you know they don't have special privileges? Like maybe they can stay up later and have a television in there and aren't supposed to let any of us know."

"If they had special privileges," Anne said self-importantly, "Sister would have told us, to ward off exactly this kind of speculation."

Anne was fast on her feet, Grace saw. She was probably on the right track, wanting to be a lawyer someday. "So what do you think they're doing down there?"

"What any self-respecting senior would be doing the spring before she graduates — smoking a few joints and flipping through *Playgirl*."

"Anne! You know, you are absolutely — banal!" It was a new word Grace was trying out and she was unsure of its pronunciation. Anne, she could tell, was

14

unsure of its meaning, but seemed to catch on that she had been insulted.

"Oh, I really don't give a shit what they're doing. Probably just talking about boyfriends, which is what we're supposed to be doing, remember? I thought you were going to listen to my problem."

"Yeah, go ahead," Grace said, still distracted by the seniors' daring misdeed.

"Well, Rick wants me, next Saturday night, to go over to his friend Bobby's house. Bobby's parents are not going to be home, and Bobby is having his girlfriend over and asked Rick to bring me if he wanted." Grace waited for Anne to go on. "Well?" Anne asked.

"Well, what? Do you go? Is that all you want to know? Of course not. You know what they have in mind, and there'd be nothing and no one to stop them."

"I know that."

"So?" Grace searched Anne's face for some sign of solidarity, but Anne looked away. "You don't mean you're, I mean, you can't possibly be seriously considering —"

"You know, Grace, Rick is a junior. How long do you think he's going to keep putting up with me slapping his hand away when he goes for the zipper on my jeans?"

"I can't believe what I'm hearing." Grace's voice had dropped to a raspy whisper. Not only was she taken aback by Anne's recklessness, but she realized in one scalding moment how far ahead Anne was when it came to boys. Grace had been kissed, she had been grinded up against at dances, but she was light-years away from being on the threshold of going all the way. "That's not enough of a reason to do it."

"I think I want to," Anne said calmly.

"So what do you want from me? Permission? You've obviously made up your mind." Grace flicked the flashlight off. She was on the brink of tears, wondering what she was going to do without Anne for a best friend.

"Hey," Anne said softly. She fished the flashlight out of Grace's lap and turned it back on. "Don't cry, silly. I'm not really going to go. I mean, even if I do go, I won't let him do anything. I'll threaten to scream and call the police."

Grace was concentrating on regaining a normal breathing pattern. Next time the subject came up, as she knew it would, she would have practiced not being so openly shocked. What scared her most was the knowledge that, if Anne's day was approaching, then her own could not be far behind.

"Tell you what," Anne said, her tone conciliatory, "let's go see if we can hear if Linda and Joan have a television in there."

"Are you serious? You don't think I'm going to go sit outside their door, do you? I mean, we might as well go stick a firecracker under Sister Mary Alice's mattress with our names on it."

"Nah, they'll never hear us. Besides, if they catch us, they'll know we caught them. Come on. How are you going to be a reporter if you can't do something as simple as this, Grace? Once you're a reporter, you're going to have to do things like this all the time, steal people's suitcases for top-secret documents, hide in people's closets to bug their rooms. Unless you're not really serious about it."

A swell of wounded pride made Grace head for the door. "Well, let's go then."

Grace didn't breathe once. She could hear the suction of their palms against the shiny wood floor as they slithered down the hall. Joan's room was easy to find; it was the last one on the right. Sister Mary Alice had pointed it out in case anyone had an emergency in the dead of night.

Grace took the position closest to the door and Anne crouched beside her. Her knees began to ache after only a few minutes and she could hear an occasional sneeze and cough through the flimsy doors down the hall. But Joan's room was mysteriously quiet. In the half-light from the window high above them, Grace could make out Anne's frown. Grace gave an exaggerated shrug. Her face felt sweaty with fear.

Just then Grace heard an unfamiliar sound, a groan somewhere between pain and pleasure. A bolt of terror shot through her. What if the seniors had both been stabbed by an intruder who had slipped in through an unlocked window? They'd have to go in and save them, but how would they explain having been outside their door? Just as Grace was about to panic, she heard Joan's voice, hushed and plaintive.

"You have to leave now. This is all wrong, what we're doing. What we're feeling."

Linda's voice was strange, more clipped and urgent than usual. "You're just coming to this conclusion now, after almost a year?"

"I've had time to think."

"Well, you think too much. Come here, at least you can't think when you kiss me."

Anne's hand flew to Grace's forearm; only

paralyzing fear kept Grace from shrieking as Anne dug in her nails. Grace beat Anne's hand away and listened again.

"I just can't anymore. I want to be a nun."

Linda laughed once, a mirthless sound. "I thought you wanted to become a famous novelist, like the founder of your precious magazine."

"I still do. Why can't I do both?"

"Because there are no famous nuns. Only famous priests."

There was a silence. Grace turned to see Anne chewing vigorously on a cuticle as she stared wide-eyed at the door. Linda's voice came again.

"Besides, open your eyes. There are lots of nuns who feel what you and I feel for each other. What do you think Sister Patrice and Sister Agnes Marie are all about?"

"Stop it! I don't want to hear it! It's not what you think, anyway. They're not even special friends. If they were, they'd have been sent to separate convents by now."

"The church can't afford to do that anymore. There aren't enough women lining up to become the nuns of tomorrow, barring you and gross Stephanie Karinski from two years ago, that is. Besides, what do you think is so special about all those special friendships, anyway?"

"I don't have to listen to this. I want you to leave now. I want us to be just friends, the way we used to be." It wasn't hard to tell, even from out in the hall, that Joan was near tears.

"Don't you love me, Joan?" Linda's voice was

muffled, tender. "You never used to want to be a nun before you loved me. It's okay to be afraid, but please don't hide behind bad excuses."

"I'm not afraid," Joan said. "I'm just not like you. I could never be like you. This has all been an experiment for me. And it's failed."

They heard nothing for a long moment. Then Linda: "You don't mean what you're saying. You're too upset to even know what you're saying. Don't you think I know this doesn't fit into your neatly ordered plan for the future? But life is like that. Some things you choose, some things choose you. Either way, you have to deal with them."

"It doesn't have to be like that. You don't have to give in to every urge you have. Especially when it's wrong."

"Wrong according to who?" Linda's voice was skirting hysteria now. It had the panicked sound of someone who knew she was helpless. "You would literally give up your soul, wouldn't you, just to conform to someone else's idea of a normal life?"

"No, you're wrong. I'm going to become a nun because it's right for me."

"Don't expect me to buy a line like that. And I wouldn't expect Mother Superior to, either. This is just the kind of rumor that can get the convent doors slammed in your face, proper little Miss Joan Sweeny."

It happened before the girls had time to budge, or maybe they really couldn't move, or really didn't want to move, hooked on having to know the outcome. But suddenly the door swung open and

Linda, sweet-smelling in gray sweat pants and a T-shirt, was towering over them like a California redwood.

"Oh, great. Holmes and Watson. Get the hell back to your rooms, now!"

They raced down the hallway without a word and slammed their separate doors safely behind them. Lying rigid in the darkness on the narrow, uncompromising mattress, Grace replayed Linda and Joan's argument in her head a hundred times. Exhausted by confusion and some peculiar sense of despair, she finally drifted off to sleep just as the sky was turning light gray.

In the morning, there was a knock on Grace's door before she had finished getting dressed for Sunday Mass, which began in half an hour. She opened the door to find Anne, still in her terry cloth robe, slouching beside Linda, who looked military-fresh in pressed slacks, a pale yellow blouse and white blazer. Grace saw a spray of freckles across the bridge of Linda's nose that she hadn't noticed before. "We're having a small unofficial meeting, Miss Molino," Linda said. "Now." She smiled. Grace glanced quickly at Anne's face for clues, but she only looked as scared as Grace herself felt.

Her mind was racing as they headed down the hall, their small parade attracting curious stares from the other sophomores who were rushing back and forth between the bathroom and their rooms, desperate not to be late. Already Grace's heart ached over how much she would miss these friends, now that her fate was sealed. In the cool hallway, she shivered, still damp from her hasty shower, and a film of nervous sweat made her feel clammy and conspicuous. She was trying hard to come up with excuses for Sister Mary Alice about why they had been in the hallway last night, but she knew none of them was any good. She would not buy the murderous intruder story. Then Grace changed gears, trying to cut her losses, and started to consider what to tell her parents about why she was being expelled from school. But by then she realized they weren't turning the corner toward Sister's room at all; they stopped abruptly at Joan's door, and Linda pushed it open.

Joan, her hair in order and her navy dress crisp, was standing by the window, arms folded across her chest. The room vibrated with tension. Grace thought she might pass out. There was something so adult, so womanly about Linda and Joan, that the sight of Anne's childlike, slumped shoulders in her robe seemed suddenly ludicrous. Joan glanced once at Linda, and Grace felt her own cheeks go scarlet. There was a palpable intimacy between them, and though Grace was on guard for feelings of disgust or fear, she felt none. Instead, something inside her swelled with a disturbing and painful mix of awe and envy.

Joan cleared her throat. "Linda told me that she found the two of you outside my door last night after lights-out. Is that true?"

Linda effortlessly hopped up on the bed and made

a snorting sound. "I don't think they're in any position to deny it." She turned and smiled cheerfully.

Joan sighed, as though she were being taxed beyond her limits. "Is there any point in asking what you were doing, besides taking the huge risk of getting into an incredible amount of trouble?" Grace was staring hard at the floor, praying that Anne would think of something to say. She didn't. "You realize, don't you, just how much trouble you could be in if we reported you?"

Grace's heart was pounding hard in her throat. Was it possible she had heard right, that Joan had said *if?*

"Fine. I don't want to hear your childish reasons. The point is, we all know the walls here are made of paper so it's possible you heard some conversation that confused you." Joan spoke each word slowly, as if she were using a foreign language she had just learned. "Even though it's clearly none of your business, I feel it's my responsibility to tell you that we — what you heard — was Linda and I rehearsing a play. Linda, of course, was speaking the male part." She turned back to look out the window while Linda kept dragging her hand through her hair.

Grace held her breath while the lie hung heavily over their heads. Whether Joan thought she really was fooling them, or if this was her diplomatic way of asking to be spared, Grace couldn't be sure.

When Joan turned back to them, her face was set. "We're not going to report you, because we agree that you're both basically good kids. But," she said, glancing quickly at Linda, "you mustn't say a word to anyone, especially Sister, about what you heard. It's a surprise for the senior play."

"No, of course we won't," Anne said, finally making herself useful, Grace thought.

"Of course not," Grace chimed in, her own voice so stiff with fear she barely recognized it. "Thank you very much."

"All right, enough already," Linda said. "Get back to your rooms and make sure you're not late for Mass." She was rubbing her hands together vigorously and smiling, like a football coach anxious to get the team out on the field.

Grace and Anne didn't dare look at each other as they raced down the hall. But there was between them a shared energy, like sprung inmates who knew they had just gotten away with murder. Why then, Grace wondered, didn't she feel completely off the hook?

Grace and Anne walked the few blocks to Mass together, hanging back from the rest of the crowd. "Jesus Christ," Anne said the second they were out of everyone's earshot. "Did we luck out."

"I suppose." Grace shivered slightly in the still morning air.

"I guess you didn't buy the 'rehearsing a play' line either, huh?"

Grace shook her head, strangely on the brink of tears. "It's so sad," she managed.

"What? That they're breaking up?" Anne had lowered her voice, though they were nearly a block behind the rest of the group.

"No," Grace said quickly. "That now Joan can't become a nun."

"Are you *serious?*" Anne screwed up her face in disgust. "Joan has no idea what a favor Linda has just done her." She stuffed her hands into the pockets of her plaid coat. "You're letting this retreat business go to your head. Do you think the nuns sit around all day singing 'I Believe?' They have to do things like kneel through the night in a pitch-black room and flog their backs raw with leather whips."

"Get out, they don't do that anymore." Despite herself, a chill ran down Grace's spine.

"How do you know?"

It was true — Grace didn't have any current sources. Still, that was a detail she couldn't concern herself with now. "Do you think Joan's right?" she asked hoarsely. "That what they're doing is wrong?"

"Well, you sure would never catch *me* doing it with another girl," Anne said. "But Linda and Joan are definitely cool, and if they love each other, you know, *that* way —" she said, shrugging, "then I don't think anyone has the right to stop them."

"But it's a sin," Grace said, incredulous. "You know, like they can kick you out of the church, let alone the convent."

"Your problem, Grace, is that you've never been in love." Anne wound her hair around one wrist and flicked it over her shoulder. "I'd do whatever I had to do to be with Rick. I'd rather break everybody's rules to live my life my own way than not live it at all according to someone else's."

Grace began several dozen questions in her head and then, losing nerve, abandoned them. All through Mass, the rich voices of the priest and the choir, the dazzling colors of the stained glass, the intoxicating smell of incense, seemed far away; Grace sat and stood and knelt purely by rote. It was as though her mind were in a painful cramp, trying to sort out the boundaries of love that the church said were proper and good, and others that were irreconcilably evil. She would have to be careful, she saw now, if sanctified love was just a minefield of degrees.

Grace knocked on Sister Mary Alice's door at exactly one-thirty, right on time for their scheduled meeting. All the sophomores were required to have a private session with her before the weekend was out.

Sister opened the door and smiled. Grace froze, realizing all at once that she had never been alone in such an enclosed, private space with a nun before.

"Come in, Grace, please," Sister said, sounding slightly impatient. "Have a seat." She gestured toward a wooden chair near the bed, the same sort of bed that was in all the girls' rooms. Sister's room was different in every other respect, however. It looked occupied, as though a life was led here, while their own rooms, Grace realized now, were merely visited. Bookshelves above a desk were filled with religious titles and Bibles. There was a small night table in addition to the dresser, both of which had plain lace doilies atop them, and several statues — St. Jude, St. Anthony, and the Blessed Mother, Immaculate Blessing's patron saint.

Grace sat down and crossed, and then uncrossed, her legs. Her arms presented the biggest challenge. She tried folding them across her chest, and then settled on gripping the sides of the chair. Sister Mary Alice sat at the desk, perfectly at ease. She smiled again. "Are you getting much out of the retreat so far, Grace?"

"Oh, yes. Uh huh."

"That's good. We all know you're a very bright and sensitive student. All your teachers expect greatness from you. I understand that a cousin of yours was a nun, Grace, may her soul rest in peace."

"Yes, that's true." In a spasm of panic, Grace wondered how the nun could possibly have known that, unless somehow she had seen her journal, with its comments about the beach outing she had planned for both of them. Then she remembered with relief that her mother had thought it a good item to mention in her essay for application to Immaculate Blessing.

"You know, it's no secret that fewer and fewer girls your age are expressing interest in the convent, Grace. I just want you to know that I remember — because it was not so long ago for me, after all — how difficult it is to dare to be different. And it's often easier to be different in some respects than others. Being different in a spiritual way seems to me, even throughout history, the hardest. What I mean is, it appears to demand the heftiest price in terms of worldly acceptance and reward."

"Yes, I think that's true," Grace said, no longer sure what she was agreeing to because the nun had covered so much.

"Anyway," Sister said, smiling. "Here I am doing

all the talking, and you're the one I want to hear from. Is there anything you'd like to discuss?"

Grace couldn't argue that the question came as a surprise. All the sophomores had been coached about it in religion class, and been warned not to confuse it with their confessions to a priest. This was supposed to be a freewheeling session, in the spirit of Vatican II, in which the girls were free to explore their spiritual doubts and concerns. And yet, Grace's mouth went dry. Inside her, a question fluttered and remained trapped, like a butterfly beating against the inside of a glass jar. She looked at Sister's smooth, unworried face and, for a tantalizing moment, saw her as equal parts young woman and young nun.

"Well," Grace began, methodically tearing back a cuticle. "I wanted to ask, what I was wondering about is whether, I mean, whether there are ever any circumstance when it's wrong to, you know, love someone."

Sister's pleasant social smile ebbed and she leaned back solemnly in her chair. She looked at Grace as though she had caught wind of a bad odor, one both familiar yet feared. "What do you mean by love, Grace?" she asked. "And what do you mean by someone?"

Grace frowned and studied her knuckles as the moment dragged on in silence. When she looked up, she was horrified at the possibility that the nun might see something more than innocent admiration in her eyes. The feeling terrified her, but there it was, a sturdy renegade weed in the garden of her otherwise model Christian girlhood. It wasn't until last night and the encounter with Linda and Joan that Grace first understood that such stirrings might have a place in the world — if not the Catholic one she knew, then some other one to which she hadn't yet been banished.

"Never mind," Sister Mary Alice said. "You're a sophisticated girl, Grace, and I'll get right to the point. It isn't as though I haven't seen this kind of thing before between students. I must chalk it up to your age and your close quarters with other girls. You know, of course, that love between family members or between platonic friends is blessed in the eyes of the Lord. And you know that love between husband and wife is also sacred. But when two women or two men feel that kind of love for each other, it's a very grave sin, and they must never act on it."

Grace's back was sweating, her blouse sticking to it like a watery blister.

"And if you're aware of any girl or girls at Immaculate Blessing who feel or act this way, it's your duty to tell me about them immediately, for the sake of their souls. Do you understand, Grace?"

There was something of the righteousness of the old nuns about her just then, and though Grace couldn't have said why, she felt betrayed and inconsolably lonely. "How can any kind of love be a sin?" she blurted, knowing it was more an accusation than a question. Later, she would find it hard to remember exactly where she had gotten her courage.

"Some love is false, Grace," the nun said sharply, "and does not suit the purposes Our Lord has intended for us. Sexual love between two women is unnatural, unholy and unfruitful."

Grace nodded and got up. The distance between her chair and the threshold of Sister's room seemed suddenly greater than before. She realized there would never be a movie or beach outing for her and Sister Mary Alice during which they would exchange ironic observations about the world. Linda had lost Joan, Joan had lost the convent, and Anne had either to lose her virginity or lose Rick. Why, Grace wondered, did the church profess to be about love when its rules were responsible mostly for keeping people apart?

The following month, Grace and Anne went to see the seniors graduate. Parents and other spectators collected outside on the lawn behind the auditorium and watched as the graduates, with their starched white robes flowing behind them, came pouring out of the building in triumph after the ceremony. Grace couldn't remember seeing a sky so regal and blue or a lawn so robust and green. Occasionally a white mortarboard sailed high above their heads, and everyone craned to see where it would land. The clicking of Instamatic cameras filled the air like crickets on a summer night as each senior posed first with mother, then father, then both parents at once.

"There's Linda," Anne said, sounding a little breathless, the way people do when spotting a celebrity. And Linda was now a celebrity in her own right: three top colleges had offered her athletic scholarships, and everyone was predicting fame and fortune for her. She was just thirty feet away, close enough for Anne and Grace to hear her laughing as she threw her arms around the shoulders of two former teammates while her father took a picture of the trio. The two girls grabbed Linda's mortarboard and began tossing it between them as Linda leaped high off the ground, trying to intercept it. Finally, all three of them ended up cross-legged on the grass, rocking with laughter.

Clear on the other side of the lawn, Joan was standing with her parents, shaking Sister Mary Alice's hand. Two weeks ago, when the principal had made the announcement that Joan Sweeny would enter the novitiate, some of the girls in Grace's homeroom class had giggled but most, Grace was sure, felt hugely relieved. There was a feeling that at least one girl every few years should join, and since Joan had volunteered, everyone else was unofficially spared. Grace had thought she would be happy for Joan, might even envy her discovering the convent's secrets and its world of hushed voices and dramatic rules. But when she saw her step stiffly across the lawn to the parking lot, the only rules Grace could think of began with never, never, never.

– 2 –

Ha-le-*lu*-jah,   ha-ah-le-*lu*-jah-ah,   ha-*le*-a-looo-jah,"
Grace sang, along with two hundred other students,
all assembled at Mass for the former principal of
Immaculate Blessing who had died in the convent
nursing home over the weekend. The summer had
passed quickly but uneventfully, and Grace was not
unhappy to be back at school. What made reentry
less painful was the fact that she was now a junior,
with all the privileges and respect afforded that year.
With September nearly over, she was still quietly

thrilled with her navy and black junior skirt, stiff and prickly with newness.

Sister Mary Alice stepped up to the pulpit and solemnly opened a Bible, out of which the tails of many different colored ribbons were dangling. "The Lord is my shepherd, I shall not want," she read in the same melodic speaking voice she used for commanding classes. "Though I walk through the valley of the shadow of death, I will fear no evil: for thou art with me. Thy rod and thy staff will comfort me."

Anne kicked the heel of Grace's shoe. When Grace looked up, Anne wagged her eyebrows. "Thy *rod* will comfort me, I'm *sure,*" she hissed, leaning closer.

Despite herself, Grace's lip twitched with barely suppressed laughter. She looked around for Meg, to see if she, too, had caught the double entendre. But Meg, assigned to a different homeroom, was seated far on the other side of the church, many pews behind them. "Surely goodness and mercy shall follow me all the days of my life," Sister continued. "And I will dwell in the house of the Lord forever."

Grace, thinking back to her first meeting with Meg, joined the rows of uniformed girls traveling up the center aisle to the altar to receive Communion. Meg had come over to their table in the cafeteria to ask Anne about a homework assignment for their social studies class. Then, eager to drop the subject of school work, Meg had leaned back and scanned the other faces at the table. Smiling, she announced that the bow-shaped barrettes Grace was wearing would never do. She had leaned over and deftly unclipped them, spilling Grace's hair across her cheeks. "Much better," Meg announced. Grace had blushed deeply, feeling both grateful and mortified that she had been singled out for this girl's attention. As soon as she got home she had promptly thrown out all her barrettes.

Some girls were never really girls at all, Grace felt. They started out in life as young women, and Meg was one of these. Alongside Meg, with her buxom figure and frosted hair, Grace knew herself to be lank-limbed and clumsy. There was about Meg the intoxicating aura of drama, and sheer proximity to Meg's everyday crises — the twenty-year-old in her neighborhood who had asked her to run away with him, the smarmy drugstore paperbacks she kept stuffed under her mattress — made Grace feel her own life was more daringly lived.

Even Meg's home life was ripe with some quiet scandal Grace couldn't quite name. Her father, Mr. Heinz — whom Grace met when she went over to their small, dark house in Queens Village — reminded her of the men who lived on subways. He was always wearing a mixed batch of clothes in varying degrees of unbuttonedness, and sometimes only half his face was shaven, or only the front of his hair combed. He came and went to some unknown job at irregular hours. The rest of the time, he sat on the enclosed porch, staring, his cigarette burning into a long, fragile stick of ashes.

Mrs. Heinz was attractive in a worn-out way; certainly it was still possible to imagine her as the source of her daughter's sensual good looks. Her eyes were green, like Meg's, but gone muddy. She had a thick German accent that Grace — having heard such accents only on TV movies about Nazi Germany —

was incapable of separating from sinister intent. When she spoke, her words were like successive cracks of rifle fire.

To Mrs. Heinz, Grace observed, life was so completely a series of restrictions that it was inevitable to break one of her rules, although Meg seemed to break more than many others might have. Boys over eighteen were off-limits; Meg claimed never to have dated one younger. Coming home after midnight was forbidden, driving in friends' cars was prohibited, reading books by Jacqueline Susann and her ilk was officially banned, and going to dances more than once a month was patently disallowed. Meg managed to do all these things and more. Her mother found out about enough of the transgressions to wear her fingers raw on rosary beads and to keep intensifying the threatened punishments to the point where it would have been illegal to carry them out.

Yet so rarely was any punishment carried out that Grace wondered if Mrs. Heinz, too, wasn't a little susceptible to her daughter's charm. Grace had never come across anything like it — a bold hybrid of the coquettish and conspiratorial — that communicated a whole world of nuance. Meg had a way of tilting her head and smiling, and without her needing to ask, Grace found herself doing things she never would have dreamed otherwise: hiding Meg's Marlboros in her own locker when Meg was on probation for smoking in the bathroom (the nuns would never have searched the locker of a model student like Grace) or taking the bus into Jamaica to help Meg shop for jeans while telling her own mother she was staying late at the library to study. To Grace, Meg seemed part of the unpredictable promise of life fully lived, and Grace considered her friendship an overdue pleasure.

The rousing chords of the church's organ marked the final hymn of the Mass, "Turn, Turn, Turn." Their voices rising sweetly up into the steeple never failed to have its effect on Grace: a blush of joy and pride warmed her cheeks. Even Anne was standing tall beside her, her chin tilted up, lost in some private reverie.

Outside, on the church steps, the huge crowd of students broke up quickly as friends found each other and rushed off in different directions. The September day was sunny but blustery, and Grace zipped up her jacket.

"Where are you off to?" Grace asked Anne.

"Meeting Rick at Sacred Soldiers. We're going bowling," she said, studying herself in a compact mirror she had fished out of the pocketbook she had suddenly taken to carrying all the time. Grace preferred to stuff the essentials — tokens, a comb, some cash — in her pockets or a zippered compartment of her bookbag. "How do I look?"

"Fine," Grace said dismissively, but Anne was evidently too absorbed with brushing her hair to catch the subtle reproach. Grace, who still eschewed makeup, privately thought that Anne, since the summer, was overdoing the eyeshadow and mascara bit. Though she felt faintly guilty about her opinion as it applied to Anne, Grace chose to leave makeup to those girls who put the goal of pleasing a boy above other, more independent pursuits, such as trying to earn early entry into the National Honor Society. Lately, Anne was less and less the friend who, only last year, bragged that she could scale a fence faster than any girl in Queens, with the possible exception of the basketball team's varsity string. These days, Anne seemed content with inspiring Rick, a senior at Immaculate Blessing's brother school, to loyalty and possessiveness.

"Well, I've got a Shakespeare paper to write," Grace said, turning her back to the wind.

"Why don't you come with me today, Grace?" Anne grabbed her arm. "Just for a little while? I've asked you every day this week. Rick's friend is dying to meet you. And he's *so* cute. Your type, too. Very brainy. He wants to be a lawyer like his dad. Just think, we could double-date."

Grace scowled into the sunshine, watching it bounce off the turquoise and red panes of the church's stained-glass windows. She'd heard all this before but still hadn't been able to articulate her fear and reluctance. Double-dating with Anne, Grace knew, would be like doing a few friendly laps around the ice with Peggy Fleming. But before Grace had a chance to answer, Meg's voice was suddenly behind her.

"Hi, guys," she said. "Guess we lost another penguin suit to the big bowl of holy water in the sky."

Anne, Grace noticed, not for the first time, stiffened slightly in Meg's presence. She suspected that Anne was jealous since Meg was slowly but surely filling up the space in Grace's life left by Anne's increased attention to Rick.

"Well, I have to go or I'll be late," Anne said, snapping her compact shut. "I'll call you tonight," she shouted over her shoulder to Grace as she bounded down the steps.

"What's with her?" Meg asked.

"I think she's in love," Grace said snidely, and then blushed at her betrayal.

"Oh, that," Meg said. "No wonder she's in a bad mood."

Later that night, as Grace was tossing and turning in bed, she thought over the day's events. Anne had called to say the bowling date with Rick went terrifically well. She had let him beat her at all three games, and as usual, they had a date for the movies Friday night. Grace had written a decent first draft of her *Othello* paper and had added playwriting to her list of lofty ambitions. She began to imagine a play of her own, in which she and Anne and Rick and Meg all starred. She didn't have all the details of the storyline worked out, but she liked what she had so far. Anne was a beautiful and rebellious princess who had lost her fortune thanks to a reckless affair with a shiftless count, played by Rick. Meg had the part of a hardworking and noble peasant who caught the attention of the dashing and eligible prince soon to take the throne. And because she was short on male actors, Grace herself took the part of the prince. But she was unable to move the plot forward beyond the point where she took the startled Meg into her arms.

Grace rolled over to face the wall, dragging the quilt with her. She shared a bedroom with her grandmother; each had a twin bed on either side of a white dresser. In the summer, Grace's father put an air-conditioner in the window in front of her grandmother's bed, requiring the beds to be turned

37

sideways in order to distribute the cool air evenly. Whenever Grace wanted to go to sleep, she had to scramble over her grandmother's bed to get to her own.

From across the room, Grace could hear her grandmother's steady breathing threatening to boil over into a full-fledged snore. But Grace had resigned herself to the close quarters. Her parents were the ones who constantly fantasized escape, specifically to the shimmering promise of Long Island. It had become a weekend pastime for them to pack her and her brother, Mark, into the car and drive out to remote parts of the Island to look at model homes Grace knew they couldn't afford. She had never seen such places as these: Smithtown and Levittown, long stretches of flat empty land with raw wood houses in small bunches, like random oases. The houses were long and low with two-car garages that could be entered from a den, with lots of two- and three-step staircases that led from one room up to the next. Hard plastic runners covered the plush carpeting and marked narrow trails past roped-off rooms featuring highly polished furniture. When they returned to their house facing the expressway — the same one, Grace was often told, that had carried John F. Kennedy and, another time, the Pope, back to the airport — Grace's mother would pretend she was walking a balance beam through the railroad-style layout. "And now, if you carefully put one foot in front of the other," her mother would say, laughing, "you can get from the living room to the kitchen, a breathtaking five feet away."

It was on one of these house-shopping excursions that Grace realized not everyone did what her family did on Thanksgiving. Her father would drag half the living room furniture into Grace's bedroom and the other half into the den, and open up an aluminum table over the soft, clean stretch of carpet where the couch and cocktail table normally were. Even so, the long table only barely fit. Grace's father, at one end, would be squashed against the television screen, and her mother would complain of the draft she felt being pressed so close to the window. Mark and various relatives sat on the side but as the smallest, Grace got the center seat, so that her legs were pinned between the table's support bar and the underside of the tabletop. Had she ever needed to get to the bathroom in a hurry, she contemplated glumly, she would have had to take the turkey with her or leave her kneecaps behind.

It was the faithful reporting of all such indignities suffered at the hands of their parents that cemented Grace and Meg's friendship. When Grace slept over at Meg's, the two girls would share either the living room couch or the twin bed in her small upstairs room and wait until they heard Meg's mother sigh and shuffle around the house before she finally went to bed. Then they'd be giddy with their temporary, unchaperoned independence, struggling to stay awake as long as possible to savor it. The air would be thick with whispered secrets and the smoke from Meg's clandestine cigarettes — she'd take a puff and then frantically fan the air with her hand. Or Meg would unearth her dog-eared copy of *The Love Machine* and read Grace the titillating portions which, from what Grace gathered, was the better part of the book.

But tonight Meg was home at her house, and

Grace was in her own. Next door were the five Angelino brothers who had been her constant childhood companions until the Summer of the Two Undershirts. As they had all progressed deeper into adolescence, the effort to stave off the day when the boys would exile her completely to the arid unfamiliarity of teenaged girlhood had made Grace's life complicated. The summer after the eighth grade marked the end of her being asked to join in as a fellow adventurer in their roughhousing games, and the beginning of her being encouraged to stay behind and cheer. There had been a new, abrupt silence when she came upon them sitting outside on the front stoop, and dark, unfriendly laughter that would trail her as she walked away.

Grace traced her troubles to her changing body, and set out to get things returned to normal. Her plan was to camouflage her budding breasts by wearing two undershirts. On ninety-degree August days that summer, she felt she couldn't have been more uncomfortable in an iron lung. But she was determined to avoid bras as long as possible. She knew that boys were always trying to remove bras from girls, whereas no one ever heard of any self-respecting boy copping a feel off a girl in an undershirt, let alone two. And as long as she wasn't yet a full-fledged teen girl, Grace would be able to keep the friends she had always known, doing things she had always loved — climbing in the construction-site ditches around the corner, outdoing each other with wheelies on their bikes, or having relay races around the block.

It wasn't as though she were a tomboy, Grace assured herself. After all, unlike the hard-core tomboys she knew of, she did not disdain Barbie dolls. On the contrary, she adored them, although she knew it was probably for all the wrong reasons.

Grace's world of Barbie and Ken (and Barbie's sister, Melanie, and Melanie's oversexed boyfriend, Joe) was a regular revolving door of sexual treachery. Melanie truly loved Joe, but when he went off to be with the guys, she'd seduce the stable Ken, who was driven mad with guilty lust in the presence of his wife's wild little sister. Barbie was hopelessly faithful, but when she and her sister were affectionately reconciling, time after time (the adultery having been discovered, usually in some sordid fashion), Grace felt a definitely other-than-sisterly thrill in Barbie and Melanie's hard, plastic embrace.

It was a drama Grace played out over and over again, though its source, and the drive behind it, was a mystery to her. It in no way reflected any of the real-life marriages she had glimpsed, her parents' own included. One day during the Summer of the Two Undershirts, in a gesture of overestimated maturity, Grace gave her entire Barbie menagerie, with all their dark, lustful secrets, to the nine-year-old Angelino girl next door. About a month later, she spotted the dolls in the Angelino's backyard, lying amidst the pebbles, legs splayed, cheeks scuffed, hair chopped off, plastic breasts indented. In a spasm of mourning, she rushed over and collected them, and retired them to shoeboxes in her closet. But they never looked like more than dolls to her after that. It was as though the life had been literally beaten out of them.

* * * * *

On the first Friday night in October, Grace found herself in a movie theater, sitting directly behind Rick and Anne, and next to Rick's best friend, Glen Reilly. The seating arrangement had been the result of Rick's extreme fussiness about where to settle, and after he had paraded the four of them up and down the aisles, scrutinizing the place as if he planned to buy it instead of sit in it for two hours, there were no longer four seats left together.

Grace had finally agreed to the arranged date with Glen, so worn down was she by Anne's persistence. When Glen had shown up, Grace admitted to herself that he was everything Anne had promised. He had blond wavy hair, hazel eyes and a swimmer's V-shaped torso. And he was rumored to be in the running for valedictorian at Sacred Soldiers of Christ.

So far, things had gotten off to a bad start. Rick insisted on seeing *The Return of the Pink Panther,* though Grace had lobbied hard for *Cries and Whispers,* which was playing as part of the Bergman festival at a theater in Flushing. Rick had considered it only for a moment before Anne assured him that it was not a porn flick.

Under other circumstances, Grace would have been happy to see *The Pink Panther,* but she objected to being overruled by a boy who smelled of a vinyl Yankees jacket and a recent meal that evidently involved ketchup. She also took offense at the fine black stubble sprouting over his top lip, messy as an untrimmed lawn, that masqueraded as a mustache. And yet it seemed to be these very qualities that were holding Anne in thrall.

Grace's irritation with Rick hadn't left her much

time to form an opinion about Glen beyond the fact that there was a calm steadiness about him that she generously interpreted as seriousness and depth. As soon as the credits left the screen, he reached over and took her hand. His palm was broad and sandpapery, and struck Grace as pleasantly mature.

The movie was barely into the rudiments of a plot when Rick, sitting directly in front of Glen, zeroed in on Anne's lips. Their silhouettes were locked together so long that, though Grace tried her best to ignore them, she was hopelessly distracted. It seemed to her that Rick was trying to inhale Anne's entire face, and his efforts were making Grace's blood pressure skyrocket. Here they all were, stuck with the movie of his poor choice, and he clearly had no intention of watching it at all. Glen's hand in her own suddenly seemed to take on darker intent. What, for instance, would she do if Glen expected the same performance from her?

Grace knew she was not on totally firm ground in the kissing department, though some of the blame, she felt, belonged to Tony, the Sacred Soldier's track star who had been her initiator early last year. Though he never asked her out, he always cornered her at dances, and they'd spend most of the night in a clammy, slow-motion embrace, no matter how fast the music the band played. During the songs, he'd mashed his lips against hers and try to wedge an urgent tongue between her teeth. Stunned, Grace would steadfastly lock her jaw. And Tony, with his brontosaurus-like neck, would raise his head back up again, heaving a sigh of what Grace later recognized as frustration and not passion, leaving her to wipe her soppy chin against his already damp polyester shirt. But Tony, with the patience of a dentist, would be back again in another ten minutes.

"Are you enjoying this?" Glen leaned over to whisper.

Grace started. For a moment, she didn't know if he was referring to her humiliating flashback, the theatrics of Anne and Rick, or the actual movie, whose plot she had, by this point, completely lost track of. "Oh, yes, yes," she said, nodding vigorously.

But Glen was studying her face suspiciously, like a prosecutor with an untrustworthy witness. "Because if you're not, we could go someplace else and talk."

It seemed too good to be true, but soon they were seated in a booth in a brightly lit diner a few blocks away. Glen had ordered a cheeseburger, and Grace, not inclined toward a second dinner, got a hot fudge sundae.

Glen offered her one of his french fries, but she declined. She was nearly choking on her ice cream as it was, desperate for the conversation to take a meaningful turn.

"I guess you don't know much about me," Glen said, rhythmically clacking open and shut the top of the silver milk pitcher on the table. A waitress breezed by in a blur of starched white and whisked their plates away.

"Just the ugly rumors," she said.

Glen stared, clearly horrified. Then he smiled, and let out a high-pitched laugh that drew stares from a nearby table. "Hey, I get it. That was really funny." He dragged his hand over his face and shook his head. "I guess I'm a little nervous."

Grace felt a cramp in her chest, and feared the

worst. Could a person have a heart attack at fifteen? "It's okay. I'm nervous, too."

Glen was clacking the pitcher so vigorously now that his thumb was dotted with drops of milk. "Well, I bet there's one thing Rick didn't tell you about me." Glen looked up sheepishly.

Grace shrugged. "I don't know. What?"

"I'm telling you because I feel it's important to be fair." He was frowning, and Grace's stomach flip-flopped. "I'm thinking about becoming a priest." He looked out the diner window, and Grace thought she saw him shiver.

"Okay," she said. There didn't seem to be anything else to add. Inside her, a jumble of reactions was fighting for dominance but already, a melancholy strain of awe and respect was gaining ground.

"It's my dad who wants me to be a lawyer," Glen said, "and who knows, you know? I mean, I really might. I just might become a priest, though, too, is the thing."

"Uh huh." Grace thought her face must be hot enough to fry an egg on. She longed to find the words to tell him that she understood, that his wanting to be a priest was very special, that admitting it was very brave, that her muteness had nothing to do with him and everything to do with her. Real conversation with a boy, she realized, was something she had little practice at. There had always been a basketball between her and the Angelinos, or the fine points of bicycle gear repair to debate.

"So," said Glen, drumming his fingers on the white table, "I guess I should take you home."

"No," Grace said, unable to meet his eyes. "I mean, not unless you want to."

45

"You're not freaked out, you mean?"

"Did you want me to be?"

"No, I —" He blushed. "A lot of people, a lot of girls, I mean, don't understand."

"Yeah, I guess," Grace said. Glen smiled, and reached across the table to take her hand. But it was not the kind of grip she expected from a boy considering the priesthood.

– 3 –

Grace waited outside the school for Meg's last
class of the day to end. It was Tuesday, their early
day, which meant that at one-thirty, when Meg got
out, they would take the bus down Hillside Avenue
into Queens Village to Meg's house. No one would
be home and Meg would smoke, laugh more loudly
than her mother considered ladylike, and tell bawdy
stories of boyfriends gone by. They'd play whole
albums' worth of old Lobo stuff, parts of *Jesus Christ,
Superstar* (from the Broadway show neither of them
could afford to see) and Cat Stevens. But Carole

King's *Tapestry* album was their favorite. Grace would listen, not daring to breathe lest she make the slightest distracting noise when Meg leaned forward on the living room couch, shut her eyes, and sang along. She had a sweet voice, trained on hymns but full of the instincts of youth and sensuality.

It was a mild, late October day — autumn was making its last stand. Grace loved the needle-sharp outline of bare branches against the slate-colored sky. She imagined herself the captain of a ship, sailing to some unnamed, heroic destiny. Or she was a famous poet, thoughtfully wandering barren streets, on the brink of yet another soul-wrenching verse. She was —

"Grace! Hey, Grace! What are you doing out here?"

Grace whirled around to see Anne striding across the courtyard. She glanced at her watch; Anne was boldly cutting class and shouting about it to boot.

"Good God, Anne, keep it down," Grace rasped as Anne caught up to her.

"No problem, I've got a legit excuse. I told Marie Regis I got 'my friend' and had to go to the nurse. What are you doing hanging around? Wasn't your last class a while ago?"

"Yeah. I'm just waiting for Meg."

"Hanging out together again today?"

Grace nodded.

"Mind if I wait with you? I'll only be hanging around at Sacred Soldiers till Rick gets out."

"Have a seat in my office," Grace said, smiling, as they slid to the sidewalk, their backs skidding down the brick wall.

"Glen'll be getting out soon, too, you know."

"I know. I talked to him last night. But he's got a

meeting. Photography Club." Thank God for Glen's clubs, Grace thought. They kept her safe from Anne's reproaches.

Anne nodded and then fell silent. Grace wondered if Anne, too, was privately pleased that the two of them were a team again for the moment, unfettered by their new attachments. Grace was about to say so when Anne spoke.

"We talk about doing it all the time now."

"Who talks about doing what?" Grace tried to keep her impatience in check.

"Me and Rick, dummy. You know, doing *it.*"

Grace steeled herself. The topic no longer shocked her the way it had last year at the retreat when she and Anne had first discussed it, but it was still a vast, frightening prospect. For Grace, sex was safely locked away in fantasy. She could not imagine revealing herself to a boy as thoroughly as sex demanded.

"We've come pretty close already, but, you'll be happy to know, I'm always the one to stop it."

"Oh yeah?" Grace scrambled to her feet. "Why would I be happy to know that? You think it matters to me one goddamn way or the other?"

Anne looked up, clearly startled. Then, to Grace's horror, she began to cry. Her shoulders bobbed jerkily as she hid her face in her hands.

"Jesus, I'm sorry," Grace said. A sudden strong gust made her wish for her warmer jacket. "I didn't mean that the way it sounded. I just meant that I'm sick and tired of hearing that I'm the last of the Righteous Sisters or something all the time. People don't know what I'm thinking. Nobody knows what I might do."

Anne abruptly stopped crying. "No shit," she said. "Really?"

Grace smirked. "Eloquently put, Anne, as always."

The two girls had just settled down to giggle when a white car, trailing an Eagles song as it went, cruised to a stop down the hill not far from them. A figure in a royal blue satin jacket, tight jeans and short blonde hair jumped out from behind the wheel, and deftly hopped up onto the hood of the car to lounge, her face to the sky.

"Somebody's boyfriend. Marie Regis should see this clown. She likes the shy, retiring type," Anne said. "A fine example for the community of young Christian women."

"Uh huh," Grace said, only half listening. Though she wasn't sure why, something about the figure on the hood was eerily familiar. She felt riveted to the cold sidewalk, unable to stop staring. "Anne," Grace whispered. "That's nobody's boyfriend. That's a girl."

Anne tucked her hands under the sleeves of her coat and shook her head. "Grace, get glasses or get laid if you can't see that that's a guy."

"Anne, pay attention. Look at the hips — they're too slender and rounded for a guy. Narrow shoulders. I can just *tell*."

Anne squinted hard as the figure crossed its legs at the ankles and began tapping one foot in time to the music. "Shit on a brick, Grace. That's not just a girl. That's Linda Amato."

"Shhhh!" Grace said, suddenly seeing that Anne was right. "Do you want her to hear you and give us the retroactive beating of our lives."

"Shhhh!" Anne hissed back, slapping at Grace's arm. "Would you stop acting like the CIA or something? Act natural." Anne began to whistle, and yanked a weed out of a crack in the sidewalk.

The bell, ringing clear out into the courtyard, sounded the end of the period. They scrambled to their feet and dusted off their skirts. Within seconds, the mahogany doors swung open and a gaggle of uniformed girls swelled forward. On the hood, Linda continued to tap her foot to the music.

By the time Meg reached them, Grace was a bundle of raw nerves, unable to hide her strange excitement. She explained to Meg in a frantic whisper what was happening. Even Anne seemed to have forgotten her mission to meet Rick, caught up in having to know which Immaculate Blessing girl Linda was waiting for. Each girl who brushed by their trio was studied carefully as possible in case she was the one who ultimately got into Linda's car.

Finally, a girl did stop, and when Linda saw her, she jackknifed to attention. She wore a senior skirt and a white blazer that the wind was blowing open, but otherwise revealed no clues to her identity. She was not on the basketball team, nor was she an athlete of any sort. She wasn't anyone of any particular distinction, it seemed; not part of the academic, artsy or rowdy circle. She was, however, very pretty. Long, straight blonde hair hung down her back and a sharply etched, thoughtful profile revealed, Grace thought, a quiet and admirable self-possession. Grace watched her intently as she shuttled into the front seat beside Linda. Then the car pulled away with a screech, turning heads all the way up the hill.

"Well, well," Meg said, "too bad none of the sergeants were here for that act." Grace was too preoccupied to cringe, as she usually did, at Meg's less-than-reverent reference to the nuns. She was remembering how Linda, a senior, earned the nuns' grudging respect. Her popularity with the senior class, if not with the whole school, was a kind of sainthood, the nuns had recognized. The girls, they seemed to know, needed a hero among them.

"Has Mr. Divinity groped you yet?" Meg asked, propped up against the couch as she sat on the floor near the stereo. Mrs. Heinz, who worked as a seamstress in a dress shop on Queens Boulevard, wasn't home yet, and the house was uncommonly peaceful.

"I wish you wouldn't call him that."

"So what do you call him? Sweetie pie?" Meg was smiling her high-beam smile, the corners of her mouth curving mischievously. A distracted glance might convince someone she was already a woman, with a cigarette poised naturally between her fingers, and her fingers running frequently through the lightened shock of hair that dipped over her forehead. "Huh? What do you call him?" Meg asked again. "Anybody in there?"

Grace smiled weakly. She did not want to think about Glen, not now, and, she thought sometimes, not ever. "I don't call him. He calls me."

Meg laughed her contagious laugh, throwing her head back so that her pale neck arched vulnerably. When she looked up again, Grace saw Meg studying her face for a reaction, scanning for any reflex that would betray the effect of her small performance.

"Is your mother going to let you come to the Sacred Soldiers dance Saturday night?" Grace asked.

"Probably if I push it. But I don't know if I want to go. Anne'll be with Rick, you'll be with Glen. And I'll be with the rest of the rejects waiting to get picked up."

"You won't be waiting long," Grace offered, though she found it hard to imagine Meg liking any of the clean-cut boys who frequented the dance. Meg went for guys slightly older, slightly off the beaten track, slightly reckless. The current focus of her attention was a guy from the local public school, Lenny, whom Grace had met briefly only once. His brown hair inched over his shirt collar and he wore his jeans so tight Grace wondered how he sat down without splitting them wide. He seemed to be on the brink of failing out of school, and his older brother was rumored to be a small-time pot dealer.

"Sometimes I wish you'd meet someone from Sacred Soldiers," Grace said. "It'd be great if we could all go to the prom together in June." The Sacred Soldiers' senior prom was the most prestigious social occasion of their set, and Grace had lately taken to fantasizing about having Meg along when hordes of them would stay out all night long, ordering their chauffeured limos to drop them off at Jones Beach to watch the sunrise. "You could always meet us after the prom itself," Grace said, "even if you went with Lenny. We're probably going to a disco in the city, then the beach, and then a diner for breakfast. You could meet up with us at any point."

"Hah! I won't be going anywhere with Lenny, that's for sure. Over my mother's dead body, anyway."

"She's met him?"

Meg nodded and smiled wryly. "She gave him the speech about how she had once wanted to be a nun and had the same hopes for her daughter." Meg tipped over from laughing so hard. "I always know she's really freaked out by one of my boyfriends when she gives them the nun speech."

"I think my mother likes Glen but she gave me the I - never - let - any - man - but - your- father - touch - me speech."

"Oh really, before or after she married him?"

"She didn't say," Grace said, and they both snickered. "Sometimes I try to imagine being married."

"To Glen?"

"Well, it helps to have someone specific in mind and I don't have that many other candidates."

"So you're planning on this being a long relationship?"

"Well, I —" Grace started, feeling suddenly defeated. The prospect of still dating Glen by June and the prom — let alone till after college — seemed unlikely. She had grown to like his easy-going manner and she loved to hear stories of his family trips all over the country and even to Europe. Still, there were worlds of difference between liking him and dating him for so long; that implied lust, grand passion. Her stomach flip-flopped again with some unnamed fear. Did other girls really want to be groped by their dates, or did they just pretend to? What was wrong with her that she wasn't burning up with desire every time he kissed her?

"You know," Meg said sagely, "marriage isn't everything everyone tells us it's cracked up to be. The husband part especially."

Grace folded her arms across her chest. They had never talked about Meg's parents' marriage. Sure, they had both bitched about Meg's mother, but her father was still shrouded in mystery. Sometimes Grace imagined he was a counterspy working for the Russians, someone who needed to seem as unlikely a candidate for espionage as possible. But mostly, when she passed him on the porch where he sat, listless and unfocused, she knew that the truth about him, whatever it was, was not glamorous or even complicated.

"I was thirteen, I remember," Meg said, "because it was only a couple of weeks before my birthday, and I had just started Immaculate Blessing. I was upstairs alone — they were both at work. I had just started smoking and I used to steal cigarettes out of my father's pack when he wasn't looking. That's how I got started on Marlboros."

Meg shifted, then crossed her legs, yoga position. "In fact, I could use another coffin nail right about now," she said. She reached behind her and tapped one out, narrowing her eyes slightly as the first ghostly puff of smoke drifted back against her face. "So I had gone into their bedroom to get a cigarette and I heard him come in downstairs. I knew it was him because it wasn't five-thirty yet and my mother always got in exactly at five-thirty," she said, saluting. "I could also tell because of his step, that shuffle he's got, like the heels of his shoes are too heavy to pick up off the goddamn floor."

Grace felt her stomach constricting. She could tell by the sound of Meg's voice that some dark, adult transgression was about to be revealed, and Grace was suddenly unsure if she had the courage to hear it. "I was really looking forward to that cigarette," Meg was saying, "so I took it anyway and I lit it with the matches he kept inside the cellophane. I figured he'd collapse into his chair on the porch and just rot there until dinner like he usually did."

"Where does he work, anyway?" Grace asked, loathe to interrupt but not able to contain her curiosity.

"Sometimes he's a janitor, sometimes he's a truck driver, sometimes he's a handyman for some shithole apartment somewhere. He never has any job for more than a year, anyway. I don't even remember where he was working back then, if he even was."

"Sorry, go ahead," Grace said, clutching an embroidered throw pillow from the couch.

"So where was I? Oh yeah, so I'm taking a nice long toke on this cigarette when I hear him coming up the stairs. And I panicked. I tried to think how I could put it out without starting a fire. I had a million stupid ideas — to crush it out on the dresser or smother it in the drapes. I remember I even thought about sticking the lit end in my mouth."

She gave an exaggerated shiver of revulsion. "I was still spinning around the room when I saw him in the doorway and he saw me and there was no hiding the cigarette. 'Daddy,' I said — because I still used to call him Daddy back then — 'what are you doing home?' I said it like we were going to have a nice, normal conversation or something. He didn't say anything at first, just came into the room and I saw his stupid face get all scrunched up and red. He grabbed my wrist — the one with the cigarette at the end of it — so hard you could hear the smack of his palm against my skin. He squeezed, and held the lit end right up under my eye.''

Grace clenched her jaw till it ached.

" 'Whaddya call this shit?' he said, or something like that. 'I knew I couldn't expect much better of you.' And then he said I'd be into drugs in a few years, and then get myself knocked up and be good for nothing pretty fast.''

"I just can't . . .'' Grace began, but a swell of violent protest made it hard for her to speak. She wanted to tear around the room, throwing things off shelves. Only occasionally had she even heard rumors of this kind of cruelty. She fought back the urge to throw herself across Meg like a fortress, as if protecting her now could take them back in time and undo the damage.

"So I dropped the cigarette because I couldn't clench my fingers, he was squeezing my wrist so hard. 'You want to end up like me?' he said. He was screaming in my face, and his breath stunk the way it does when he's drinking, and I thought I'd vomit right there. 'Why should we break our asses to send you to that snooty school? You really want to be down in the gutter like me?' ''

Meg took a quick, deep drag. "I thought he was going to squeeze my hand right off my wrist — burst the veins and I'd bleed to death right there on the rug with the cigarette and he'd tell my mother I must have killed myself. I scratched him pretty good

57

and I think he was shocked. He let go and stepped back. I didn't even see his hand come up but he smacked me so hard across the face my cheek felt like it was on fire. Next thing I knew I was up against the wall. And he had my hands pinned high over my head, so high I thought he'd pull my arms out of the sockets. And he was rocking my wrists back and forth so they were making this crackling sound against the wall, and that's when he shoved his knee between my legs and pushed them apart."

Grace didn't think she could bear to hear the rest. She buried her face in the pillow, her eyes hot with tears.

"So he's spitting pretty hard now in my face and he's screaming, and he's saying how it didn't surprise him anyway that *that school* couldn't make a lady out of me either, that all I ever really was good for was one thing, and I'd probably been giving it away to all these guys already, anyway. And then —" Meg sucked in her breath as if she'd been struck — "he starts slobbering all over my face and he grabbed my breast and dug his fingers in, hard. I thought I was gonna pass out. And then he slammed his body into me, and I thought, 'This is it, if I live, I'll kill him. I don't know how or where or when, but I swear to God I will kill him with my bare hands.' And he was grinding so hard against me I thought he'd push me clear through the wall, and I'd have been happy because then the house would fall down and we'd both die, and that would be worth it because then at least *he'd* be dead. But there was nothing at all there between his legs, just something soft like a big sandwich baggie full of mush. And then he let me go and walked out of the room and I just slid to the floor and cried till I got sick. I didn't even hear my mother come home."

Grace's whole body was trembling. Fighting back a wave of nausea, she waited for Meg to go on. Surely here was the part about justice, about how Meg's mother, in her religious fervor, must have put the fear of God into her husband and set things right.

"My mother came upstairs when it was already dark. I was in bed by then. She stood in the doorway and told me I'd missed dinner and I was stupid to get myself so upset about a boy breaking a date with me, and besides, I hadn't asked her permission to go out with anyone anyway. I said, 'Are you crazy, what the hell are you talking about?' 'Don't you use that language with me, young lady,' she said. 'Your father told me all about your boyfriend so don't try to deny it.' So I sat up and screamed back that there wasn't any boyfriend, that my father the scumbag had attacked me and — here I yelled so loud so not only could he hear me downstairs but the whole freaking neighborhood could hear me — he couldn't even get it up, the limp son of a bitch." Meg cupped the ashtray in her lap and ground out the stub of her cigarette.

"Good God," Grace whispered.

"Yeah. So I thought she was going to pass out, she turned the color of chalk. She said I would go straight to hell when I died unless I apologized to them both this second and prayed for my soul for the rest of my life. And I told *her* to go straight to hell. None of us talked to each other for weeks, and when we did again, nobody mentioned what happened."

Several minutes passed before Grace's head had cleared enough to speak. "How can you stand it, knowing she believes him over you, and nothing was done?"

"I just can't wait till I'm old enough to get the hell out of their stinking house," Meg said, her voice shaking. "Get my own goddamn house with people who love me." She reached for Grace's hand and squeezed it hard.

"What are you, her psychiatrist?" Mrs. Molino asked just as Grace was hanging up the living room phone, which she had carried into the den to huddle with in a secluded corner. Lenny had stood Meg up and Meg, desperate to see that her mother not be so easily proved right about his character, had spent the better part of the evening holed up in a drafty gas station phone booth around the corner from her house, pouring her heart out to Grace. When she got back home, she told Grace, she planned to tell her mother she'd had a great time.

"What were you doing, listening to my entire conversation?" Grace quickly and nervously reviewed some of their more highly charged exchanges, scanning for incriminating evidence. Meg had declared that, while cute boys made her insides go to mush, she found them several levels below girls on the evolutionary scale. They were untrustworthy and cruel, shallow and stupid, and knew nothing of the real loyalty possible between friends such as Grace and herself. Grace felt almost high listening to Meg's pledges of allegiance, though she hated Lenny for making Meg so miserable.

Grace didn't share any of this with her mother. Lately, their antagonism had become a routine thing. No dialogue passed between them that did not involve sparring, threats or venom. Grace was furious that her mother had made it clear that she considered Meg a bad influence. Meg lived in a lower-class part of Queens, Mrs. Molino accused. Her mother was some kind of religious fanatic, her father no doubt an alcoholic loser, and ever since their friendship had begun Grace had grown ornery, distant and argumentative. Is that what she was paying a small fortune to this exclusive high school for? To put her in contact with girls like Meg? Or was Grace just going out of her way to find misfits?

"I have every right to listen to any of your conversations with any one of your friends," said Mrs. Molino, her face taking on the familiar purplish hue that signaled she was working herself into a rage. "Or is there something you're hiding from me that you'd rather I didn't know?"

Grace began to tremble with the adrenaline of her own anger. But she was tongue-tied by all the things she longed to say: that she should really give her mother something to worry about, like getting pregnant or hooked on drugs or flunking out of school; that where someone lived or what kind of job her father had didn't count for anything in her book; that lots of the snooty girls with assemblymen fathers from Hollis Hills and the Estates had the values of vipers, as far as she was concerned, and that she was entitled to her own damn privacy as much as any other adult.

But Grace could get none of these ideas out. "I'm gonna get my own phone," she shouted instead. "And then you won't be able to eavesdrop on my life."

"Fine," her mother shouted back. "And you can pay for it yourself, too."

"Fine, I work," said Grace, already calculating in her head how much of her after-school Baskin-Robbins salary would be siphoned off to the phone company. But it would be worth it.

"Fine," Mrs. Molino yelled after her. But Grace had already stormed off and slammed the door to her room, and she didn't care at all if her mother didn't talk to her ever again.

At the start of the first meeting of the staff of the literary magazine, Sister Mary Alice asked Grace to stay behind after the meeting ended. Grace spent the whole meeting tormenting herself with black possibilities. She was going to be kicked off, and she should have known it when she joined *Voices* this past September, anyway. There were so many other talented girls on staff it was arrogant to think she could keep up. Not to mention the history of talent that had paraded through before her, including Joan Sweeny, and, fifteen years before her, someone who had gone on to publish novels. The very idea made Grace weak with awe and envy.

Now the last of the girls were filing out, and she

and the nun were alone in the stuffy classroom. It had snowed all week, and crystal patterns had frozen over the windows. The heat hissed rhythmically out of the radiators, and the late afternoon sun shone weakly on the bulletin boards, decorated with orange and brown construction paper quotes from Psalms for the upcoming Thanksgiving holiday.

"Thank you for staying, Grace," Sister said from behind the desk. She wore a green turtleneck knit dress with a delicate gold crucifix hanging just below her throat. Grace focused on the blackboard behind her, on which everyone had scrawled their ideas for photographs, cover art, and names of possible students — aside from themselves — to approach for story and poetry contributions.

"I've read your poetry, Grace," Sister said.

"Oh," Grace said, struggling for nonchalance, though a bolt of apprehension paralyzed her in her seat.

Sister came out from behind the desk and leaned against it casually. "You're one of the most talented students I've worked with in a long time, Grace," she said, "but I find your themes depressing and unchristian."

This set Grace reeling. The heat from the radiators hummed on and she thought she might pass out or hyperventilate. "I don't know what you mean," she said dumbly, though of course she did. In fact, she had agonized about whether she had the guts to let anyone, let alone Sister Mary Alice, see the poems, but her private infatuation with them allowed her to overcome her hesitation. She hadn't even let Meg see them, but she knew her motives for that, too. The poems were mostly about their friendship, only thinly veiled, and while Grace had no shyness about telling Meg what true, great friends they had become, the poems were somehow too intense. There was always the chance that Meg didn't feel the same way.

"Well, really, Grace," the nun said, "one of the poems even intimates suicide at the prospect of separation from a loved one," Sister Mary Alice said. She seemed clearly amazed, and even a touch admiring, Grace noted, that she was capable of such sentiments. The ability to shock was thrilling, and Grace was instantly smitten by the feeling.

"And another," Sister continued, "while certainly evocative, makes liberal use of metaphors that clearly point to sexual passion — and I have to think you're just too astute for that to be an accident or coincidence. Frankly, Grace, I'm the moderator of *Voices* because I believe in the pursuit of the literary, but I find much of your subject matter unsuitable to occupy not just the magazine, but the thoughts of someone as intelligent as yourself."

Feelings of shame and indecent exposure would flood Grace later, but for the moment, something inside her soared. She had struck a real nerve, and that power was intoxicating. Later, she promised herself, she would be able to savor her victory. For now, she had to appease Sister somehow. She thought of the psychology textbook from the local library she had spent last summer reading and now, some of its arguments returned to her.

"I don't think I'm writing about anything that typical teenagers don't feel," she said. "I think we need to read about real things we're going through.

That's what the title of the magazine means. And after all, we did read *Romeo and Juliet* in your class last year, Sister."

"Well," Sister Mary Alice said, striding slowly to the window. "Your point is shrewdly made, Grace, but it's pompous, to say the least, to compare yourself to Shakespeare." She turned to face Grace. "What is art in the hands of masters can be smut in the hands of dilettantes."

It was a direct hit, and all of Grace's confidence evaporated like butter in a sizzling pan.

"I merely want to suggest," Sister continued, "that subjects such as lust and suicide might not be bringing out the best in you, Grace, or your work. Isn't there some place for joy and innocent pleasures?"

Grace didn't miss the conciliatory note in Sister Mary Alice's voice, and she let down her guard a notch.

"You know I'm fond of you, Grace, as any teacher is of her best students. And I also want you to know that, inasmuch as any of these poems might be autobiographical, should you need someone to talk to, you can always come to me. Or, of course, any of us, as well as a priest or one of the school counselors."

"Yes, thank you," Grace said, getting up. "I'll certainly think this over, Sister." The lightheaded feeling had returned and she felt an overpowering need to escape.

"One more thing, Grace," Sister said. "Your talent remains unquestioned, as well as your organizational and leadership skills. I'd like to see you listed as editor on this year's masthead, if you think you can reconsider the emphasis of your work."

"Thank you, Sister," Grace said, backing out of the room. "I'll give it serious thought." It wasn't until she had bounded down the stairs to the courtyard that she registered the first stirrings of uneasiness about what she was being asked to agree to.

– 4 –

I think Anne is going to go all the way with Rick soon," Grace whispered, a slight tug of guilt ruining the rush she felt delivering such juicy news. "So far, she told me, they've only done some major fooling around."

"And you believe that?" Meg asked. They were on the living room couch at Meg's house and had been talking for hours. Grace guessed it was about two a.m. She could make out only Meg's silhouette in the darkness next to her.

"Of course," Grace said. "Anne has no reason to

lie to me." But she blushed self-consciously, worried that some elaborate joke was being played on her.

"Well, I think she's crazy. Rick is a sex animal and once he gets what he wants, he's going to break her heart."

Grace considered this, and though it made sense, when she listened to Anne talk about Rick, and how they felt about each other, she was less sure. "One of the guys who lives next door told me once that guys give love to get sex and girls give sex to get love." Grace chewed thoughtfully on a cuticle. "It doesn't seem fair. Why does everyone have to play all these games?"

Meg shrugged. "I hate it, I really do. Why do all the good people get hurt? Why is honesty always the worst policy? Why are the cute guys always the most rotten? Why do birds suddenly appear —" Meg said, breaking into song. The two girls started to giggle uncontrollably. Meg took advantage, poking Grace in the side, till she was laughing at a fever pitch.

"Stop!" Grace cried out, curling up defensively.

"Well, the first guy I sleep with," Meg said, "I'm going to have to be in love with enough to marry."

Grace shivered. "What do you think? Is there one guy out there who's meant just for you, or do you just kind of make it work out with any guy who's in the right place at the right time?"

"God, how could you even wonder?" Meg said. "There's definitely some guy out there right now who's got a little tag on his heart with my name on it. And he might be in China right now, even, and something will happen to make him come here to Queens Village. Or he might even be a little older and married to the wrong girl so he'll have to get an annulment. And I have his name on my heart, too, and we won't rest till we find each other."

"Sounds nice," Grace said.

"You don't believe that?"

"I don't know," Grace said. "I don't know what I believe."

"That's because you haven't been in love before."

"Oh, and you have? What happened? Some angel switches the tags periodically?"

A wounded look flashed across Meg's face, but then she burst out laughing. "You can be in love before you meet the one guy you're going to spend the rest of your life with, dummy. It's kind of like a warm-up exercise. And then, no matter how much you thought you were in love the first or second time, the last time just blows you out of the water." Meg made a sound like an explosion and pretended to collapse on her pillow. "See?"

"I don't know," Grace said. "You have to make me a promise, though. Before you sleep with a guy, you have to tell me about it first."

"Of course I'll tell you. How could you think I wouldn't?"

"No, I mean *before*. This way you can't get caught up in one of these things that just gets out of control one night. If you know you have to discuss it with me first, you'll have to stop and think."

"Can I run to a pay phone?" Meg said, a chuckle gurgling to the surface.

Grace smiled. "See, you don't mean it. You'll come back from a date one night and tell me it just happened." Grace felt an inexplicable sense of loss at the thought of Meg and some boy-man sealed up against each other in passion.

"No way. Here, I'll prove it to you." Meg bolted up from the couch and ran through the shadows into the kitchen. Grace heard her rifling through some drawers and cabinets.

"Shhhhh," Grace hissed. "You'll wake your mother."

Meg came running back and knelt in front of the couch with a legal pad and pen. "I hereby swear," she said as she wrote, "that I will tell my best friend, Grace Molino, well in advance before I have sex with a guy." She held it up for Grace to squint at in the dim light of her glowing cigarette and the windows across the room. "And I'll even add, 'a guy I love enough to want to marry.'" Meg signed her name with a flourish.

"Date it," Grace added warily.

"Is it the twentieth of November?"

Grace nodded. "You better put that someplace your mother won't ever find it."

"I am — you keep it." She folded it up and handed it over to Grace. Then she squeezed back onto the couch. "You're not going to have sex with Glen, are you?"

"Highly unlikely," Grace said with a nonchalance she didn't feel.

"I'm glad," Meg said, nestling her head against Grace's shoulder and yawning. Grace didn't ask what she meant. Instead, she wrestled one arm free and tentatively rested it around Meg's shoulders as she relaxed into sleep. Grace could feel the warmth of Meg's body, smell the sweet scent of her scalp and freshly shampooed hair just inches away. A prickly brush of desire raked over her, keeping her paralyzed in the same position, afraid to awaken Meg. If Meg were awake, Grace reasoned, she might see clearly on her face what she was helpless to explain and terrified to admit. And that would ruin everything.

The bell rang, signaling the end of Grace's trigonometry class. Everyone bolted up in unison, shuffling toward both exits. Once the doors were thrown open, bursts of conversation and the squeak of rushing rubber soles ricocheted off the green walls of the hallway. Grace's mood was black with thoughts of tonight's homework and having to work later at Baskin-Robbins. At least the air in the hallway was free of the chalk-dust smog of the overheated classroom, and Grace took a deep breath, feeling her mood lift. She almost didn't notice Meg leaning in the doorway. "Hey, what are you doing here?" Grace asked. "Don't you have a class now on the third floor?"

Meg slipped a folded piece of looseleaf paper into Grace's notebook. "Read it when you're alone," she said, smiling tremulously, and made off around the corner toward the stairwell.

"Hey —" Grace called after her, but then, consumed by curiosity, she headed directly for the bathroom. Smoke from contraband cigarettes hung heavy in the air, and gaggles of girls clustered around the sinks, alternately complaining and laughing. Grace pushed into an empty stall, her heart tapping anxiously at her rib cage. Holding her breath, she folded open the page.

"In case I didn't tell you last night," it read, "you have a very comfortable shoulder. P.S. You should probably tear this up. Love, Meg."

A rush of adrenaline made Grace feel trapped behind the stall's black door. She hurried out into the hallway, remembering vaguely that she was headed for a European History quiz. On her way up the stairs, she checked and rechecked to make sure the note was safely inside the cover of her textbook, and she stepped on the backs of several girls' shoes in her distraction. She had no intention of tearing up the note, not now or later. In fact, she reread it so many times over the next several hours that she memorized not just the message but the shape of Meg's large-looped handwriting.

By the time she headed home on the subway, Grace had reviewed the note and its motives from every possible angle. It was the P.S. — Meg's advice to destroy a note she nonetheless took the risk to present — that Grace focused on. Without that, she might have tried to tell herself that the shoulder sentiment was innocent. The potential opportunity for both salvation and destruction was making her a little breathless. Could it be possible, Grace wondered, that she was not alone with whatever strange energy it was that had kept her awake all night, watching the rhythm of Meg's breaths?

The Thanksgiving meal that had taken Grace's mother and grandmother since early morning to prepare had been devoured by the family in a mere twenty minutes. Down went various parts of turkey, stuffing with chopped gizzards, white onions, cauliflower, cranberry sauce and Grace's favorite, sweet potatoes. Mrs. Molino was noisily cleaning up, relentlessly scraping pots and dropping plates into the sink, turning the water on full blast and shouting directions at Grace and her brother.

"Phyllis, go sit down and the kids and I'll clean up," Mr. Molino said. "You've been slaving in this kitchen since dawn."

Mrs. Molino dragged the back of her hand across her forehead. She did look beat, Grace admitted. She didn't know what drove her mother, what force compelled her to such frantic perfectionism. "Sure, if you can get them to stay long enough."

It was out then; her mother was upset because both Grace and her brother had dates, something that had never been permitted before on a holiday night. Grace suspected that her father had intervened on their behalf. She'd have been perfectly content not to see Glen tonight, but since Meg was with relatives in New Jersey, it was Glen or staying home.

Mrs. Molino untied her apron and handed it to her husband. "Good luck," she said, disappearing from the kitchen.

"Dad, I have to pick up Eileen at seven," Mark said, holding his watch up to his father's nose.

"Yeah, yeah, get out of here," Mr. Molino said, slapping his son playfully on the back of the head. "And I guess your boyfriend is coming soon, too?" he asked Grace as he was tying on the apron.

"Dad, that's *Mom's* apron," Grace said, laughing as the turkey head jutted up under her father's armpit.

"Sometimes you make do with what you've got,"

Mr. Molino said, plunging his hands into the sudsy water.

Grace dried for a while as her father washed, both of them in silence. She loved her father mutely, blindly; he was capable of no wrong in her eyes. She couldn't imagine her mother without him, or vice versa, so much a unit did they seem, so precisely and comfortably fit. And though she had no idea of its source, a voice inside her told her that she herself was jut not cut out for such a fit with any man. For her, there would be something else, but what that something else exactly was, she had no clear idea.

Glen was idling his father's Lincoln under the railroad trestle across from Jahn's Ice Cream Parlor, where he and Grace had just downed butterscotch sundaes. He had gotten his learner's permit only last month and Grace held her breath a few times during turns when he had seemed to aim the car like a missile directly at oncoming traffic.

"I'm so stuffed," Glen said, sliding his seat back from the steering wheel. "And I thought I couldn't choke down another bite of anything after all the food I ate at my mother's."

"I never get sick of ice cream. I think it's genetically impossible or something. Even at work, I eat the stuff every chance I get when the store's empty."

He laughed, and his smile lingered in a way that made her insides go warm. He looked so handsome in his maroon sweater, so grown up with the streetlight glinting off his class ring. Suddenly Grace had a vision of them in their own house, where she was making dinner for her parents who were coming over. Glen appeared smiling in the doorway, snow in his hair, their blonde child on his shoulders. He knelt in front of the fire she had just built in the fireplace, and warmed the child's little hands between his own. Then he smiled up at her and she leaned down to kiss him. Melancholy made her shiver.

"Cold?" Glen asked. He reached across and slipped an arm around her shoulders.

"Can't we die from breathing in all this carbon monoxide?" Grace asked. There it was again, the claustrophobia she felt when he moved too near, too intently.

"No, silly. Only if we were in an enclosed place."

"Oh." Grace wondered quickly if Meg knew that. Meg was forever having fights with her mother and bolting out of the house to hide somewhere for an hour. Grace imagined Mrs. Heinz calling her house tearful one night, unable to find Meg after a particularly ugly fight. Grace would race over, and know instinctively that Meg was in the car, in the garage, unsuspecting. Grace saw herself fling the door open wide and carry out a limp Meg, lay her down on the lawn and breathe life back into her lungs.

"Hey," Glen said, turning Grace's face toward him by her chin. Suddenly he was kissing her, and the car was silent except for the slippery sound of their lips against each other's. Soon, his tongue came forward like a burrowing squirrel. The muscles of her neck constricted against a swell of laughter building there. She held her eyes wide open, hoping to sober herself. She began to pinch her wrist hard. She tried to imagine her grandmother's funeral, or a car wreck involving her parents and brother. Nothing helped, and the laugh was gaining momentum, moving like a current, steady and swift. Glen was wriggling closer, angling his body against hers, when Grace's laugh broke free, bursting onto his face like a crashing wave. She bent over and gripped her stomach, feeling horrible even as she gave herself over to unbridled laughter.

"Hey, what the hell is so goddamn funny, huh? You don't like the way I kiss or something? Huh?"

The laughter died inside her as suddenly as it began. Glen was slumped against the far door, angrily raking his hand through his hair until Grace feared he'd come up with a clump of blond curls between his fingers.

She reached over and touched his arm. "I'm really sorry. I was just — a silly joke my father told at dinner just popped int my head, and it's like, you know, when you're in church and it's real quiet and someone farts. I just thought of it at the wrong time. I'm really sorry."

Grace saw his shoulders relax a notch but he wouldn't look at her. His face, she could see in the half-light, was beet red. His arms were folded tightly across his chest.

"I think I'm also punchy from eating so much," Grace offered. She felt rotten, as if she had tormented an eager puppy.

"Yeah, me too," Glen said, turning the key in the ignition. The car coughed to a start, and Glen wiped the fog off the windshield with his sleeve.

As they drove in silence toward her house, Grace twisted her silver bracelet round and round on her wrist. She strained out the window to see a star. It was never really dark in Queens, not like it was when her family had gone to visit some of her father's friends who lived upstate. If she had seen a star, Grace thought, she would have wished that she could feel what she was supposed to feel with Glen. As it was, dread lay heavy on her like a wool blanket.

− 5 −

Grace rang the convent's buzzer at ten o'clock sharp. Having arrived early, she had spent several minutes outside the brick building, pacing. It was a dry cold Saturday morning; her nostrils stung with every inhalation.

Several more minutes passed before she had the courage to press the buzzer again. Was it possible that Sister Mary Alice had forgotten their appointment? Highly unlikely, since Sister had reminded her only yesterday of the importance of studying carefully old issues of *Voices* in order to prepare herself for her possible role as editor. Grace turned to look down the quiet block. A cornflower-blue sky was visible through a tangle of bare branches, and a light dusting of snow from the night before gave the streets a dignified, virginal look.

The heavy wood door creaked open behind her and Grace turned around so quickly she lost her balance and stumbled. But the old nun in the doorway didn't notice. She was Immaculate Blessing's librarian. No one liked the suspicious way she handled the books students had chosen to borrow. She, along with all the other older nuns, still wore the traditional black habit and robe. Behind her thick glasses, one eye was squeezed into a perpetual, watery wink. Everyone had called her Cyclops behind her back so long that Grace wasn't sure what her real name was.

"I'm here to see Sister Mary Alice," Grace said, her stomach suddenly taking wing.

"I know," said the old nun, smiling a sweet, toothless smile. She ushered her into a tiny foyer, then disappeared up a long, dark staircase. Standing alone on the worn gold carpet, Grace heard the distant ticking of a clock, the tinny hiss of a teakettle boiling. How strange to find the convent in an unguarded moment, abuzz with the sounds of the nuns' own particular family life. Still, it was bound to be an endless, uncomfortable afternoon, Grace thought, anxiety making her fidget. She could have been shopping with her birthday money for a new snow jacket or listening to albums with Meg.

Just then, Sister Mary Alice began descending the stairs, and Grace was hit by such a bolt of loyalty and respect that she couldn't imagine having wanted to be anywhere else. Sister, in a blue and brown print dress, had gotten up, showered, and dressed just to be with her, Grace marveled.

"Good morning, Grace," Sister Mary Alice said, looking her over the way a farmer would a valued workhorse. "Have you had breakfast?"

Grace nodded.

"Let's get started, then," Sister said. "This way." She led the way to a damp, musty basement with green cement walls. Unlike Grace's own basement — which was cluttered with board games she and her brother had tired of, her father's bowling trophies and fishing gear, her mother's old gowns and magazine collection, and everyone's off-season clothing — this room was stark and barren except for one wooden cafeteria-style table. Two tin folding chairs sat catercornered at one end.

"I'll give you these to begin," Sister said, opening a small cabinet and spreading out a handful of old issues of *Voices* on the table. "In the meantime, I'll be mimeographing some things that came out of our last staff meeting. Make yourself at home and I'll be back shortly." Sister walked briskly out of the room, exactly like she did at school, Grace noted with regret; she'd been hoping that the great mysteries of Sister's life behind these walls would reveal themselves in small ways.

Grace settled into one of the chairs, its metallic chill touching her skin even through her heavy corduroys. A mildewy smell rose up off the stack of magazines in front of her. What, Grace wondered, would Sister normally be doing on a weekend morning? Did she ever sit cross-legged? Did she ever eat an ice cream cone, or watch a football game on TV? Did she ever call an old friend from high school and gossip about people they used to know?

Restlessness crept over Grace and she got up and peeked down the hallway where Sister Mary Alice had headed. There was a washer and dryer, peeling and rusted at the edges, and a cabinet, the sort that belonged in a pantry to hold cans and jars of sauce and vegetables. Grace heard the churning and whirring of the mimeograph machine from some hidden recess. From upstairs, delicate female laughter and the murmur of animated women's voices floated down to her, the way conversation from the beach wafts out unevenly to swimmers.

Grace returned reluctantly to the table and slowly turned the rough-stock pages of the issues. She began with the year before, although she remembered it well. The cover featured a close-up photo of a robin redbreast, its nest soft-focused in the background, a real coup of a shot taken by a senior right on Immaculate Blessing's courtyard lawn, the lawn that only the seniors were allowed to use. Grace paused next at the staff box, where Joan Sweeny's name appeared in italics at the very top. She flipped some more pages, hardly noticing what was there, but stopped at a poem of Joan's titled "The Calling." A densely detailed angel, the work of a junior, illustrated the upper right-hand corner of the page. It had been months since Grace had read the poem or even thought of Joan at all, and she felt her heart thumping in her throat as she read the words again. Their meaning seemed to change before her eyes, the way tiny chips of colored glass in a kaleidoscope rearranged themselves to make a new image. The parts were the same, but the picture struck her totally anew:

I hear Your voice softly calling me
Not down the usual path.
Alone in my longing, outcast
Until I see Your Face
Do I have the courage to love You?
To forego the common rewards:
A wedding dress, a bassinet,
At the altar of Your uncommon love?

"How are you doing here?" Sister Mary Alice appeared in the doorway. Grace jumped, and quickly turned the page. Not quickly enough, though, because Sister came around behind her and turned the page back. "Ah, Joan Sweeny. A well-crafted poem about her call to God. You admired her, didn't you?" Grace nodded as Sister dragged the other chair over and sat down. "Yes, a good many of the underclassmen did. And she was admirable. I hear she is a model novice."

Grace felt suddenly as though the air had been sucked out of the room. The effort to breathe made tears come to her eyes. She didn't dare look up from the page. "Yes," she managed at last. "She's a real role model." The muscles in Grace's chest tightened. She felt as though she needed to brace herself, as though the chasm opening up between them, even as they sat together so casually, almost intimately, was quite literal. She wondered if she ever dare tell Sister how wonderful she thought she was, how brave and bright, and how she saw her only half alive here, like a beautiful flower in the shadow of a mountain.

Sister pushed forward the stack of papers she had carried in, still wet and smelling vinegary from the machine. "I've blocked out some of the ideas suggested at the last meeting," Sister said, and Grace leaned over in earnest. For the rest of the morning, they were united in their diligence, and Grace was surprised when her hunger signaled that it was time for lunch.

Back upstairs, Sister paused outside a small chapel room. Sun poured in through two large stained-glass windows and bathed the polished pews in warm light. The kneeling pads were made of plush red velvet, and at the front of the room, a large gold cloth banner read, "Rejoice! He is coming!"

"I thought you might want to say a prayer before you went home," Sister said, smiling like an anxious hostess. She closed the door after her and left Grace in the room alone. Grace silently said a Hail Mary, wondering how anyone dared speak above a whisper in the room. A strange excitement started a flutter in her throat as she glanced around, trying to envision a Mass peopled only by nuns, their strong profiles slightly upturned in concentration. At first Grace thought it was only her imagination, but then she realized that from somewhere — upstairs, down the hall — came the sweet siren song of women's voices joined in a hymn. The voices were young and earnest, the conviction genuine, the emotion palpable, and Grace felt a spray of goosebumps ride up and down her arms and neck. Nowhere in her mind were thoughts of God. Instead, freedom, in full and graceful leaps, was dancing dizzily in her breast.

When the curtain parted on the auditorium stage, there was a collective sigh of appreciation from the packed audience. Grace and Meg, seated in the front row, were among the most appreciative. Over a hundred girls, dressed in the gold and white robes of Immaculate Blessing's choir, stood regally on staggered bleachers, their faces glowing in the bright spotlights. But, it seemed to Grace, nervous with excitement for the brave performers, the spotlights didn't account for all the glow from the stage. The girls, formerly ordinary in their everyday habitat, seemed transformed into poised and radiant young women, innocent of their own glamour.

Sister Margaret McClancy, the stout and stern nun who had been training Immaculate Blessing choirs for nearly thirty years, bowed slowly for the opening applause, her self-important manner whipping the parents, students, friends and alumnae into a more frenzied state of anticipation. Then she turned her back on the audience — a position she would maintain for the next hour and a half — and held up her arms. With military precision, the orchestra struck the opening notes of the first hymn. Suddenly the whole auditorium, warmly decorated with pine cones and red ribbon at the end of each row of seats, vibrated with the robust voices from the stage. Grace felt the hair on the back of her neck stand up. The choir moved from Christmas hymns — "Angels We

Have Heard On High," "O Holy Night," "What Child Is This?" — to school favorites, "I Believe" and "Ave Maria." All around, there was the sound of the tearful blowing of noses.

For the entire performance, Sister Margaret McClancy tirelessly beat the air with her arms, and even with her back to them, Grace felt sure the old nun was frowning. Only the other nuns addressed her casually as Sister Marge; the students were required to use her full name. Privately they called her The Bulldog. Many girls who joined early on, imagining afternoons of campfire-style singalongs, dropped out well before October, bringing back with them tales of joyless drills, liberal insults, and fiery temper tantrums. Still, the nun earned back the students' grudging respect for pulling off such a magical evening each Christmas.

The concert ended to stirring applause, and as the audience filed out, the choir sang the school anthem, normally a deadly number that, in the glow of good will, sounded almost catchy and triumphant. While the crowd inched toward the back doors, exclaiming and shouting Christmas greetings across the aisles, Meg and Grace stayed in their seats. Grace didn't want to be seen by Anne and Rick, who would surely report back to Glen that she wasn't there with her parents and brother, as she had told him she would be.

All the girls had left the stage now, and a crew of freshmen began to disassemble the bleachers. Grace turned to Meg and saw that she still had tears in her eyes. "Hey, the sad part is over," Grace said.

"I wanted to be in it this year," Meg said.

Grace was stunned for a second, and then felt

grossly stupid. How had she not realized that Meg, who loved singing, would have been filled with envy?

"Well, you'd be perfect. I bet you'd even get a solo. Why didn't you try out?"

Meg kept staring up at the stage and for one horrible moment, Grace was terrified that Meg would say she had, and been turned down. But Meg only shrugged. "My mother said I didn't have the discipline. Mostly I was afraid. I was afraid The Bulldog would say I wasn't good enough, or that even if I did get in, she'd humiliate me in front of everyone. Or that she'd put me next to some girl with a really outrageous voice and I'd feel like shit, and everyone would think I was really average, or worse than average."

"Everyone's afraid of that, but you have to get over it. Shit, you're just as good, if not better, than most of these people." Grace had never seen Meg, who was always so cavalier and confident about her problems, look so vulnerable. "Wow, I mean, I can't believe you didn't tell me this sooner. I'd have made sure you tried out. I'd have come down here with you and coached you and waited outside and everything. I just thought you were such a great singer that if you weren't in the choir it was because you didn't want to be. And even when you said you wanted us to go together tonight, it didn't hit me. I just thought it was in the holiday spirit and everything."

"I wish I had told you sooner. Because now it's too late." Meg stood up and they headed wordlessly for the doors; they each had to call their fathers to pick them up.

"Well, it may be too late for this year," Grace said. "But maybe she'll need some new people for the spring concert — I mean, I know that one's not as big a deal, but then you'll be all in place for next Christmas."

"I might not be here for next Christmas," Meg said, pushing a dime into the phone and dialing. Grace thought her heart had stopped. A tingle crept down her whole body and splotches of colors danced a nauseating pattern in front of her eyes. From far away, she heard Meg saying something into the phone. She leaned against the cool brick wall and regained some equilibrium.

"What are you talking about?" Grace asked in a tone far calmer than she felt.

Meg hung up. "Call your father first and then I'll tell you."

Grace struggled to sound normal on the phone. "Now tell me what you're talking about," she said as soon as she hung up.

They went outside and stood on the concrete steps at the end of the courtyard, facing the traffic. The air was still and cold, and the sky dotted with stars.

"My mother isn't sure we can afford this place next year," Meg said, her voice breaking. "My father isn't doing so hot this year. And we still owe them money from last year. Tuition's going up next year and he says the place costs as much as some colleges, anyway. That I don't need it."

Grace was so angry that for a moment she couldn't speak. "Well, that's *ridiculous*," she said finally. "There must be *something* they can do. A loan, or something. This is a *Catholic* school. It'll be your senior year! How could they be so heartless? Isn't the school trying to work something out?"

"Don't you think I've thought of all those things? They said they'd think about it if I could get my grades up to scholarship level. You may have made the Honor Society, but I didn't, remember?"

Grace was silenced. She walked down a few steps and watched, as her vision blurred with tears, the last of the crowd get into cars and drive away. She forced herself to breathe evenly, in-out, in-out.

"I'm sorry," Meg said, suddenly on the step behind her, her hand on her shoulder.

Grace whirled around. Their faces were just inches apart. Grace's heart lurched painfully. She stepped down to the sidewalk.

"It was a rotten thing to say," Meg continued. "I was just mad as hell at everyone. At myself, but not you."

"Yeah, it's okay." Grace stuffed her hands in her pockets.

"Anyway, don't worry about it. I'm just feeling sorry for myself. My mother says this every year — 'Well, next year we won't be able to afford that place' — and I'm still here, aren't I? It's just their way of keeping me in line, I think. I swear, though, sometimes I wonder why I want to be here, anyway. The prestige was what got me in the beginning. But all these nuns are so creepy and mean. How dare she, that Bulldog face, act all that sweet and wonderful to the parents every year at the concert and then torture everyone as soon as she's got the students alone?"

"Yeah, you tell her, the old dog breath. Get in there at auditions and blow her away!"

"Oh, here's the great provider now," Meg said, as her father's boxy black car slowed to the curb.

Grace walked over and said a cursory hello to Mr. Heinz. Sometimes he responded, but not always. Tonight he actually smiled, or moved his lips in a way that approximated a smile.

"Well, goodnight," Meg said to Grace, glancing sidelong at her father. Then, opening the car door, she whispered, "I know why I want to be here this year, though." And it might have been an accident, but when she leaned over to kiss Grace goodbye, just for a moment the corners of their lips met.

After meeting outside Sacred Soldiers, Glen and Grace walked toward her house, side by side. While Anne and Rick headed off toward the subway for an ice-skating date, Grace refused to be talked into joining them, pleading that her paper on a proof of the existence of God was due before Christmas break.

"Which proof did you choose?" Glen asked, cupping her gloved hand inside his own.

"The teleological," Grace said, worried that she'd pronounced it wrong. "And then we have to defend our choice and say why it appealed to us. And then say where faith fills in the gaps." The class was exciting to Grace, acknowledging, as it did, that there was a world in which reason and intuition worked together, instead of at odds.

"We had a class like that last year," Glen said. "But Brother John made us come up with our own theory after we'd read all the classic arguments. It didn't have to be a formal philosophical proof or anything, just whatever one thing made us think there had to be a God.'

"Really? What did you say — or is it too personal?" In fact, to Grace, God was a deeply personal issue. She couldn't understand how people who didn't believe in God got up out of bed in the morning. If life was just one long senseless march to death — and ended flatly there, without rewards and punishments for how one conducted her life — she couldn't imagine how she'd get through it. Sometimes she'd work herself into a terror trying to imagine the ultimate blankness of a death that lasted an eternity.

"Well," Glen said, "the thing that always got me was that you could never *show* someone God, you could never look at him. And the people who claim to have seen him or talked to him are always written off as crazies, anyway."

"Uh huh," Grace said encouragingly.

"So I tried to think, well, there are plenty of things that exist that we can't see — wind, electricity, sound waves. But there you have evidence of the direct effect, sort of the outline of the thing. So I thought about the ant farm I had one summer when I was a little kid. I thought about how, every day, people walk around and step right over ant families, step right over these incredibly complicated societies, and don't give them a second thought unless one of them is crawling in their picnic. And the ants don't have the slightest idea we exist."

"You mean," Grace said, "we could be like ants and this whole other kind of life, like God, could be stepping around us right now and we're just too small to see it?"

"Uh huh, exactly," Glen said, nodding earnestly.

Grace was moved by his simple but apt analogy. "Is that why you want to be a priest?"

A rosy blush spread quickly over his cheeks. "If you really want the truth," he said, taking her hand again, "I haven't thought about the priesthood much since I met you."

Grace's stomach somersaulted. She hadn't the slightest idea how to react. None of the things she imagined she should say sounded right: *I'm so flattered, thank you.* Or: *I feel the same way.* Instead, her mouth felt full of sawdust.

At her stoop, Grace stalled for time. She didn't want to invite him in. How could she ever explain to him how of two minds she felt? His ant theory had touched her and made her feel warm and trusting, and yet not a drop of that spilled over into erotic feeling for him. After ten minutes of small talk and scuffing his feet, Glen stood on the step above her, pulled her as close as he could in their bulky winter coats, and kissed her goodbye. From behind the safety of the porch window, Grace peaked through the blind and watched him walk slowly away.

"Grandma?" Grace called when she got upstairs.

"In here," her grandmother said. Grace went in to the den and watched her drape a fresh shirt across the end of the ironing board. Big blue veins stood up along the backs of her hands, pushing up through the skin like limbs under delicate bed sheets. Her grandmother smiled, then expertly placed the iron down with a hiss of steam. She went to church every

Sunday, and sometimes during the week. She didn't lecture her own daughter for not going to church anymore, but she was disappointed, Grace knew. Mrs. Molino, as Grace had been told many times, had been unofficially excommunicated for confessing that she used birth control. Her mother had believed in forgiveness, but the priest had curtly explained that forgiveness did not apply to a blatant disregard of one of the most basic tenets of church doctrine. Grace tried to tell her mother that the church would probably look the other way now and take her back, but Mrs. Molino said it was too late; they had abandoned her when she needed them and now she had learned to live without them.

"I have to write a paper on one of the proofs of the existence of God."

"Boy, that sounds hard."

"How come you believe, Grandma?" Grace asked. "I mean, don't you wish you had some proof?" Her grandmother was the only person Grace knew, aside from priests and nuns, who talked about God with absolute certainty, as though he were a person she knew directly, someone she might pass on the street and greet.

"Oh, I don't know a thing about any proof. I don't need to," she said. "You only need to prove a thing when you don't really believe it. And something can be true even if you can't prove it."

Grace considered this for a moment, feeling vaguely disturbed. Then she headed for her room to change. It seemed to her just then that the human race was just a bunch of blind pups, wandering around making feeble and pointless attempts to explain the world and their own nature. In truth, forces beyond their control moved around and within them all the time, and the best they could do was accept it all without making a fuss.

— 6 —

It kills me we won't see each other at all over Christmas weekend," Meg said, running a brush through her freshly dried hair as she sat at the foot of her bed. She had on the red-and-black checked flannel nightgown that had grown so familiar to Grace. Her skin was still rosy and glistening from a shower.

"I know," Grace said, lying on her stomach on the bed. "That's why we have to exchange presents now, even though it's only the night before Christmas Eve."

Heat from the radiator had been hissing loudly for the last half an hour, and even in her own brushed-cotton pajamas, Grace was grateful for the extra warmth. They had just come in from a long walk in the new snowfall, and already the icy air had formed a thin crust over the powder-soft surface. The stars had seemed to grow brighter and dimmer by turns, and bare tree branches cast a network of pencil-thin shadows over the drifts.

Meg got up abruptly and began rifling through her desk drawer. "What are you looking for?" Grace asked.

Meg turned around with a satisfied grin, holding up two tall red candles in little wooden stands. She lit them with the lighter she kept hidden with her cigarettes, then flicked off the overhead light. Plunged into semi-darkness, Grace felt her stomach flip-flop with anticipation. She hoped more than anything that Meg would like her gift.

"Here." Meg held out a red square box tied with green ribbon. Grace sat up and felt herself blush clear to her eyebrows. She swallowed hard as she pulled the ribbon open.

"I'm going to love it, whatever it is," Grace said, carefully peeling off the paper. She thought she'd burst from having Meg's eyes on her, hungry for a reaction. Grace was never good at presents. She didn't know how to say she really liked something, and she didn't know how to hide it when she didn't.

Grace joggled the box's cover off and stared: it was a watch, with a rectangular silver face and a ribbed silver bracelet band. "I love it!" Grace squealed, throwing her arms around Meg's neck. "It's beautiful."

Meg lifted the watch out of the box and hooked it onto Grace's wrist. "It looks great on you. I knew it would."

Grace admired the watch, a little stunned that Meg had gotten her something so wonderful. "Now you," she said, holding out her small box. She had bought a roll of special green foil paper just for Meg's package. A tiny white bow was perched on top. Meg had the wrapping ripped off in seconds and popped the box open.

"Oh," she said, "my God." Even in the half-light, Grace could see tears in Meg's eyes. She watched as Meg reverently slid the silver band out of its felt slot and slipped it onto her finger. It fit, as Grace had hoped. She had tested the size by secretly trying on Meg's other rings when she wasn't looking.

Meg reached over and wrapped Grace in a deep hug, rocking her slowly. The perfect oval flames of the candles blurred in Grace's vision, and her body was pulsing with adrenaline. She felt she could run a marathon, bound effortlessly straight up the side of a building, burst unscathed through a brick wall. Meg kept rhythmically rocking, and Grace felt the sweet burn of swallowed tears in her own throat.

"I love you," Meg said in Grace's ear, so quietly Grace wasn't sure what she heard. But Meg pulled back and looked at her so intently that Grace knew she wasn't mistaken. "So much," Meg said simply.

There was no way of knowing who moved first, no way to determine which one of them had inclined slightly forward. Like the hands of a clock, there was no way to see their progress, only that the time had changed. But somehow Grace found her lips on Meg's, and Meg's on her own, both suddenly and slowly, strangely and naturally. For one long, lingering beat, neither of them moved, paralyzed by the fact of their lips together. Then they kissed, a hungry, innocent, knowing pact that made Grace lightheaded and clammy, that made the soles of her feet tingle and the bottom of her stomach drop out. They were tipping backward and Grace heard the whistling of December's breath against the windowpane, eager to find its way inside. But nothing could reach them, no other light or sound, no protest, no doubt, no caution.

Meg had fallen asleep hours ago, but Grace lay awake on her back, watching the sky go from dark to light gray, all the while peeking down at Meg, whose cheek was sealed against Grace's shoulder. Periodically, Grace glanced over at the candles to make sure the room didn't go up in flames. Not that it would have surprised her to have died just then. Life was suddenly so unbearably good, so sweet, that it hardly seemed possible that God would ever give her more moments like this one. Surely this kind of happiness had to be spread around. Surely she had used up her quotient.

Meg was making a low purring sound, and only her lips, parted slightly in a pout, betrayed the total innocence of her sleep. It was those lips Grace had spent half the night kissing. From their tender-shy beginnings, the kisses had turned deep and fierce, had become stomach-pounding, dizzying, demanding. Grace had felt the way she did when she lay out on a raft at the beach, waves rippling underneath her and moving her away from the shore in a hypnotic rhythm.

But as amazing as their kisses were, Grace knew that it was some unspoken restraint that had kept them confined to kisses alone. The whole while, she sensed, a larger hunger had been clawing to break free. It was as if she were straining against a gathering of energy in her arms and hands that wanted to take her further, but her towering fear held her back.

Meg stirred, and then opened her eyes. She gave Grace a dewy, little girl's smile. Grace blushed till her temples grew moist. She was suddenly tremendously grateful that she hadn't fallen asleep and let her hair get tangled or her eyes grow narrow and dim with sleep. "Are you sorry?" Grace blurted, no longer able to keep her torrent of feeling to herself.

"Why, did I hurt you?" Meg said, smiling mischievously. She stretched up and, unbelievably, in the near daylight, kissed Grace again on the lips. But there was no time to marvel. Meg was breathing rhythmically again in sleep, and this time, raw and jittery from the lack of it, Grace followed.

By eleven-thirty, Meg and Grace were settled into a booth in the diner around the corner from Meg's house. Mrs. Heinz had pounded on their door in time to get them up for ten o'clock Mass; she herself had gone to an earlier service. There had been no time to talk, and no safe place, because Mrs. Heinz — to Grace's ferocious irritation — was briskly moving about the house, up and down the stairs, cleaning and muttering, starting little spats with Meg for no reason. During Mass, Grace had heard precious little of anything that was said. She and Meg had kept sneaking each other shy looks, and whenever they both stood up, Meg would curl her hand around the smooth wood of the pew in front of her and press firmly against the side of Grace's hand. Grace's heart thumped like a hammer in her throat — what if someone saw them? — but she didn't once move her hand away. She felt as though some electrical current were running back and forth between them and she didn't dare short-circuit it.

In the diner, Grace looked cursorily at the menu; there was no time to waste. She was expected home soon, to tackle all the studying for midterms she had left untended all weekend. She had no idea how she'd get through it all. She was hopelessly preoccupied with the events of last night: What should they call what they had done? Would it happen again? Did she want it to? Did Meg? What did it mean that it had been so amazingly terrific to kiss Meg, nothing like it was to kiss Glen? Was this something she could be confessing, or rejoicing about? Would her mother be able to tell something had changed? When the waitress strolled over, both girls ordered hurriedly.

"I've been thinking," Grace said.

"Thank God somebody has," Meg said, smiling broadly and twirling her new ring round and round on her finger.

"What does that mean?" Grace asked, her chest tightening.

"Just a joke. Don't get paranoid on me," Meg said, reaching across the table for Grace's hand, but then quickly withdrawing it. They both began to giggle uncontrollably.

The waitress came over with Meg's coffee and Grace's glass of milk. She paused to smile. "Boy talk, huh?" she said, her hands, mock-reproachful, on her hips. This started a fresh fit of laughter. The waitress shook her head and walked away.

Suddenly Grace was sober. "No really, I've been thinking this over and it really makes perfect sense."

"Uh huh," Meg said, slurping coffee out of the too-full mug.

"What I think is," she said, crouching over the tabletop to whisper, "what we did was just — I mean, what happened was like, the physical expression, you know, of what we feel for each other *emotionally*."

"Oh, obviously," Meg said. "I mean, it wasn't like we spotted each other on the street the day before or something and I thought, my God, I just gotta kiss this chick."

Fresh peals of laughter started again, and by the time they died out in painful sighs, the corners of Grace's eyes were wet. "Right, exactly," she said. "I mean, to most people, it would seem pretty weird."

"If I'd never been hot for a guy in my life before, maybe it'd seem weird to me, too."

"Exactly," Grace said. "To put it mildly."

"Exactly."

"But what we have is no ordinary friendship," Meg said. "What we have is —" Meg turned to look out the window at passing traffic — "power. Together, we have power."

Grace swallowed hard and nodded solemnly.

When her English muffin and Meg's scrambled eggs came, her courage completely left her, though all her questions remained. She didn't dare risk raising them. For Meg, it seemed, the issue was clearly resolved, probably not to be brought up again. It was crazy, anyway, just crazy. Already, the world was returning to its normal proportions. Homework would still loom, Glen would still pressure her, she and her mother would still fight. Whatever window she had passed through last night — when for those few tantalizing hours all the old rules had been suspended, all the old definitions ignored — had been firmly shut again. She was partly grateful and contented. She bit into her muffin with the hunger of the newly absolved. It was easier to believe nothing really had changed.

The smell of cauliflower and turkey necks boiling on the stove floated through the house like a rich incense as Grace lay curled on the couch, taking stock of her Christmas presents. On the floor lay a few pieces of balled-up wrapping paper and crushed bows that had escaped her mother's careful eye as she tried to clean up everything in the wake of the morning spent tearing open gifts. Her father had given her mother a plush royal-blue robe with a fifty-dollar bill in each pocket; her mother had given him an assortment of matching shirts, ties and socks. Grace's grandmother had gotten perfumed powders, slips, and a string of good imitation pearls that she would no doubt put away and save for special occasions like wakes. Mark had already headed to the basement to practice beginning chords on his new electric guitar.

Grace felt giddy with good fortune looking over her own booty: a green snow jacket, several sweaters and pairs of jeans, a Bee Gees album, a mood ring that had turned a deep blue on her finger, a Kahil Gilbran book, a Thoreau calendar with a nature photo and quote for every month, and a pair of gray suede boots that she had already fantasized a new and exciting life around. She would wear them to dances and win admiring looks from everyone. Meg would never have any reason to question her coolness, and Sister Mary Alice would feel certain she had moved beyond the influence of Immaculate Blessing and begun her worldly life of hedonism and sophistication.

If only every day could be like Christmas morning, Grace thought, turning over on her back and taking in for the millionth time the look of the house dressed for the holiday: holly and Christmas lights framed the large painting hanging over the television, and Christmas cards, suspended from loops of red ribbon, hung from floor to ceiling on the wall by the bathroom. Tacked onto the front door, a Santa face with a fleecy white beard played "Jingle Bells" when the string under his chin was pulled. And finally there was the tree, bursting with shiny balls and looming over a miniature Christmas scene, crowding the small den with its sentimental power.

All last night, she and Mark had sat at the foot of the tree, half hypnotized by the blinking colored lights, trying to guess what each brightly wrapped package concealed. Now that they knew, what remained to look forward to was the orgy of food at four o'clock, especially the desserts — her grandmother's chocolate cream pie, petit fours her aunt in Florida always sent, apple pie à la mode. Her father would have his favorite fruit cake, a gooey, tangy concoction Grace couldn't even stand the look of.

Now would be a good time to call Meg, Grace thought. Her mother and grandmother were busy as surgeons, hunched over a huge field of vegetables to be peeled and chopped. Her father had been sent out on a crisis mission for more milk and eggs to use in breading the cauliflower. Grace went into her bedroom, looking again at the watch Meg gave her resting on top of her dresser. Grace had shown it to her mother, hoping Meg's generosity would redeem her in her mother's eyes, but Mrs. Molino had only snorted, asking where Meg had gotten the money.

Looking at the watch triggered memories of that night again, not that Grace needed even the slightest prompting. Thinking merely of the startling fact that they had kissed at all — and so well, for so long — still set her stomach quivering in awe, though she must have reminded herself already hundreds of times a day. From there she greedily dwelled on the details: the taste of Meg's lips, the memory of Meg's hand at the back of her neck, pulling her closer, her little sounds of pleasure, their breathing going shallow and labored by turns. She remembered the cool, porcelain-smooth feel of Meg's cheek, the way they kept their bodies sealed against each other so that Grace knew their breasts were touching, if only through the safety of cotton and flannel. That thought always resurrected the raging monster of desire that seemed to have no conscience, no fear at all, that planted in her mind all manner of fevered imaginings, things that embarrassed her even to think of, let alone ever have the courage to carry out.

She dialed Meg's number, and after a few rings, Grace heard an odd clicking sound and then an operator's voice: "I'm sorry, the number you have dialed has been temporarily disconnected."

Grace dialed three more times before she convinced herself she had made no mistake. She replaced the receiver gently and sank to the bed, her eyes stinging. What did that mean, temporarily disconnected? It wasn't like out of order, Grace knew. She felt numb, and brought her book and calendar into her room and began reading both with a growing sense of doom. Life was like that, cruel and unsparing. She was being punished for what she knew, deep down, was perversity and dementia. She would return to school next week and there would be no sign of Meg anywhere. Her family would have moved suddenly, without a forwarding address. She would never see Meg again. Grace's throat was burning. She couldn't remember what it felt like to have been so happy and contented just an hour ago.

When her phone rang, Grace leapt for it so vigorously that she nearly sent it flying off the dresser top. "Hello?" she shouted.

"Hi," a small voice said. It was Meg. Meg, really Meg.

"I just tried to call you. Your phone's dead.

What's going on? I was afraid you'd left town and I'd never see you again. Where are you?"

"God, and merry Christmas to you too," Meg said, laughing. "I'm in the phone booth around the corner. The phone company finally disconnected us because we haven't paid them in a couple of months. It sucks, I know, but my mother'll scrape together some money for them soon. It's not the first time it's happened. She always pays them last because the electricity and the heat are more important. I offered to get a job after school again but they keep telling me they're paying a fortune for Immaculate Blessing so I can concentrate on my homework."

"Jesus, why didn't you tell me?"

"I don't worry about it. It's their problem," Meg said sullenly. "The bitch of it is that she's putting a lock on the phone."

"What?"

"She says I'm the one who runs up her bill. They put this little bolt in one of the finger holes so you can't dial. You unlock it with a key that she's going to keep. Every time I want to make a phone call, I gotta beg her for the key."

"Oh, great," Grace said, angry but hugely relieved that her worst fears had not, for the moment, at least, been realized. Still, the threat of Meg's not being able to stay at Immaculate Blessing reasserted itself.

"Are you having a good Christmas?" Meg asked.

Grace rattled off her litany of gifts. "How'd you do?"

"Not bad. A lot of clothes, which I need. And

Lenny came by last night and gave me a Pink Floyd album."

"Pink Floyd? Is that who he thinks you listen to? Some drugged-out head music?" She felt fury at the mention of Lenny's name but for some reason could vent it only on his taste in bands.

"He let me hear some of their stuff when I was over there last week —"

"You were over there? At his house? You didn't tell me. And he came over last night, on Christmas Eve? You spent Christmas Eve with him?"

"He just came by for a little while. My mother was dragging us all off to midnight Mass. It slipped my mind, that's how big a deal it was."

"Was anybody home when you were over there?"

"Well, he was."

"Very funny — you know what I mean."

"God, look at this poor bastard dog, a stray on Christmas, running through the snow all alone."

"Meg!'

"No, no one was home, but nothing happened. Really."

"Jesus, Meg, how could you? He calls only when he feels like it, he stands you up, he tells you about other girls he's seeing, he does drugs — I mean, come on."

"We made out for a little while. It wasn't anything."

Grace held her breath till her temples started to pound, trying to sort out what she was feeling.

"It scares me," Meg said finally.

"What does?"

"I think about you. A lot. I think about our night together."

Grace's mouth was dry, her heart was racing. She ought to be afraid, too, she knew, but her face was hot with joy.

"Grace," her mother called from the kitchen. "Dinner's ready. Get your brother."

"Okay, in a minute," Grace shouted back, barely keeping her irritation in check. "I have to go," she said into the phone.

"Yeah, well, merry Christmas."

"Wait! How am I going to call you?"

"You can't. I'll have to call you until she sends them something. Don't worry, I will."

"Meg?" Grace said. "Don't be scared. We want to be close to each other because we love each other. How could there be anything wrong with that?"

Grace could tell Meg was smiling. "True. Besides, I've been in worse trouble for less."

"Do you really like it?" Glen asked, leaning over the table so far that their empty dinner plates rattled.

"Of course, can't you tell?" Grace said, clasping the necklace, with its tiny brushed-gold heart, around her neck. Actually, it was a far more dainty piece of jewelry than Grace would have ever picked out for herself, but then, she wasn't entirely sure, either, how much Glen liked the wool sweater her mother had helped her pick out for him.

"Anything else here?" the waitress asked, smiling.

"No. I'll take the check," Glen said, looking handsome and adult in his new herringbone sports jacket. Her parents had noticed, too, when he came to pick her up; he shook her father's hand firmly as her mother whispered excitedly that she could have her curfew pushed to twelve-thirty for the night. She ought to have been beside herself with excitement, too, Grace knew, but she felt as though she were watching the whole scene happen to someone else, someone she didn't particularly envy.

"I want to pay for my share," Grace said when the waitress set the check down in a small plastic tray.

"No way. I told you it was part of my combination Christmas-New Year's-three-month-anniversary present," Glen said, reaching into his back pocket for his wallet. As he counted out the bills, moving his lips as he silently did the math, Grace tried to imagine them, ten years from now, an old married couple, having a routine dinner out. They would have a beautiful house, and when they got home, Glen would pay the babysitter who had watched their infant twins. The picture seemed so perfect and inviting that Grace was surprised to find herself wondering what had happened to the years between now and then. Had she had any adventures? Had she seen the world beyond Queens?

Glen drove them the few blocks to his house. He wasn't able yet to have a conversation while he drove, staring sternly out at the road in front of him, but he had clearly become a more skilled and confident driver over the last few months. When he pulled the car into the driveway, Grace saw that the house, with its flower pots under the front bay window, was dark.

"Aren't your parents home?"

"My parents? No, uh, they're visiting my grandparents for the weekend."

Grace heard the forced casualness in Glen's voice, and knew she'd been set up, though she was sure Glen would be wounded to hear her describe it that way. She nearly wished she could find him a girl to stand in for her during these moments, a girl he wouldn't have to apologize to.

Grace had never met Glen's parents before, or been to his house. When he pushed open the front door, she stepped into a large, airy living room with a white rug, beige leather couches, and a glass-top cocktail table. A small, conservative tree with red satin balls stood on top of the television, which had wooden panels that closed over the screen. It was not a house where an aluminum table would be produced from the basement for Thanksgiving dinner.

"You didn't tell me you were rich," Grace said. Glen took their coats and threw them down on the couch, where they slithered off the leather and landed on the rug.

"Because I'm not. My room's upstairs." He was so matter-of-fact, taking the stairs two at a time, that Grace was reluctant to protest.

Upstairs, the house was less intimidating. A tiny bathroom had damp towels hanging crookedly from racks, and the pile on the carpet was worn flat in the center of the hallway. Glen stepped into his small room and sat down on the bed. There was a desk under the window, and his closet door wasn't completely closed against the clutter of tennis rackets, sneakers, books, and balled-up jeans.

"Come here and let me see how the necklace looks up close," he said, holding out a hand. She walked over, and though he tugged at her arm, she wouldn't sit down. "Come on, Grace."

"Is that all you ever think about?" she said, pulling away. Her heart was beating hard now. She knew, in this predicament, the only thing she had to stop him was reason.

"You've never given us a chance at all," he said, his voice pinched with rejection. "If you just relaxed. I mean, don't you like me at all?"

She looked over and saw that there was a film of tears in his eyes. She sat down next to him gingerly. "I like you a lot," she said, her mouth going cottony. "I'm scared, that's all." It was not completely a lie; she was scared, but for reasons different from the ones she expected he imagined.

He took her hand, twisting to face her. "I know, but don't worry," he said, suddenly as eager as a car salesman. "It isn't scary at all. We'll go slow. Let's just take our shirts off —" He bolted up and switched off the light, unbuttoning his shirt as he went. In the dusk, she could see that his cheeks were flushed. He pulled his T-shirt over his head. Wordlessly, he took her hands and placed them on his bare shoulders.

"No, not if I'm expected — it's not the same," Grace said, putting her hands in her lap. "Guys have their shirts off all the time." She was angry that he was so willing to take advantage of her vulnerable position. But he didn't answer, and when he reached over and gently put her hands back on his shoulders, she didn't pull away.

He sat up very straight and didn't take his eyes off her face. She hadn't the slightest clue what he expected her to do, so she simply let her palms slide slowly down his chest, hairless and solid. She held her breath the whole way, and when she reached his waist, she pulled her hands away again.

"That felt really nice," he said. "Now you."

It had gotten too exhausting to say no, not just to him, but to herself, to whatever part of her was finally more afraid not to try. This was the whole point of love, she reminded herself, and even girls with morals were supposed to secretly crave the boy they were saying no to. She also knew, as Glen fumbled at the buttons of her blouse, that next time she would have to let him go further, and the next time, even further. It would be impossible to regain lost ground. She fought against a low-grade panic building in the hollow of her stomach, and sat impassively as he tugged her blouse free of her skirt, then expertly snapped open her bra.

At the last minute, she didn't allow him to completely take off her bra. Instead, she pulled it up to her throat, and stared hard at the ceiling as he fell on top of her on the bed. His earlier restraint abandoned him completely at the sight of her breasts; he seized on them as if he were afraid they might otherwise get away. She felt him panting against them, crushing them underneath him as he began a rhythmic thrust against her legs, which she had clamped together. As she watched him bucking against her, he reminded her of dogs she had seen get a death grip on a guest's leg and mortify their

111

owner. Suddenly, he jumped off and bolted from the room. By the time he returned, wearing different pants, she was all dressed again and ready to go.

Midterms greeted the juniors the week they returned from Christmas vacation. There was a feeling of unreality in the air, a hushed tension, as everyone moved solemnly through the halls. When the bell rang, signaling the end of Grace's European History final, she joined the rest of the group gathered outside the courtyard. It was a benign winter day; fresh snow lay on the ground but there was no bite in the air.

"I could have filled up the whole blue book with the first question alone," said Terry Cusack, a pasty-faced girl with a long auburn braid whom Grace normally never spoke to. "I mean, I have a cramp in my hand. She had to be kidding!" A few of the other girls grumbled in agreement, but Grace didn't have the energy to complain. She was just glad it was over. Her trigonometry final was tomorrow. Everything else paled by comparison.

Grace lingered anyway. Meg's chemistry exam was breaking next period and there was a chance she'd finish early. They both had to get home and study but they hadn't seen each other that morning and Grace felt uneasy and lonely. She kicked at the snow and listened half-heartedly to the conversation.

". . . oh, she's such a brown nose anyway," Terry was intoning again. Grace had missed which student they were crucifying now. "She thinks she's going to get extra points for smiling at her."

"With Sister Maria, she probably will," someone said. Dark laughter rippled through the group.

"Anne! Anne!" Grace called out as she spotted her friend hurrying down the courtyard steps, eyes to the ground.

"I definitely blew it," Anne said, mock-collapsing onto Grace's shoulder. "My French exam. In fact, I'm sure I set a new record. I'll just have to live with it," she sighed. "I'll never be able to order white wine with flair."

"I'm sure you did just fine," Grace said, steering Anne around the crowd. "You always think you failed something and then you ruin the curve for everyone else. You'll probably do better than I did on my Spanish."

"I've never done better than you in anything." Then she grinned and pulled a white ski cap over her hair. "Well, okay, when it comes to guys."

"Great. Let me know when the grades come in. What'd Rick get you for Christmas?"

"I'm wearing it," Anne said, unzipping her jacket to reveal an ankle bracelet around her neck.

"Jesus — two wings and two hearts. Engraved, too. You're practically married." Grace was impressed. Ankle bracelets had clout, and the more hearts and wings — the bars of gold surrounding the hearts — the more clout the necklace had.

"Yeah," Anne said, fingering it and trying to angle her head down low enough to see it around her neck. "I know you think he's a jerk, but he's really . . ." Anne shook her head and looked away. He's really very sweet."

A car pulled up to the curb behind them just then, "Rocket Man" blaring on the radio. Everyone

113

turned. This time, the car was close enough that Grace could clearly see Linda Amato at the wheel.

"Oh, don't look now," Terry Cusack said, dropping her voice to a raspy whisper, "but here come the lezzies."

The group exploded in laughter. "The lezzie brigade," someone else chimed in.

Anne nudged Grace hard with her elbow. "Hah, they should only know."

"What's that supposed to mean?" Grace said, as all her nerve endings snapped to attention.

"I mean our retreat adventure and nearly getting our asses kicked the hell out of here on her account," Anne said. "Or had you forgotten?"

"It's not right to be spreading rumors about people —"

"Rumors, what are you talking about — rumors?" Anne said, following Grace, who had headed away from the group. "It was plain as black and white, or yin and yang, as the case may be. You need to have that kind of thing notarized or something?"

"Okay, okay," Grace said. "but we were *there*. We're allowed to talk about it. They weren't. They don't deserve to have their gossip justified. They haven't got the slightest idea what the hell they're talking about."

"Hey — everybody likes Linda, anyway. No one meant any harm," Anne said. "What's it to you?" She grabbed Grace by the shoulder. "I'm asking you a question."

Grace turned and stopped, pounding her heel hard into the snow, over and over. "It's just — oh, shit, nothing. I'm just grouchy. You taking the train

114

back? I've got another chop-buster midterm tomorrow."

Anne looked at her steadily for several beats. "You sure?"

Grace nodded. Then they headed down the hill together to Hillside Avenue. Grace was grateful for the company. She wasn't sure why, but suddenly she didn't feel safe anywhere.

— 7 —

Grace and Meg stood in line waiting to get into Sacred Soldier's gymnasium for the first dance of the new semester. Even the hailstorm earlier hadn't kept away the crowd of Sacred Soldiers boys and Immaculate Blessing girls.

"So you're not supposed to dance with any guys?" Meg asked as they were squeezing through the door with the rest of the crowd.

Grace smirked. Glen was away for the weekend on a family tour of Washington, D.C. "I don't know, we didn't go into details. I think he was hoping I

116

wouldn't come at all." They joined the line for the coat check. "Did I tell you he invited me to come with them?"

"And stay in his room?"

"Very funny. No, I would have had a room with his sister. But I told him I asked my mother and she wouldn't let me."

"Good ol' Mom. She sure can come in handy sometimes."

"Well, if I had really asked her, she probably wouldn't have let me anyway," Grace said. They got their coat tickets and made their way down the harshly lit hall, past glass-encased displays of basketball and track trophies.

"Maybe she would if she had known you were going to spend the weekend with me instead."

"Don't get me started. I want to have a good time." Grace's face heated up all over again remembering how, yesterday, her mother had been in her room dusting when the phone rang. Grace didn't get to it soon enough, and her mother had answered. When she heard it was Meg, she gave the phone to Grace and announced, so Meg could hear, "It's her again. What happened, you're renewing your surliness lessons?"

But Grace gave herself over to a tingle of excitement when she stepped inside the gym. It was huge and dark, far darker than the nuns allowed Immaculate Blessing's cafeteria to be during their disastrous dances. Colored lights moved in swirls around the dance floor, which was slick with polish and gave the place a faint, waxy smell. The band, Stardust, a local favorite, had already begun pounding out a song by BTO. Swaying girls gathered under the

117

stage by the lead singer, a muscular young man all in black, with hair as long as theirs.

"Come on, let's dance," Meg said, taking Grace by the wrist and leading her onto the dance floor. In her black corduroys and a red knit sweater, Meg fell naturally into the rhythmic step. Grace, stiff and self-conscious, kept her eyes fixed alternately on her new gray boots and on a point in the distance over Meg's shoulders, so she could pretend to be absorbed by who was here, and with whom.

The band switched to a faster song with a driving bass line. Dancers all around were warming up rapidly. Grace, now damp with fear over looking awkward, took some comfort in watching several boys nearby doing box steps or breaking into spastic contortions.

"Let's do the bump," Meg said, grabbing Grace's hands. Grace was flooded with relief that she was reasonably good at this, having been taught by Anne over the summer. They turned in opposite directions and began to swing their hips in time, bumping against each other for several beats, then clapping, and starting again facing the other direction. "Down, go down," Meg shouted over the music, and they bent their knees and snaked their way to a crouch, meeting hips all the way. When the song was over, the crowd cheered the band on.

Grace recognized the first lazy piano notes of "Color My World," and a shriek went up from the group near the stage. Singles shuffled dejectedly to the sidelines, and Grace spotted Anne and Rick strolling confidently to the middle of the room.

"Hey, hi," Grace said, tapping Anne on the shoulder. Anne and Rick turned in unison, clamped

118

together at the waist by Rick's arm. Anne looked terrific in a royal-blue jumpsuit, her dark hair full and shiny down her back.

"Oh, hi! Behaving?"

"Badly, as always," Meg answered.

"Catch up with you later," Anne called as Rick, in the black satin shirt Grace recognized as Anne's Christmas present, pulled her onto the dance floor with a parting wave.

"He's such a dud. He's not even that cute. What does she see in him?" Meg led the way into the cafeteria. It took a moment for them to adjust their eyes to the normal light, and then they each bought a can of soda and claimed two chairs against the wall. "My God, that's Tom Impelizato," Grace said, straining forward in her seat. "And he's *alone*. I used to borrow Mark's yearbook and just stare at his picture." Tom, the star center of Sacred Soldiers' basketball team, had nearly gotten kicked off the team several times after brushes with the police for drinking and brawling.

"I thought I was the one who went for the wild type," Meg said, pouting into her compact mirror and reapplying her strawberry lip gloss.

Grace could hear the band's lead singer warbling the love song's repetitive lyric before trailing off to make way for the lethargic flute solo. That was usually the signal for the dancing couples to slow to a mere shuffle of bear hugs and sloppy kisses. And she realized all at once that she was not following Tom with her eyes. The flash of interest in him had seemed like a reflex, some holdover from another lifetime. Now it was extinguished simply, like a match being blown out.

She turned to Meg. "Speaking of the wild type, how's Lenny?"

Meg crisply snapped her compact shut and dropped it into a tiny purse that was clipped to her belt. "History," she said. "He stood me up again this afternoon."

A rush of adrenaline made Grace's cheeks hot. "I'm sorry," she said, struggling to sound sincere.

Meg leaned over to whisper in her ear. "Like hell you are." Goosebumps sprang up along Grace's arms as the two girls bent over together, laughing.

When the music turned fast again, they got up and started to make their way back out toward the dance floor. But suddenly there was a hand on her shoulder from behind. She whirled around.

"Grace! Surprised to see me?"

It was Glen, and surprise was not nearly a strong enough word. She was shocked speechless.

"I got bored with D.C.," he said, leaning over to kiss her on the lips, "so I convinced my dad to let me come back on the train by myself. I called your house and your mother said you did go to the dance — so here I am!" He was grinning proudly at her, as if he'd just announced that he'd accomplished some Houdini-like feat.

"Oh, well, that was *nice* of your mother," Meg hissed to Grace.

Grace felt her stomach go sour with dread. "Glen, uh, this is Meg. Meg, Glen." Grace felt Meg stiffen alongside her.

"Nice to meet you," Glen mumbled, and then grabbed Grace's hand. "Come on, let's go dance. And Rick told me he was gonna be here with Anne, too, so maybe we can find them." He started to tug her toward the dance floor.

"Wait!" Grace said to Meg's retreating back. But she had pressed into the crowd and out of sight in a matter of seconds. Panic and anger collided in her chest and gave her the courage to tear her hand free of Glen's grip. "What do you think you're *doing?*" she demanded. "You can't just barge in like this — you can't just, just *materialize* and expect me to drop everything just because you changed your plans at the last minute."

Glen's eyebrows shot up into his forehead. People brushed past them roughly as they packed the dance floor again. Finally, he laughed. "You're kidding, right? I mean, you're just here with some girl, right? I mean, unless you two have dates waiting for you somewhere." He scowled suspiciously at her.

"No, we *don't* have dates waiting somewhere. But I made plans with *her.* She happens to be my best friend, and I just won't drop her off to wander the dance alone now."

"I thought Anne was your best friend," he said, frowning. "Anyway, what's the damn big deal? I'm sure she's here to meet a guy, so let her go meet a guy. Really, you're too conscientious." He seized her hand again and tried to steer her into the swaying crowd.

"Well, of *course* she's here to meet a guy!"

"Okay, then, so forget about it. Aren't you glad to see me?" He wrapped her in a hug and started to kiss her hard.

She pushed him away. "Glen, *no.* I won't do it. I won't abandon her. You'll have to spend the night with the two of us, then. Now come help me find her."

He blinked at her in disbelief. Then his face became a red fist of anger. "Look, Grace, you're my *girlfriend,* and if you expect me to spend the night babysitting your friend instead of spending it alone with you, then maybe you shouldn't *be* my girlfriend."

His shouting had attracted the attention of a few onlookers and Grace fervently hoped Meg — but not Anne — was among them.

"There's a principle involved here," she said, her voice shaking with barely suppressed rage. "And if you can't see what's the right thing to do, then maybe *you* shouldn't be *my* boyfriend."

She was pushing through the crowd in the next moment, not allowing herself a second to feel contrite or to wonder at her recklessness. Even if he had been calling after her, she wouldn't have heard him over the boom of the music and her own panting. She rushed into the painfully bright hallway and headed directly into the bathroom. She had to find Meg.

She burst into the bathroom, startling one of the girls by the mirror into dropping her lipstick onto the counter. But Grace barely noticed. Meg was sitting on a cushioned bench, smoking.

"Shove over," Grace said, her heart still pounding with adrenaline.

"Where's your other half?"

Right here, Grace thought to say, but she couldn't, not here, not now. "I got rid of him. Told him I had other plans."

Meg took a deep drag and blew the smoke out in a long, deliberate breath. "You're not serious."

Grace thought she saw her bottom lip quiver slightly. "I absolutely am. I'm sorry you missed it." She quickly replayed the scene.

"That's crazy. You can't get away with that. You gotta go be with him." But there was no force of real persuasion in Meg's voice.

Just then, Anne pushed through the door. "*What* is going on, Molino? Glen just turned up — I thought you said he was away this weekend — and tells me, if I see you, to tell you that he left, so you can, and I quote, 'fulfill your obligations.'" She looked from Grace to Meg impatiently. "So what's going *on?*"

A slow smile crept up Meg's face and there was no mistaking the triumph in it. "Come on," Meg said, jumping up and throwing her arm conspiratorially around both Anne's and Grace's shoulders as she led them out of the bathroom. "Let me tell you the whole, sad story."

That set Meg and Grace laughing hysterically. Anne just looked on, shaking her head.

The dance ended at exactly eleven o'clock, and Meg and Grace headed out to the street to look for Mrs. Heinz. The block was jammed with double-parked cars, honking and jostling, all piloted by parents waiting to drive their sons and daughters home. Meg spotted her mother at the corner, working her way through a pack of Kents as she sat behind the wheel. They bounded into the back seat, giggling because they had finally escaped the gangly boy with glasses who had trailed them outside, pressing Meg for her phone number.

"And vat's so funny, girls?" Mrs. Heinz asked, turning around to smile, but also, Grace knew, to quickly examine them for signs of sin.

"Oh nothing, Ma," Meg said. "This car reeks," she added, rolling down the window and letting in the icy January air.

"Shut that vindow, I've got da heat on," Mrs. Heinz reprimanded. Meg obeyed, turning to smirk at Grace, who knew that Meg enjoyed pretending, in front of her mother, that she was offended by cigarette smoke.

"And so," Mrs. Heinz said, "do you have a new boyfriend now, Margaret?" Mrs. Heinz was the only one who called her "Margaret." It gave Grace a jolt of surprise every time she heard it.

"No, Ma," Meg said, rolling her eyes. "Do you?"

Grace turned to stare bug-eyed out the window. The urge to burst out laughing was getting the better of her.

"I bet *you* don't talk to your mother dis vay, with no respect," Mrs. Heinz said, glancing at Grace in the rearview mirror as she turned the car onto Main Street.

"Well, I —" Grace said, looking at Meg, totally at a loss.

"Grace doesn't talk to her mother at all anymore," Meg said casually. "They hate each other's guts." She bent over in laughter, making a kind of hiccuping sound.

"Silly child," Mrs. Heinz said, frowning into the mirror at her daughter and shaking her head.

* * * * *

It was one a.m. before the house was peaceful. Meg's brother, away at college on a wrestling scholarship in Arizona, had lost track of the time difference and called at midnight to say hello. Grace and Meg had sat up rehashing the night's events, whispering in the dark so Mrs. Heinz wouldn't hear them.

"I still can't get over how you told him off," Meg said, admiringly.

"I know. I kind of surprised myself." Actually, now that some of her bravado had worn off, she began to worry how much damage she might have done. But tonight, she wanted to push the thought of Glen away. "I think I pulled something in my neck when that jerk spun me around during that Chicago song," she said. "He was a prize."

"Turn around, I'll fix your neck," Meg said, sitting cross-legged on the bed behind her.

"Right here," Grace said, pointing. "Yeah, that's it." Meg's fingers were sure and skillful. Grace's back began to tingle under her touch.

"You know," Meg said after a few minutes, "I have a confession to make."

"What?"

"No, don't turn around," Meg ordered, holding Grace in place by her shoulders.

A jolt of fear passed through Grace's stomach. "Tell me already."

Meg paused. Grace heard her suck in her breath. "I thought about kissing you a long time before that night," she blurted. "I even wrote you a letter about it, when the phone was out."

125

Grace's throat went dry. "What did you write?" she asked carefully.

"Just that I — that I felt like kissing you. All over. Just like I do now."

Grace sat rigid with disbelief and awe. The room took on the surreal texture of dreams, because surely only in dreams did things like this, things that she wanted to hear more than anything, finally get said. Before Grace had a chance to reply, Meg swept her hair to one side and pressed her lips wetly against the back of her neck. Grace's stomach somersaulted, and a sweet low burn she recognized from her fantasies began between her legs. When she turned around, Meg's lips, tasting faintly of strawberry, were suddenly on her own, moist and open. Grace could hear her own heartbeat pounding in her ears, and a spasm of passion made her throat squeeze closed.

Meg tipped backwards, pulling Grace down on top of her. Then her hands were underneath Grace's pajama top, tracing a feather-light pattern up and down her spine, traveling out toward her sides. Grace pressed fully up against Meg, partly to reassure herself that this was really happening, and partly to answer her physical greed. When Meg pulled Grace's thigh down between her own legs, Grace knew instinctively what she wanted because, for the first time, she wanted it for herself, too.

"My God," Meg said, pulling away suddenly. "I'm going to pass out if we don't stop for a second." Meg closed her eyes and put a palm to her forehead.

Grace could feel Meg's chest heaving underneath her, and she rolled away. Then, summoning courage she didn't know she had, she kissed Meg's eyelid. "I love you," she whispered hoarsely. "More than anyone."

Meg opened her eyes, and she took Grace's face in her hands. Grace felt a new bolt of bravery; she knew she would do anything at all that Meg asked of her.

"It's bullshit what people say about this making us queer or something," Meg whispered, her voice shaking slightly. "Because I'm not queer, and I still feel this way about you."

"Absolutely," Grace said. "I mean, it's not the same thing at all. Homosexuals," she said, drawing the word out to its full five syllables, "have sexual desire for people of the same sex. Which means they feel this way about *everyone* of their own sex, and it happens even when they don't love them."

"Where'd you find all this out?" Meg asked.

"The dictionary. I looked it up. While your phone was out."

"Well, that doesn't apply here at all."

"No way."

"I don't think there's any word for what we feel," Meg said.

"Unh uh." But Grace didn't really care at all. Especially when Meg reached out for her again, tangling her hands in the back of her hair.

"You're so pretty," Meg said shyly. She was tracing a line down Grace's cheek, to her neck and then just barely under her pajama top along her collarbone. She locked eyes with Grace. "Is this making you feel," she said, her voice barely audible, "what I'm feeling?"

Grace was too frightened to speak. What could

she answer? What if Meg meant nothing, meant only
that she felt close and warm? Meanwhile, Grace felt
herself on fire from the inside, felt her thighs going
trembly and taut by turns.

"Is it making you —" Meg pressed her lips to
Grace's ear to whisper, "making you want me?"

Grace had to close her eyes; the room seemed to
be spinning out of control. She had no words. She
only pulled Meg closer to her, as if there were a
powerful force loose in the room that neither of
them could be trusted to face alone.

But Meg would not be pinned. She wedged a
small space between them and slipped her hand
under Grace's pajama top. At first Grace thought it
must be an accident, but gradually she knew it was
deliberate: Meg was working her hand, in studied
increments, up her side. Grace felt herself burning
with self-consciousness and desire. Meg paused for a
moment below the swell of Grace's breast, and then,
in one smooth gesture, moved her hand upward.
Grace sucked in her breath sharply, and then, unable
to tolerate any distance between them, pressed her
lips insistently to Meg's again. As their kisses gained
urgency, Grace felt Meg's thumb slide down and
begin to rock over her nipple, making it sharp and
hard with pleasure. How did Meg know exactly what
she wanted? Grace felt stunned with longing. But still
the questions bore through: How could they go on
from here? How could they not?

"I love you," Meg breathed against her cheek.
"That's why we're not queer. But God, you feel
good."

Grace agreed. Whatever Meg said, she would
agree.

* * * * *

"I have some really exciting news for all of us," Mrs. Molino said. She had made Grace and Mark sit on the living room couch, the plastic slipcovers squealing underneath them. Their grandmother was sitting on the loveseat, folding warm laundry fresh from the dryer. Her father came into the room and sank into the club chair.

Annoyed at being interrupted from the poem she had been working on for *Voices,* Grace wished her mother would just get on with it. She had been grinning at them from beside the television set for what seemed like hours.

"Your father and I have finally found the right house on Long Island and we'll be able to live the way we've all wanted to for so long. Everyone will have their own bedroom, there's a big backyard, the high school looks like a college campus — not to mention that you won't have to take the subway to get there —"

"You're not serious!" Grace said. It hardly seemed real, what her mother was saying. She and Mark had stopped going on the house-shopping expeditions over the last few years, and she thought her mother had resigned herself once and for all to Queens. Her mother's smile had vanished. Grace tried to feel some compassion for her but couldn't. How could she when this was clearly a premeditated act of cruelty?

"When are we moving?" Mark asked neutrally, and Grace shot him the most hateful look she could muster.

"Well, we knew it would be next to impossible to get you into another school midway through your

129

senior year," her father said, "so you'll finish out the year here, and we'll go right after your graduation."

"Oh, yeah?" Grace said. "And what about *my* graduation? What about the fact that I've been at Immaculate Blessing for three years and next year I'll finally be a senior and you're going to make me start all over somewhere else like a freshman and leave everyone I know behind." Grace was too choked up to continue for a moment. "What is it with you two, anyway?" she managed. "You're fixated on Long Island and those stupid houses, and all those stupid kids out there. You know the kids are stupid out there. Everybody knows city kids are smarter. Long Island kids don't go anywhere in life. The girls are cheerleaders and they become secretaries and —"

"There she goes again with that tone, Thomas! And what is wrong with being a secretary? *I'm* a secretary!" her mother shouted.

"Oh brother, round one," Mark said, slouching down into the couch, creasing the slipcovers as he went.

"Say a prayer, Mark," Grace's grandmother whispered.

"It's a nuthouse I'm living in," her mother yelled. "I'm telling you we're making a tremendous financial sacrifice to move us out to a neighborhood that's safer and cleaner, where there'll be lots of kids your age, where you'll have your own rooms, and a big house where you can have parties for your friends and this is the thanks I get?"

"What friends? I'm not going to have any friends. My friends are here," Grace shouted. Her face felt hot and swollen.

130

"Your friends here are what turned you into such a sour, moody, argumentative person — your friends and that know-it-all school where they tell you your mother is a dummy for being a secretary —"

"Enough already!" her father stood up to say. "We're going and that's it."

But her mother plowed on. "I can't *wait* to get you away from your precious friends. It'll be the best thing that ever happened to you. It's sick, the way you're always stuck together — if you're not over there living with her, you're on the phone —"

"Can I come back later?" Mark asked.

"Just shut up and pay attention," her mother said. "Everyone is going to love this house."

"In the name of the Father, the Son, and the Holy Ghost," Grace's grandmother was saying.

"I don't care where we live," Mark said, "as long as I have a place for my amps and guitar."

"You're not doing this for us," Grace leapt to her feet to scream. "You're doing it for yourself and you don't care how I feel at all!" She brushed past her mother and slammed her bedroom door behind her.

"For the love of sweet Jesus," Grace heard her grandmother say.

Grace sat cross-legged on her bed and buried her face in the pillow folded into her lap. Her sobs were dry and painful and her eyelids felt lined with sandpaper. She longed to call Meg but didn't dare; she knew her mother might barge in at any moment.

Gradually, she felt calmer, almost resigned, as if

she were a patriotic soldier being sent to the front, or a pioneer loading up the covered wagon and heading west. Nothing at all would ever keep her and Meg apart. How *dare* her mother think she could just step in and dictate her life. No one had ever been made to suffer so, Grace was sure. And why? Because of her mother's Long Island house fetish. For a kitchen with a built-in dishwasher and garbage disposal, her mother was ready to trade in her happiness. She could never, ever bear to be apart from Meg. The thought was unbearable. Grace's sobs came like hiccups.

Then she thought of the letter Meg had written while her phone was out, the letter she gave Grace when she was there last, the letter that was still as potent and amazing after scores of readings as it had been after the first. Grace knelt down and pried the letter out of her bottom dresser drawer, which was crammed with her own writing and other papers from *Voices*.

"Dear Grace," the letter began, in Meg's large-looped hand. "It's the day after Christmas and all I'd like is a damn phone that works so I can call you." Grace skipped over the chatty parts about Meg's family's holiday comings and goings. She knew exactly where the part was that sent a tingle from her scalp to her toes. "It scares me how much I think about you sometimes. I imagine you here with me (not there with you because your mother hates me) and we're under the Christmas tree and I'm kissing you . . . and kissing you. I don't know why it makes me feel so good. I've tried to think why but I can't. I can only *feel* why. Does this make any sense??? And then I think about touching you, and you touching me, I mean *all over,* and I just feel so full of love, and that's how I know it can't be queer and sick and stuff — because I know I'm not that way — and then I think we must have invented something pretty special between us that no one else would understand."

"Grace?" Her mother knocked lightly on the door.

"Just a minute!" Grace yelled, stuffing the letter back into the drawer and slamming it shut, narrowly missing her fingers, just as her mother walked in.

"Can I sit down?" her mother asked, sitting.

Grace moved as far away as she could without straddling the headboard. For a while, they both stared at the floor and said nothing.

"I'm not making you any promises, Grace, but I want you to know that your father and I will think things over. But the real estate people need a firm commitment by next weekend."

Hope made Grace's heart lurch, and for a second, she wanted to throw her arms around her mother in gratitude and love. But she stopped herself. No guarantees, she had said. She was still technically the enemy.

"Did you hear me, Grace?"

"Uh huh," Grace said with a loud sniffle.

"Here," her mother said, handing her a tissue, warm from her housedress pocket. "But I have to know, Grace, why you're so dead set against this."

Grace noisily blew her nose and frantically tried to think of the answer that would save her and Meg.

"I know the schools out there aren't Catholic," her mother said, "but they're just as good — that's

133

why the taxes we'll be paying are so high. They're nothing like the public schools in the city."

There was that tone again, Grace thought, like the move was already a fact. She couldn't let her guard down, couldn't afford to make a mistake now.

"I know it'll be hard at first," her mother went on, "being the new kid in town, but it's different out there. People are friendlier. And you won't be so far away that you couldn't ever see your friends from here again. Dad could always drive you, and there's the railroad. But I think if you just gave it a chance, you'd see there was no reason at all to come back into the city."

The room was swimming in front of Grace's eyes again, and she thought her chest would split in half from holding back the sobs trapped there. But she would not allow herself to cry in front of her mother.

"Grace, I — it breaks my heart to see you so miserable, and I just don't understand it. I want us to be a family, to want the same things —"

"*Why* do we have to want the same things?" Grace said in a strangled voice. "We're not the same people." Her mother blinked at her, like someone knocked off balance. Grace regretted her words; she hadn't meant to sound as though she didn't understand at all what her mother was saying. But she didn't have the energy to defend herself and also apologize.

"I don't know when you grew so far from me, Grace." Her mother got up and turned her back, her voice wobbly. "I don't know why it's so repugnant to you to want the same things I do. And I don't know where you got the idea that I want to hurt you. Why can't you see that I'm doing this because I love you, and because it would be a good thing for all of us?"

Grace hugged the pillow tightly against her, trembling. She willed herself not to cry, willed her mother not to take a step closer. More than anything, she couldn't bear her mother's compassion, couldn't bear the possibility of her kindness when she was willing herself to hate her. Because Grace felt her mother had made it clear: Grace couldn't love both her and Meg at the same time.

"If this is all over that stupid girl, Grace," her mother said, angry again in the face of her daughter's stony silence, "you just better knock it off. You act like you're the first person in the world who ever had a friend."

"What would you care? You don't have any friends. You just have us."

"And the same thing will happen to you too, when you get older, Grace, and have a job and children and a lot of other things to worry about. Don't make the mistake of thinking you'll be different. Friends don't last. But your family will always be your family."

Grace saw the debate slipping away from her and she got hold of herself. "You're the one who taught me to push myself to be the best I could, Ma. Don't you remember how great it was that night we went to Immaculate Blessing's open house together?" Grace knew she didn't have to remind her mother that *she* was the one who had been so anxious to please, the one who had cornered nun after nun to put in a good word for Grace. "Remember how you told me a good education was the one thing that you never had that you wanted to be able to give me? You know all the best colleges recruit first from Immaculate Blessing's seniors. Now you're telling me nothing is more important than an extra bathroom and a bigger backyard. But what I want," Grace said, suddenly flashing on pictures of herself in biology lab, in the social studies resource center debating the merits of a two-party system, in her Shakespeare class, writing her hand into a cramp explaining the theme of *Othello,* "is a bigger future, a bigger life. It's too late to trade all that for a football field."

Her mother stared. When she finally spoke, Grace was terrified she'd start crying. "Did I make you want all those things, Grace? Where along the way did I teach you to put your family last? How could I have imagined an education would make you think we were too small and narrow-minded for you? Don't think I'm not proud, Grace —" her mother said, her voice breaking, "— of what you're making of yourself. I just never thought your dreams would take you places where there was no room for things I wanted for you too."

Her mother gently blew her nose. Grace was torn up inside. *Mommy, don't cry!* an unacceptable voice somewhere inside her called out. But she sat silent, trapped in her own confused misery. It would take more courage than she knew how to muster to say the things that mattered most.

"Well," her mother said, "we'll see." Then she turned and walked out, leaving the bedroom door open behind her.

− 8 −

Grace's fingers were burning inside her soaked mittens. She and Glen had been working for two hours on the snowman in his front yard. The storm last night had stopped just short of dumping enough inches to get classes canceled. Still, hardly anyone had been able to concentrate all day on anything much but snowball fights, sledding parties, and the plain old high-spirited clowning that only calf-deep snow could elicit. When Glen had shown up outside Immaculate Blessing with the announcement that they were going to build a snowman together, Grace didn't hesitate.

"I think he's ready," Glen said, stepping back and narrowing his eyes critically at the snowman. He had shown an engineer's passion for getting the three balls of the body in perfect proportion, and had refused to be distracted when Grace stuffed snowballs down his back or raced away to track up the fresh snow on lawns in front of houses where no one had come home yet.

Glen reached into a brown bag he had brought along and pulled out a shiny black plastic derby. "Now all we have to do is use these two twigs as nails," he said, fixing the hat on the snowman's head, and boring the twigs into holes in the hat's brim. "How's that?"

Grace frowned. "No. Needs more of an angle."

Glen made the adjustment. "Here. You do the buttons."

In her bulky mittens, Grace had a hard time handling the big slippery buttons, but she pressed them as best she could into the snowman's stomach, hearing the satisfying squeak they made as they bit into the hard-packed snow.

"Now his scarf," Glen said, running around the snowman to wrap it, muffler-style, around its throat. "Another twig nail in the back here," he said, "and we're all set."

Glen put his arm around Grace as he stood appraising their work. "The first thing we made together," he said, grinning lewdly at her.

"Very funny," Grace said, breaking free and scooping up some snow to throw at him.

Glen pushed up the bulky sleeve of his coat to look at his watch. "Come on, let's go in and get warmed up. I can't feel my feet anymore."

He led them inside through a side door so they could deposit their snow-caked boots and wet jackets in the well at the top of the basement stairs. "Hot chocolate?" he asked.

"Okay, but then I really have to go," Grace said, sitting down at the table in the gold and brown kitchen.

"Can't you stay for dinner? My mom said I could ask you." He positioned the mouth of the teakettle under the kitchen faucet.

"No, my mother'll be mad. I have to let her know way ahead of time if I'm not going to make dinner." The truth was, the idea of meeting Glen's parents filled her with dread. First of all, it would somehow implicate her more deeply than she cared to be. And besides, they intimidated her: his father was a lawyer and his mother worked for a public relations company in Manhattan. Most of the mothers Grace knew worked at the mall; the ambitious ones had secretarial jobs.

"What do you think your parents will decide about moving?" Glen asked as he poured boiling water into two mugs waiting with hot cocoa mix.

"I don't want to think about it," Grace said. The deadline was just two days away and her mother hadn't given any clues. But she had heard her parents up late, whispering in their room.

"Well, don't worry. I'm coming to see you wherever you live. Unless you start going out with the captain of the football team or something."

"I wouldn't worry about that." She blew on the steaming mug, greedy for a sip, and made a mental note to tell Meg that one.

"I'm glad," he said, squeezing her hand.

"Careful. It still stings from the cold."

"Best thing is to warm it with body heat." Glen dragged his chair over next to hers and, to her alarm, slid both her hands underneath his sweatshirt. Her hands throbbed against his damp chest.

"Thanks," she said, curtly, taking her hands away and reaching for her mug.

"What about mine?"

Grace's throat tightened as she let the steam float like a dewy cloud over her face. "Go ahead, put them under your sweatshirt, too."

"Cute," he said, grinning, grabbing at her waist.

"Stop! You're tickling me!" Grace squealed as she wormed away from him.

His eyes were darting and he was leaning forward determinedly in his chair. "Come on, let's go upstairs."

"Glen, I really have to go."

"Come on," he said, and she heard it as an ultimatum. He held her hand on the way up the stairs. Her mind was racing. All she could think of was escape.

He led her into his room and put his *Yellow Brick Road* album on the turntable. Someone had straightened up his closet since the last time she'd been here, and in the sunlight, the room looked bigger and cleaner. "Wait here," he said as he left the room.

Grace weighed her options. She could walk back down the stairs and out the front door to the subway. That would probably mean they would be officially broken up. She could stay and insist that this avenue of exploration be stopped immediately. That would also probably mean they would break up. She could stay and get through it, and hope some combination of decency and restraint kept it within reasonable limits. She could tell him the truth, but what was that exactly? That being alone with him held for her about the same appeal as a visit to the dentist, and the only time she felt what he wanted her to feel was when she was with Meg?

"Hi, I'm back," Glen said. She whirled around. He was in the doorway, wearing only his underpants.

Grace leaned heavily against the desk. He was milky white from head to toe. Fine blond fur covered his legs from the thighs down, curling up around his ankles. Grace tried to tell herself that she was seeing no more than she had ever seen on a public beach, but there was something so intimate about the whiteness of his underwear, its thin cotton allowing a bold outline of the mysterious shape beneath, that she knew this wasn't true.

In a few long strides, he was across the room and in front of her, tugging her sweater up over her head. Panic was pounding in her ears and her face was hot with stifled protest. She struggled to cover her breasts with her arms, but he was faster, and he managed to yank down one cup of her bra and mash his lips against her nipple. A stab of pain shot through her body and she cried out.

"Shhhh, the neighbors will hear you," Glen said, smiling, obviously mistaking her cry for one of pleasure.

She tried to squirm away but he caught her wrist

and pushed her hand down below his waist. His chest was sweaty against her as Elton John wailed nasally in the background. Then she heard the snap of an elastic waistband and felt her knuckles graze a tangle of wiry hair. Grace squeezed her eyes shut tightly and tried to brace herself as if she were on a roller coaster about to careen off the track.

"Hey, anybody home?" a woman's voice called suddenly from downstairs. "Who built the great snowman? Glen? They sent us home early because of the snow —" the voice said as it headed deeper into the house.

"Jesus H. Christ on a raft," Glen said, his voice raspy with anger. Grace opened her eyes in time to see his splotchy rear end, with his bleached-white underwear hooked underneath, retreating swiftly and awkwardly from the room.

"You have to go in," Grace told Meg as they stood outside the heavy oak doors of the auditorium between classes. "It's your last chance." The tryout schedule for the choir had been posted since Monday. Today was the last day.

"I know, I know," Meg said, her hand on the brass doorknob. "If I don't try, I'll never know for sure." Grace had been coaching her all week.

"There's no reason to be afraid. You have a beautiful voice. It gives me goosebumps."

Meg turned and smiled slyly. "That's not all that gives you goosebumps."

"Stop trying to distract me," Grace said, glancing around nervously as a swell of students strolled back and forth in both directions, gossiping, exchanging papers, pausing in groups to chat. "You know you can do it, Meg. God, think of how great it'll be. By next year you'll have a solo —"

"Yeah, and you'll be at your school on Long Island."

"Stop saying that. My mother hasn't decided yet. Besides," Grace said, dropping her voice to a whisper, "I'd travel to the ends of the earth to hear you."

"Would you?"

Grace met Meg's green-gold eyes head on. "You know I would."

"I'm afraid," Meg said, looking away. "I don't think I could stand it if McClancy turned me down."

"But how can you stand not trying? How can you stand the idea that you have this talent and it's going to waste because you're too afraid to try?"

"Because I'm afraid of the rejection more."

"Are you sure you aren't afraid to succeed?"

"Don't be ridiculous." Meg folded her arms across her chest.

"I'm not. I wouldn't tell you to go for it if I didn't think you had at least a reasonable chance. And I think you're going to blow the Bulldog right off her little navy pumps. The only thing left for you to be afraid of is being heard — and being admired. I don't know, maybe that's your problem."

"Don't look at me that way," Meg said.

"What way?"

"Like I've let you down. I never want to let you down."

"I want you to want this for yourself," Grace said, nearly reaching out for Meg's hand but stopping herself. "Nobody can make you feel what you have to feel to take a risk."

"Excuse me," a sophomore said, stopping in front of them. "I need to get by."

"Oh. Yeah," Grace said, adopting the slightly condescending tone used for addressing underclassmen. She stepped aside to let the girl open the door. When she did, another girl's clear, crisp voice was riding up and down the scales. The door swung shut against the sounds.

"I'm not leaving till you go in there," Grace said. "If you want, I'll even cut my class and go in with you."

"No, I don't want you to do that. I couldn't stand it if she said something humiliating while you were there. Go to your class," Meg said, throwing open the door.

"No, no, no, *no!*" Sister Margaret McClancy was booming.

Grace saw Meg blanch but she gave Grace a brave smile and headed down the aisle before the door swung shut behind her.

The meeting had gone exceptionally well, Grace thought, not without some pride. She had spent the last few weeks visiting homerooms in the morning, asking for prose, poetry and art submissions for *Voices,* the deadline being late March. There were already several possibilities for cover art — Grace was leaning toward one of the line drawings, since last

144

year's cover was a photograph. And best of all, Sister Mary Alice had made the announcement that since there was the unusual circumstance of no seniors on staff this year, Grace was acting editor-in-chief, to be made final pending her performance. Grace considered the trial period purely a formality.

"I haven't seen any more submissions from you, Grace, since our last discussion," Sister Mary Alice said as the rest of the staff filed out of the room.

"I've been working on some things," Grace said, blushing violently, "but nothing's ready yet." After a numbing exercise toying with poems about music and nature, Grace had gone back to her usual theme of star-crossed lovers. These were only more, not less, of everything Sister had disapproved of before. Grace was beginning to despair that she wouldn't have the nerve to show the nun anything again.

"I know how dedicated you are, Grace, and I have no doubt that you'll produce something quite stirring," Sister said.

"Yes, well, I — that's my goal," Grace said, blushing a shade deeper.

"You might find," Sister went on, gathering up her papers, "that if you need some inspiration, there's little poetry more beautiful than in Psalms. And of course, there's always the Song of Solomon. 'Rise up, my love, my fair one, and come away,' " Sister recited reverently, looking out the window across the courtyard. " 'For, lo, the winter is past, the rain is over and gone, the flowers appear on the earth, the time of the singing birds has come.' " She turned and looked at Grace with a shy smile. " 'My beloved is mine, and I am his. He feedeth among the lilies until the day break and the shadows flee away.' ''

Silence vibrated between them. "That's from the Bible?" Grace said finally.

Sister nodded. "Of course. It's about God's love for his people," she said, heading for the hallway. "I realize you're trying to reach your peers with *Voices,* Grace, but I'm merely trying to make the point that there's more than one way to do that."

Do *you* love anyone, Sister, Grace burned to ask, as she fell into step alongside the lithe, sweet-smelling nun. And if you do, how do you bear not being able to do a thing about it? A vow of celibacy would be like being buried alive, Grace thought, like being shut off from what was best about being human.

"Well?" Sister said, resting a hand on Grace's shoulder as they paused at the doors to the courtyard. The hall was warm with the afternoon's fading sun, and a kind of dignity, palpable only when the stream of students wasn't rushing through the place, could be felt.

"Uh, yes," Grace said. "I'll think about what you said." A burst of January air hit her as she pushed the door open.

Anne was sprawled across her bed on her stomach, hugging a pillow beneath her. Grace sat on the floor, braiding the blue and white tendrils of the shag rug.

"Rick came over for dinner last night," Anne said. Grace looked up. "You're kidding? How'd it go?"

146

Grace knew well that Anne's mother did not believe in encouraging Anne's boyfriends, and in the year and a half that she had been dating Rick, Anne's parents hadn't said more than polite hellos to him.

Anne rested her chin on her fist thoughtfully. "Pretty well, I guess. I mean, he dropped his fork on the rug once, and he didn't really say much, but they seemed to think he was okay." She flashed Grace a wicked grin. "Then we went downstairs to watch TV and cop some feels."

"You're a certified maniac. Weren't you afraid they'd come down?"

"Nah. I was more concerned about what was coming up." She wagged her eyebrows lasciviously.

"Very funny," Grace said, continuing her line of braids across the rug like a long stitch.

"I hear you and Glen are getting to know each other," Anne said in a taunting sing-song.

"What's *that* supposed to mean?" Grace said, her face hot.

"Come on. Glen tells Rick everything and Rick tells me everything. I heard about the huddle up in Glen's room the day after the snowstorm."

Grace's mind was racing. What exactly had Glen told, and how had he told it? She felt ill over the possibilities. Had he described it as the ambush that it was, or painted it as some tryst between sex-starved lovers united at last?

"Well," Anne continued, "I thought you might want to carry a few of these around, like I do." She tossed a small foil package into Grace's lap. "It's a rubber — in case things, you know, get out of hand, so to speak."

Grace picked it up and knew immediately she

147

wanted nothing at all to do with it. "Why? Are you guys, I mean —"

"Filling those up?" Anne said in a hoarse whisper, giggling. "Not yet, but let's just say I've got plenty to confess as it is. And it sounds like you're catching up, Molino."

Grace felt her stomach clench; she didn't want to talk about it another second. Talking about it would mean having to say how she really felt about Glen — and by extension, Meg — and that was out of the question. "Just for the record," Grace said, "I don't hear anything from Glen about you and Rick."

"You don't have to," Anne said, sitting up, suddenly angry. "*I* tell you everything. And you don't tell me anything anymore. Do you think I like having to find out what's going on in my best friend's life secondhand from her *boy*friend? You're too busy telling everything to Meg, I guess, and God knows what else."

"What's *that* supposed to mean?" Grace said, trembling slightly, unprepared for Anne's anger, and unable to summon enough of her own. She felt like she was trying to run underwater.

"Come off it, Grace," Anne said disgustedly, rolling onto her back. "Everybody's noticed. It's kind of weird, you and Meg. When you're together, it's like there's this bubble around the two of you and nobody else is invited in."

"Ha! and now you're feeling left out?" Grace said, her hands suddenly clammy. She got to her feet and began to pace. "Did you forget how many times you canceled on me when you and Rick started going out?"

"It's not the same thing. At all. Besides, you're

going out with Glen now. We should have *more* to talk about than ever. But it's like you're a million miles away."

Grace's heart felt swollen in her chest. How could she begin to explain to Anne something she couldn't make sense of herself? Besides, she liked things the way they were — her and Meg's private little world. "What else does Glen say about me?"

Anne continued scowling a few moments longer and then, as Grace knew she would, she caved in to the temptation to gossip. "He doesn't know how to turn you on. He says you always act like you're getting open-heart surgery without an anesthetic whenever he lays a hand on you."

"Goddamn him!" Grace said, kicking wildly. She caught her toe on the metal leg of Anne's bed and began to howl, sinking to the floor, clutching her foot and rocking in pain. When Anne crawled over and put her arm around her, Grace allowed herself to sob, feeling a huge knot of grief in her chest uncoil.

"Is it broken?" Anne said, prying Grace's fingers. She carefully wiggled each toe while Grace winced. "I think you've cleared Code Blue."

"Very funny," Grace said, straining for a martyred tone but feeling giggles creep up on her. Soon the two were swaying in laughter on the rug, side by side.

"So what was it that pissed you off so much?"

"What Glen said. You know," Grace said, wiping her cheeks, "it would never occur to him to try to do anything to get me to like it. He just reaches over and grabs whatever's handy."

"Yeah," Anne said, "Rick used to be like that. But then," she said, laughing, "so did I. You've got to

149

get him to calm down a bit and then teach him a thing or two. They're very trainable once you get their attention."

Grace sighed, feeling the knot growing back. "No, you don't understand." She got up and sat on the bed, quickly dragging a finger under her nose. "I'm not sure it's really his fault anyway. I don't know if anything would help in my case."

"Don't be ridiculous," Anne said. "Everybody's got a sex drive, and once you get yours in gear, you're going to wonder how you ever did without it."

"I looked at the list of McClancy's cuts for choir," Grace said, as soon as they closed the door of Meg's room behind them. "They were posted right after lunch."

"I know. I saw her put it up," Meg said, sitting on the bed.

Grace watched Meg, in a black corduroy vest over a pale blue blouse, as she folded her arms tightly across her chest. Meg's name was not on the list. Grace had read it over at least a dozen times. "I — I'm really sorry," Grace said. "I feel terrible. I shouldn't have pushed you if you weren't ready. I don't understand. I could kill her, though, I —"

"Grace, Grace, stop," Meg said, covering her face. "I didn't even try out."

Grace stared, her face stony with disbelief. "What do you mean, you didn't try out? I was there, I saw you go in."

"I waited till you were gone and then I walked right back out. I lost my nerve."

Grace's mind was racing. Was this a new lie? Had Meg really tried out but was too mortified to admit she hadn't been chosen? Which was worse? "You're serious?"

Meg nodded and looked out the window. "You hate me, don't you? You think I'm a coward."

Grace was numb. She sat down next to her.

"If it makes you feel any better, you were right," Meg said. "I kept reading the list of names and thinking, I can sing better than they can. I've got a better voice than Elizabeth Healy or Nancy Maggio. But," she said, shaking her head, "I didn't feel that way before the tryouts. It's a curse, feeling this way."

"I never should have left," Grace said, angrily pounding her fist on the bed. "I should have marched you right down that aisle and — what's so funny?"

"Nothing." Meg gave her a little shove. "Just an interesting choice of words."

Grace paused, then blushed hotly. "All I meant was, I should have stayed with you, made sure I was there to support you. I —"

Meg put her finger to Grace's lips. "No. If you could have done the singing for me, I know you would have. I had to do it myself, and I couldn't. I'm not like you that way. You're sure of yourself. You don't let people push you around."

Grace stared. "You really think so?"

"Totally. I wish I . . . . You have no idea."

Grace stared at her feet in embarrassed silence. "No, you got it backwards. You're the one people want to be around, at school, at dances. When I first met you, all I wanted was to be even a little bit like you."

151

"Don't be a jerk."

"Don't make me mad," Grace said, getting up. "I hate it when you talk like that. You sound just like your mother — all the things you *can't* do. Don't buy her crap. You *are* smart. You just gotta stop putting yourself down." Grace sat back down, her throat tight with proprietary pride. She took Meg's hand.

"I couldn't stand it if you ever stopped loving me," Meg whispered.

"I never will." Fired by her conviction, Grace took Meg's face between her hands and began to kiss her more confidently than she had before. She slid her hand under Meg's vest and began to stroke her breast.

"Let's get rid of these blouses," Meg pulled away to say, her voice hushed, nearly desperate. She unbuttoned her own first, quickly unsnapping her bra, and then turned her attention to Grace's blouse, pulling it free of her skirt. As she deftly slid the blouse and her bra off Grace's shoulders, Grace felt every nerve ending in her body come to life.

Meg gently pushed Grace back onto the bed, and lay next to her, brushing her cheek, then her lips and finally her tongue, leisurely and urgently by turns, over her breasts and nipples. *How does she always know exactly what I want?* Grace screamed inside, her heart beating frantically, erotically, as if unable to contain her body's pleasure. She watched the concentration on Meg's face, and then, shyness giving way to desire, she tipped Meg over so that she could drink in the look of her breasts, larger and more womanly than her own, Grace observed with overwhelming longing.

She rolled over so that Meg was underneath her

now, and she kneeled over her so that she could brush her own breasts against Meg's, marvel at the sight of their nipples, darkened and hard, grazing each other's. And then she felt Meg's hand, warm and tentative, on the inside of her thigh. It was as if a three-alarm fire started in her groin, and she thought she might pass out. Never before had they allowed themselves to venture below the waist, and Grace was speechless again at Meg's boldness, awed by the passion she must have been heeding in order to always be the first to take such risks. She couldn't bear to meet Meg's eyes, so she inched up slightly and kissed her again, opening her mouth over her lips and tongue with greedy force.

She felt her body not as divided into limbs and torso, but as one single plane of sensation, completely at Meg's mercy. And yet, it was Meg's hand on her inner thigh that was the center of all sensation now, as Meg moved it, with extreme caution, further and further up along her stockings, under her skirt. With every inch, Grace felt her stomach constrict in a clash between fear and impatience. She was violently torn between wanting and not wanting Meg's fingers to find that secret, virginal place that pulsed with an urgency she had never before experienced.

But then, in an instant, Meg moved her hand away and pulled Grace down on top of her in a crushing hug. For another hour, they lay against each other, kissing their lips red and fondling their breasts tender. They had scared themselves — but just for the moment, Grace thought giddily. She felt sure they were on the brink of some greater, yet unknown, discovery.

* * * * *

Grace neatly trimmed the fat off the edges of her lamb chop. The bright white kitchen was steamy from the night's cooking, and her grandmother was, as usual, periodically sneaking up to quietly begin washing the pots and pans.

"Well," her mother said, tapping her glass with a fork to get her family's attention, "we've made a decision about the move."

The meat turned to sawdust in Grace's mouth, and she sat paralyzed. She watched, incredulous, as Mark continued eating, oblivious.

"Your father and I have talked about this a lot," her mother went on, catching Grace's eye and then quickly looking away. "We realized that someone was going to have to make some sacrifice, some compromise. But we thought it was important to make the decision that would make as many of us as happy as possible." Waves of adrenaline were washing over Grace's body, making her tremble slightly. "So what we've decided," her mother said, looking straight at her, "is to wait until Grace has graduated before we seriously start looking for a house again. We know you'll only be able to graduate from Immaculate Blessing once in life," her mother said, "but there'll always be another house. And . . ."

Grace barely heard the rest of what her mother was saying. Hosannas were dancing a chorus line in her head. She wanted to push away from the table like a rocket bursting through the stratosphere. ". . . I expect you to make some effort to meet us halfway . . ." Life was sweet, life was good, she would never be miserable again. ". . . to realize that we've put ourselves last here . . ." She and Meg really would go to the senior prom together, graduate together, then maybe even go to the same college and room together. ". . . some changes in your attitude as a way of showing gratitude . . ." Yes, yes, gratitude, Grace told herself, abandoning her plate and going over to kiss her parents hurriedly. Then, propelled by some energy outside herself, she was around the corner with her hand on the phone, dialing the number she knew by heart.

— 9 —

Grace watched Meg press the halved bagels flat and drop them into the toaster, like letters into a mail slot.

"Are you sure you're going to be able to get those out of there?" Grace asked warily.

"They'll be fine." Meg pushed the handle down. "My mother does it this way all the time — and God knows, that's good enough for me."

The girls laughed, and Grace leaned back happily in her chair. When Mrs. Heinz wasn't around, Grace pretended that this was their house, hers and Meg's, and now, they were preparing one of their many meals together.

"What are you thinking?" Meg said, coming over and pinning Grace's hands to her sides before she began kissing her neck mercilessly. Then she stopped abruptly, leaving Grace slightly breathless. "And what are you thinking about now?"

Grace got up and cast a sidelong glance at the progress of the bagels before slipping her arms around Meg's waist. "About how furious Glen would be if he knew. He must think I'm frigid."

Meg smiled half-heartedly, and Grace felt a nervous flutter in her throat.

"What's wrong? What'd I say?" Grace asked.

Meg went over and unplugged the toaster and began wrestling with a knife to pry the bagels free. Grace seized her wrist. "Stop that and answer me."

Meg leaned against the counter and refused to look up. "I have no right."

"No right what? What are you talking about, damn it."

"I can't kiss you anymore," Meg whispered, "not if I know you're still kissing him." It took a few minutes before the words translated from mere sounds to meaning in Grace's confused mind. "I just can't share you," Meg said, leaning against Grace's shoulder, trembling as if after great physical strain.

Grace inhaled the sweet scent of Meg's hair and kissed her warm forehead. It had never occurred to her that she could choose between them, because she had never allowed herself to admit that they were in the same category, that they applied to the same yearning — though one satisfied and the other didn't. What she felt with Meg had, until now, always seemed to exist on some alien plane; it was possible to go there, and still keep the rest of her life intact. Now Meg's simple request laid the charade bare, sent the whole house of cards tumbling.

"I won't let anything stop you from kissing me," Grace said, finding Meg's lips. Her mind was made up. Now all she had to do was take action.

Grace had been sick with dread since she got home from school. Her mother was moving around the house in a barely suppressed fury. Immediately, Grace went into her room and shut her door under the pretense of changing clothes. She feared the worst. Her heart pounding, she rifled through her bottom dresser drawer, scraping her knuckles raw against the wood in her frenzy. When she saw that Meg's letters and Christmas card, plus some drafts of her own poems with their thinly disguised references, were nowhere to be found, she sat down shakily on the edge of her bed. Her mouth was dry, her underarms damp, and tiny dots of color danced nauseatingly in front of her eyes. Numbly, she dialed Meg.

"Are you sure they're gone?" Meg asked, her voice rigid with fear in a way Grace had never heard before. "Of all the rotten, vile things to do, go digging through your private stuff —"

"What are we going to do?" Grace asked, too terrified even to cry. Already, though, at the sound of Meg's voice, the faint outlines of protest were beginning to form in her mind. Why did she have to be afraid of admitting to her mother that she loved

Meg? Because she knew now with sickening certainty that the letters were the cause of her mother's anger.

"Whatever you do, just get through tonight," Meg said. "Don't let her put crazy thoughts in your head, like signing up for shock therapy or something. And if we have to, we'll just run away. You and me, Grace."

Meg's promise in her head was the only thing that got her through dinner, waiting for the confrontation. After the dishes were washed, her mother went systematically around the house, turning down all the lights, sending Mark down to the basement to practice his guitar, and taking both phones off the hook. "In," she said to Grace through gritted teeth, pointing to her own bedroom, shutting the door behind them.

Her mother yanked open her dresser drawer so hard it nearly fell out, and clenched the familiar papers in her fist, holding them up in front of Grace's face. "Is this girl a *lesbian?*" her mother shouted, her face so inflamed with anger — her cheeks purplish, her mouth twisting, the blood vessels in her forehead standing up — that Grace barely recognized her. The word, wielded like a weapon, struck Grace like a physical assault. She hadn't expected the blow to be so swift and ugly, and she felt suddenly unsteady on her feet. All at once she was shaking with sobs.

"It's true, then, isn't it? *Isn't* it?" her mother screeched, coming closer. Grace curled up and covered her head with her arms.

"And these poems of yours — soft lips and breasts and God knows what other pornography — I suppose you're a lesbian, now, too?" Her mother was circling

159

like a vulture. "Is that right?" She grabbed Grace by the shoulders. "Sit up straight and tell me it isn't true."

To Grace's amazement, when she looked up, there were tears in her mother's eyes, too. "Don't make me not see her anymore, please," Grace pleaded, knowing it was the last thing her mother wanted to hear, but unable to fight for anything else.

"Is this how you've abused my trust?" Her mother reached for the bed as if she suddenly didn't have the strength to stand. "Is this the thanks I get for putting you first? For treating you as an adult and thinking you were able to decide on your own what was good for you? If I hadn't listened to what you had to say, we'd be living far away from this sick girl now."

Her mother went on and on, working her way up and down a scale of rage, charging her with an inexhaustible list of evils and perversities. Grace was soon numb, and though she saw her mother's mouth moving, she no longer heard exactly what was being said. Instead, she hugged herself, crying till her throat was raw, imagining that Meg was sitting at her own house, keeping a kind of vigil. Silently, she repeated like a chant Meg's promise of escape, rehearsing in her head the embrace Meg would give her when they saw each other again.

"It's not how it seems, Ma," Grace found the energy to interject at long last. "We love each other and —"

"I don't want to hear any more of this obscenity. It was bad enough I had to read it. This is what higher education is all about, this is the kind of girl it attracts? I'd like to let those pious nuns have a piece of my mind —"

"No! You can't —"

"I won't have this, Grace. I only thank God I found out about this before it went any further. And I don't want to know how far it's gone. You're never, *ever,* to see that girl again, and if I find out you're seeing her behind my back, I'll take you out of that school, and you'll have to finish at one of the city public schools —"

"You can't do that!" Grace gave herself over to a new tide of painful sobs. "I can't be without her."

"You most certainly can. And you *will,*" her mother said. "I never heard such sick, sick talk in all my life. Do you have any idea what you're saying?" Her mother was shouting again, her upper lip curled in a snarl. "I've already made some phone calls."

Grace was too shocked to go on crying. If she had called Mrs. Heinz, they were done for.

"The rectory was very helpful. I've made appointments for both of you to be counseled. Maybe Father Frank will make you see how completely sinful this thing is you've gotten yourself into."

A priest? A cold sweat broke out over Grace's body. Her mother's excommunication for confessing to use birth control was part of family lore. Some sins were unforgivable, the priest had told her. She had never been back to church since.

"You'll be meeting him together the first time," her mother said. "That was his idea, not mine. After that, it'll be one at a time. And that's the last time you'll ever be in the same room with her, alone or in public, do you understand?"

161

Grace nodded, even as she knew she was lying. But it was impossible not to disobey. There was a higher commandment she knew she had to follow: her own will. Yet she nodded and nodded, desperate for the torture to end, feeling sadder and older than she ever had. She would have to risk everything now, and her mother would know nothing about it. But no one could help her now, and only Meg had any power to hurt her. Nothing would stop them from being together, surely not something as simple as her mother's demand.

Glancing back as her hand was on the doorknob, her mother spoke again. "I know you can't imagine right now that I'm doing this because I love you," she said, her voice breaking, "and not because I hate you. You can't know, not till you're a mother yourself, how much it hurts me to see you suffer like this, but I'm only trying to spare you worse suffering in the end." She took a deep breath Grace could hear even across the room, "And if Father Frank assures me after a while that the two of you have come to your senses, that this was some kind of freak stage, then maybe, *maybe* I'll think about letting you be friends again." Her mother was out of the room before hope even had a chance to register in Grace.

That night in bed, Grace tossed and turned till her quilt was hopelessly twisted and her joints ached. Her grandmother, already humming a low-grade snore, had said nothing to either her or her mother after their fight was over, but Grace knew she had heard the crying and the screaming through the closed door. She also knew from her grandmother's scowl of disapproval that she judged her mother as being too hard on her. "You don't know a thing about it, Mom," her mother had hissed as the older woman headed for the kitchen, "but you wouldn't blame me if you did."

Grace felt literally bruised, as though she had been roughed up in a back alley. Why had it come down to blame? Was it anyone's fault how she and Meg felt about each other? And why was it a fault, anyway? What had her mother meant — trying to spare her more pain in the future? Who would she and Meg be hurting if they quietly lived together after college in the apartment Grace had already sketched a blueprint for?

The worst pain was not being able to talk to Meg now. It was the first night in more months than she could remember that she hadn't spoken to her for at least a half hour before she went to sleep. How could she ever be apart from Meg for more than a few days, let alone a lifetime? How could she make her mother understand that she didn't choose to feel this way? Everyone wanted her to love Glen this way. She would have liked to. But wanting didn't make it so.

Grace stared into the darkness. Her parents were asleep. She could see underneath her door that the living room light had been turned off. "Lesbian," she whispered softly. Was that what she was? No, it was only Meg who stirred her like this. In fact, if Meg didn't exist, she might even have grown to love Glen, might have learned to like his body and his rough, urgent touches. After all, she wouldn't have known the difference, wouldn't ever have known how wonderful it could be.

"She called me a *lesbian?*" Meg asked, disbelievingly. They were in Meg's room, having taken the Hillside Avenue bus after their last class. It was still early afternoon. Grace had called her grandmother to say that a *Voices* meeting had been called and she'd be home around five o'clock. She hated lying to her grandmother, but somehow, in her grandmother's steady gaze and small smiles, Grace felt as though she was trusted, that even if her grandmother knew she was lying, she was willing to believe Grace had a good reason.

All last night, Grace's mother had left the phones off the hook. But Grace believed that Meg knew what had happened and was suffering along with her. Miraculously, this morning Meg had sneaked out of her own homeroom and appeared outside the door of Grace's room. Grace had only had to nod across the room, and she saw that Meg understood that their worst fears had been realized. Immediately, Grace began to tremble. Anne glanced up just as Meg was stealing away, and though she eyed Grace suspiciously, she said nothing.

"Yeah, I couldn't believe it, either," Grace said, "and she called you sick and said you had corrupted me and that we had no idea how much trouble we were in, and how perverse and terrible it all was. That it could ruin the rest of our lives, and that she almost would have rathered that I was pregnant, at least that would have been normal, and not disgusting and shocking like this was." Grace had repeated the phrases over and over in her mind all through her sleepless night, but still she could not completely convince herself that they had anything to do with her. Even by this morning, it was still a shock to recall her mother using such serious language to describe something that had happened so naturally and had brought her only joy.

"It's bad. And a priest of all things!" Meg said, pacing the small room, making Grace dizzy. "Well, I guess it could have been worse. She could have made us talk to a nun!"

They both fell silent for a beat, and then burst into gales of laughter. Grace laughed till her sides hurt, incredulous the whole time that happiness was so quickly retrieved. Last night, she thought she'd never feel it again — not the way she had that morning she'd awakened in Meg's arms after the night of their first kisses. That Meg could restore her faith in goodness and hope buoyed Grace and made her more certain of the rightness of their love.

When their laughter subsided, they were in a tangle on the bed. "We have to prepare what we're going to say," Meg said, suddenly somber. "We have to convince Father Frank that we're totally platonic, so he can tell your mother."

Grace had not thought of this, and the idea of entering into yet another layer of deceit made her feel desperate and depressed. She would never be able to keep track of all her lies — to her mother, to Father Frank, to Anne, to Glen, to Sister Mary Alice. All these lies, all these people lied to. Someone would have thought she was an embezzler, a murderer. All she was doing was loving someone.

165

"Are you sorry?" she asked Meg, unexpectedly overcome with remorse. "I feel like I got you into this big mess. I'm terrified you'll tell me it's not worth it, that —"

"Don't ever," Meg said, seizing her hands. "Don't ever," she said again, pulling her close. Grace could feel Meg's heartbeat, could smell the mix of musk and Marlboros rising faintly off her skin. "Haven't I convinced you yet how much I want you?"

Meg didn't wait for an answer, instead began kissing her steadily, unbuttoning her school blouse, pushing her bra away. Grace hooked her arms around Meg, pulling her blouse free behind her, sliding her hands up to unsnap her bra and ducking her head down to bury her face in Meg's cleavage, fragrant and already slightly dewy. A bright flame of joy burned inside her. No one would ever be able to keep them apart, she thought feverishly.

Grace tumbled over Meg, and this time, she was the one to slide her hands past Meg's hips first, bunching her skirt up and rubbing her open palm over her stockinged thighs, circling each time higher and higher toward the place of her keenest fascination. But by this time, Meg had joined her, hiking Grace's skirt full over her hips, pushing her legs apart with her own knee, and angling one hand along her inner thigh with new boldness.

"Oh, my *God*," Meg breathed into Grace's neck as they wrestled closer, sweaty and frantic. "I wish I could . . . what I want to do to you . . ." she whispered. And then her fingers were there on that place that was rushing with some wild current, and Grace felt her face go scarlet with surprise and the most deeply rooted passion she had ever felt. Nearly

166

blinded with pleasure, she groped her own hand further up Meg's thigh, and found the same miraculous place, found her warm and wet, clear through stockings and underwear.

But Meg didn't leave her a second to marvel; she began to yank down Grace's pantyhose, dragging her underwear with it. "Wait!" Grace said, a full panic of scalding self-consciousness upon her.

"Shhhhh," Meg blew into her ear as she touched two gentle fingers between Grace's legs. Grace went rigid with concentration and tears sprang to her eyes. But it was too much, too overwhelming, too revealing, too new and too strong a sensation to take in all at once. The whole world revolved around Meg's fingers on her, around the flicks and strokes, inexpert but thrilling nonetheless, and yet, the fire seeped slowly out of her and was replaced by a still awe, an aching love that demanded expression now, even over the demands of her body.

Grace pulled away just enough to be able to look Meg full in the face. "Do you remember," she started uncertainly, "when we talked about how you would know who you were going to marry? You said it was fated. But we were only talking about guys, then, and I didn't know, I mean —"

"I know — yes, your name is on my heart," Meg said, burying her face in her neck, and Grace, her body and mind equally fevered, found she didn't have the words to respond.

Father Frank was surprisingly young and frail, as she and Meg shuffled nervously into his small office in the rectory, just across the courtyard from Immaculate Blessing. He held the door open for them, smiling cordially, as if they were paying a mere social call.

"Can I get your girls anything — water, perhaps?" he asked when Grace and Meg sat down on two hard plastic chairs, the kind used in Immaculate Blessing's resource centers. His voice shook slightly — Grace heard it distinctly — and it struck her that he might be as ill at ease with their predicament as she and Meg were.

"Yes, Father, I'd love some water," Meg said, in the demure tone she reserved for all exchanges with nuns or teachers she was aiming to charm, or was genuinely terrified of. Grace wasn't sure which was the case now.

"You'd *love* some water?" Grace leaned over to Meg to say with a smirk when Father Frank left the room. Grace felt reckless in her new outlaw status. Never before had she been singled out by a priest or nun for anything but praise. "Since when have you ever *loved* water?"

"Maybe he'll bring us holy water, and we'll just drink it and be cured," Meg said, doing Grace's irreverence one better, as usual. "Except nobody ever asked me if I wanted to be cured. What I want," Meg whispered, leaning away at the sound of approaching footsteps, "is to make love to you."

Grace was completely electrified. They had never used such adult words before. It was as if the accusation freed them to face the possibility in all its full-blown glory. Sweat broke out across Grace's back just as Father Frank reappeared in the doorway, carrying a tray with a water pitcher and three plastic glasses.

"Here we go," he said, uncertainly placing the tray on the desktop before he shut the door. He had a pleasant-looking face, with melancholy eyes, and thin, grave lips. His light brown hair was combed and parted with obvious care. Grace was grateful that he was wearing a reassuring black robe, and not laymen's clothes the way many young priests did, showing up in neatly pressed corduroys and plaid, short-sleeved shirts, with only a stiff white collar across their throats to distinguish them from ordinary men. Father Frank rolled the desk chair over to their two chairs, and handed them each a glass of water.

His office was nicer than Sister Mary Alice's had been on the retreat, Grace observed. There was a rust-colored carpet, lush portraits of Christ, wooden shelves stocked with hardbound books. But then, this was probably one of the offices where young couples about to be married met for pre-canaan counseling, Grace reminded herself. No one had much occasion to visit the nuns' quarters.

"So," Father Frank said, stretching the word out as though he hoped it could fill the space of several minutes.

Grace caught Meg's eye over the top of her glass, and a jolt of nervousness made her feel suddenly ashamed and absurd.

"We're here today," the young priest said, leaning his elbows on his knees and rubbing his hands noisily together, "because Grace's mother expressed deep concern about the nature of your friendship." He looked over the top of his fingertips at them, his forehead furrowed. Grace sat stock still. "Now, uh, I'd like to say a few words about friendship, first, before I hear from you girls."

Grace watched him carefully as he began to talk about Christ's friendship with the apostles, King David's friendship with Jonathan, and Ruth's friendship with Naomi. Hope fluttered in Grace's chest and she blushed when she felt Meg's eyes on her. She had been prepared for the priest to deliver a chilling lecture about abomination, not a homily on the rewards of same-sex friendship. She was nearly reeling in her seat just as his speech took on a totally new direction.

"Uh, the important lesson here, though," he said, clearing his throat, "is that true and selfless friendship puts the other first. It puts at its center the higher good, the will of God. And that will is always to go forth and give witness to his mercy and goodness. Some friendships lose track of these goals, and no matter what wrong path they take, what they have in common is that they forget that all love is made possible by God, and therefore all love must be godly."

Grace was moved by the young priest's conviction. She sneaked a glance at Meg and saw that she, too, was listening respectfully.

"So," he said, again making the word torturously long, "what we have to find out is whether your friendship would be pleasing in God's eyes. Your mother, Grace," he said, nodding at her again, as if she might have forgotten who she was, "expressed specific concern that your friendship had placed too much emphasis on the, uh —" Grace held her breath, "— physical." She breathed out, grateful that he hadn't said "sexual." His glance darted wildly around the room. "Well, let me ask, then. How much of the time, when you're together, would you say you feel the need to be, uh, physical?"

Fear crept up Grace's spine on clammy hands. Something about this conversation struck her as distinctly less wholesome than anything she and Meg had ever done together. To her great relief, Meg rushed forward to answer the question.

"I'd say about fifty percent of the time," Meg said with utter confidence. For a second, Grace was stung, feeling that a hundred and fifty percent was closer to the truth. But then she read in Meg's encouraging nod that this was simply to mislead Father Frank — trusting Father Frank who had told such nice stories about invigorating Bible friendships.

"Yes, I'd say that's about right," Grace said nonchalantly, as if the subject was supremely inconsequential to her, as if she had not obsessed about such matters nearly day and night since she and Meg first kissed.

Father Frank leaned back and was nodding thoughtfully. "And the rest of the time?"

Now Grace had the hang of it. "Oh, we talk about the interesting classes we're taking, or our boyfriends, or Meg's wanting to be in Immaculate Blessing's choir, or some poem I'm writing about spring grass. You know, the usual."

Grace saw Meg's eyes widen in alarm, and she was afraid that perhaps she had gone too far, but Father Frank was crossing his legs comfortably and smiling. "Well," he said, "I think that maybe what you need to do is just think some about that other fifty percent of the time, and just try to work it down to, say, twenty percent, by the time we meet next week." He stood up, rubbing his hands on his upper arms as if he were cold. "See you next week, then." He opened the door.

"Thank you, Father," they both said at once. Grace did not remind him that her mother had made it quite clear that she expected him to see them separately after the first meeting. Instead, they headed down the hallway, silently relishing their small, warped victory, and listening to the echo of their footsteps as they made their way to the front door. Once outside, they slapped their gloved hands together and jumped as high as they could before running all the way to the bus stop two blocks away.

Glen unbuttoned his winter coat so roughly that Grace expected the buttons to go flying across the room. He sat back on the floral couch on Grace's porch, his arms stretched proprietarily across the back. "Okay," he said, "what did you want to talk about?"

Grace had rehearsed her short speech four nights straight and by now it seemed like old news. Yet here was Glen, without a clue, smiling eagerly at her like a puppy who spots his master with a ball. How could it be that they were so out of sync that he didn't even suspect any unhappiness on her part? It was as if they were in two different relationships. Looking at him smiling, she felt profoundly sad that all the potential had completely drained away. On the surface, he really was all she could have hoped for in a boyfriend. But the surface, she knew, wasn't what counted at all.

"What is it?" Glen leaned forward. Grace could feel her lips pinching in a sulk. She hated that she couldn't force her face to disguise her feelings. In her rehearsals, she was never able to imagine Glen's reaction. All she imagined was rushing to tell Meg that no one would ever come between them now. Next to that, the thrill of Immaculate Blessing's junior prom, the cafeteria table chatter, all paled, and she wondered how she had once thought they were all worth it. It wasn't that she liked Glen any less as a person; she still felt he was good, smart, and, despite his hormonal outbursts, sensitive. It was just that she had no place with him. It was barely even personal.

"I've been thinking," Grace said, looking out the window through the slats of the blinds at the expressway in front of her house. "About us." Her stomach was churning like a washing machine in the heavy-load cycle.

"Yeah, what about us?" Glen asked, sidling over and crunching her against him with both arms. "The same things I've been thinking?" He was aiming his lips at her.

"No, that's exactly the problem," she said, shoving away from him and immediately regretting how forcefully. He looked bewildered, the way someone would slamming into a wall he hadn't anticipated in the dark. "I just don't, I mean, I feel like we just don't — *click.*" Grace looked at him hopefully. In her rehearsals, Glen had understood the word like a code, and its pronouncement was final. Meg had suggested it because one of her past

173

boyfriends had used it on her, and it had impressed her as sophisticated and irrevocable.

But Glen just frowned. "What are you talking about?"

"You know, I mean, we just don't *click*," Grace said more loudly, as if he hadn't heard. She felt like an actress whose leading man was badly missing his cue and embarrassing everyone.

"You mean, you want to break up?" He laughed.

She glared at him. Why was he being so rude, torturing her this way? Why was he refusing to understand?

After a moment, he leaned back into the couch, deflated, like a balloon after the wind has been let out. "I don't believe it," he breathed. "I don't understand." He shook his head. "Why?"

Grace got up and stood at the window. It was too hard a question to answer. Though he couldn't know it, he was asking her why she felt more for Meg than she did for him, why loving Meg the way she did meant she could never love him the way she was now afraid he was beginning to love her. "I can't tell you the truth," she said, feigning interest in the passing cars, "and I don't want to lie."

"And what the hell does *that* mean?" he yelled, jumping up and seizing her by the wrist. "What can't you tell me?"

Grace had not imagined resistance. She certainly could not fathom anger. It occurred to her now like a revelation that his pride was wounded, that he would have to explain this somehow to his friends, to himself. She shook her head. She had said too much, she saw that now. "I can't explain it, that's all. I just don't know how else to say it but that some people hit it off and some people don't."

He blinked at her slowly. "Like chemistry, you mean?"

"Yeah," she said, relieved by his calmed and interested tone. They might have been having one of their conversations about God, and for a moment, she felt a vague stirring of regret and loss. She had never stopped to imagine what it might feel like to see him at Sacred Soldiers with his arm around another girl. But the loss she really felt, she realized, was knowing that she would never be able to put her arm around Meg in public. It was another new pain; it seemed there were more every day. Loving Meg was costing her more than anything before in life had, and yet it had never occurred to her to question it. It was just her fate, and all of it simply had to be endured. Glen's kind tone made her wish for a second she could confide in him. After all, she had no one to ask about these things.

"Chemistry," he said, sitting down gravely as if just being given a doctor's grim diagnosis. She could see him thinking it over, judging it equally for credibility with his friends and for the feel of truth for himself. "I guess that isn't the kind of thing you can work on, huh?"

She smiled awkwardly and shook her head. And not the kind of thing you can prevent, either, she thought.

He looked about to say something. Then he stood abruptly and buttoned his coat. At the door, he raised his hand briefly and was down the steps before she had a chance to say good-bye. She watched him kicking snow all the way down the block, her face pressed to the cold storm door, till he had disappeared from sight. He didn't look back once, and, she thought, she could hardly blame him.

– 10 –

The smell of burnt coffee in the diner was as strong as incense at High Mass. Blasts of icy February air rushed in with every customer who pushed open the door, jangling the brass bells hanging above it. Anne and Grace had each ordered chicken noodle soup and hot chocolate, and Anne was aiming her cheeks over the steam rising up from both.

"Ahhh, this is better than a facial," Anne said, angling her face from side to side for maximum effect.

"And cheaper, too," Grace said, blowing on a

spoonful of soup, her stomach rumbling. Just as she got a steaming mouthful down, she noticed Anne frowning distractedly. "What's the matter?"

"Nothing," Anne said. "When you said 'cheaper,' it just reminded me. Rick told Glen not to feel too bad he didn't have a girlfriend for Valentine's Day because at least he'd save some money."

"Shit, Anne," Grace said, clapping her spoon down on the speckled table. "You promised you wouldn't do this to me."

"I'm sorry, I just still don't *understand*."

Grace leaned back into the red booth, letting out a sigh slowly till her temper was under control. Part of her wanted to lash out — what was it to anyone if she and Glen broke up? But when she looked up and saw Anne's face, pinched with genuine concern, her anger ebbed.

"I mean, I know what you told me," Anne went on. "I guess it's just one of those things. But I feel like there's more to it than you're telling me." Anne plunged her spoon into the depths of her soup bowl. "I guess you'll tell me about it when you want to. *If* you want to."

Grace felt a tingle of apprehension. What exactly did Anne suspect? Should she tell her? But she couldn't. It was too much to explain casually over soup, and besides, she hadn't figured enough of it out herself.

"For what it's worth in the flattery department," Anne went on, "Glen's still pretty devastated."

Grace's forehead was damp. She felt pressure on all sides. In some ways, breaking up with Glen hadn't relieved any of it. His absence seemed to make her more conspicuous. Her friends at the cafeteria table didn't understand why, since the breakup was her idea, she didn't want to be fixed up or wasn't anxious to be back at the dances as a free agent.

"Look," Grace said, "did Rick or Glen set you up to grill me?"

Anne fell back against the seat as if shoved. Indignation washed across her face. "That's really a new low, Molino. We're supposed to be best friends, remember? We used to talk about everything. Big and little. And this is pretty major stuff here and you act like I don't have a right in the world to ask you about it. Did it ever occur to you that maybe I give a damn about how you feel?"

Grace stared hard into her soup. She didn't dare look up for fear that she would cry. Finally, she trusted her voice and even managed a smile. "I'm fine, Anne. Really. Thanks for worrying about me, but there's really nothing wrong. I just have nothing else to say about Glen."

"Well, whatever it is, I'm sure *Meg* knows all about it."

"You know, Anne, you've been pretty preoccupied yourself the last year and a half. You always made it clear Rick came first."

"Does that mean Meg doesn't have a date this Friday, either?"

Friday was Valentine's Day, and though they hadn't talked about it, Grace knew she and Meg were counting on a special night together — without her mother's knowledge, of course. Since the meetings with Father Frank, their longing for each other had only gotten more insistent. Denying what they felt each week was like trying to keep a beach ball under water — the more they held it down, the stronger the force driving it back to the surface.

"We're hanging out together Friday, if that's what you mean." Meg hadn't told her own mother a thing about Father Frank, and oddly, he had overlooked calling Mrs. Heinz himself.

"Well, I have big news," Anne said, wriggling closer to the table to whisper. "This Friday is *it*. Rick and I are going all the way."

The news really didn't surprise Grace. It had seemed inevitable since the night during their sophomore retreat when Anne had first brought it up. So much had happened since then, it seemed almost like another lifetime.

"Where are you going to go?" Grace asked, unexpectedly mournful. It was as if Anne were crossing over to a place firmly out of her reach. Would they maintain enough in common to stay friends?

"That's where you come in," Anne said, leaning as far as she could across the table. "Rick's arranging to get a room at the Turnpike Motor Lodge."

"Oh God, not the old Lodge and Lay? The Bedbug Boudoir? The pay-by-lay-away?" The two girls burst into noisy laughter, and Anne accidentally sent her hot chocolate rocking. The motor lodge was well known for its breathy radio commercials advertising waterbeds and mirrored ceilings for "romantic interludes with that special someone."

"No one knows about this but you, and I told my mother the four of us were going to a movie and rollerskating, and then I was staying over at your house."

"What are you talking about? The four of who? You don't mean your mother still thinks I'm going out with Glen?"

"I had to, Grace. She gets much more nervous if she knows it's just the two of us. And you don't have to tell your mother anything. My mother will never call and check. But I just wanted you to know in case you ever call and get my mother on the phone or something, you can say you had a great time with all of us on Valentine's Day. Get it?"

"Yeah, I get it, no problem," Grace said. The irony was that Grace was telling her own mother that she was staying over at Anne's. Anne was often her alibi, in fact, without her even knowing it. But she couldn't ask Anne directly because that would have meant having to explain why her mother had forbade her and Meg to see each other in the first place.

"Are you nervous?" Grace asked. "I mean, not about getting caught —"

"A little, I guess. Not that we haven't already had our close calls."

"Yeah, well, just keep those foil things handy. Because I don't feel like going to an abortion clinic with you next."

Anne nodded solemnly. An Irish girl they both knew only passingly had just been asked to leave Immaculate Blessing after the nuns got wind of her abortion. It was an ugly and isolated incident, and all the students felt badly for everyone involved.

Anne shivered, but then seemed to recover. "I'm

not thinking about stuff like that." She smiled wickedly. "I'm in *love,* and I can't wait to be with him — totally. I never want us to be apart."

Though Grace couldn't say so, she knew exactly what Anne meant.

"At least getting pregnant is one thing we don't have to worry about," Meg said, her hands behind her head on the pillow.

It was the evening of Valentine's Day and Meg's parents had gone straight to bed at eleven after playing cards at a friends' house. Grace allowed herself to relax and assume she had gotten away with the lie about her whereabouts; her mother would never call anyone's house after eleven at night.

"On the other hand, I guess we can't have kids," Meg added.

"Would you want to?" Grace asked, leaning on her elbow, wedged between the wall and Meg's side.

Meg reached up and pushed Grace's hair behind one ear. "I want to do everything with you. I want us to graduate together, go to the same college, have an apartment together, get married, have our parents over for Thanksgiving dinner, have babies and raise them together. And then get old together."

Grace's throat squeezed shut with emotion. Her eyes filled with tears, but she was no longer embarrassed to cry in front of Meg. It was amazing to hear Meg planning their whole life together, when Grace herself lived in fear that each day would be somehow snatched away from them. Amazing but also frightening, because Grace was beginning to

worry that Meg's dreams were too big, that all the
things she wanted for them were perhaps not
possible. How could they be, when Grace's own
parents didn't even allow them to see each other?
Grace was terrified that Meg would only be
disappointed.

"I know what you're thinking," Meg said, smiling
slowly, that half-little-girl, half-knowing-woman smile
that made Grace irrational with optimism. "Always
worried about the details. Here's how I figure it —
girls have girl roommates all the time in college, so
no one will suspect anything there. And after school,
we'll have some kind of private ceremony of our
own, and then I'll sleep with some old boyfriend and
get pregnant. And if our parents don't come for
Thanksgiving dinner, screw 'em."

They giggled into each other's neck, working in a
few quick kisses, but Grace was having trouble
beating back a creeping melancholy. "Won't you miss
a big church wedding? And what will we tell people
when they ask who the kid's parents are? Jesus, what
will we tell the *kid?* I mean, we won't have the
church, neighbors probably won't talk to us — my
God, my parents will probably have a contract taken
out on your life —"

Meg was laughing hard again, leaning up on her
elbow. Her shoulder looked creamy smooth, and
Grace thought she would risk everything, throw
down her life, to defend just that shoulder.

"You're such a worry wart," Meg said. "What are
you going to be like when you're thirty?"

Thirty — was it possible they'd still be together
then? It was almost too unbearably wonderful to
think of so many years of happiness promised to her.

And yet, it was impossible to conceive of any life without her.

"Besides," Meg continued, "no one has to know unless we want them to. No one knows now."

"But that's not true. There's my mother and Father Frank. And Anne's been making cryptic comments. Besides, I don't know if I want to lie all my life."

"Well, we can't exactly announce to people that we're in love with each other," Meg said. "Jesus, they'll call us lesbians."

Grace's growing impatience with Meg's disdain of the word finally got the best of her. "I'm starting to think maybe I don't care what they call us. You're the only person I'll ever love, and if that's what people want to call me, fine."

"Stop talking crazy, Grace. We're not dykes. They're all fat and ugly with short hair and they want to be men. You, on the other hand, are beautiful."

Meg pushed Grace down into the sheets and they kissed till they lost track of time. Along the way, they each wriggled out of their pajama tops, and the sight of their breasts sealed against each other's, dewy and warm, sent tremors through Grace's body. When Meg put her mouth on her nipple, Grace had to bite her own lip to stifle her cries of joy. In her lightheaded abandon, Grace felt as though she were shedding some skin, and the self she glimpsed underneath was strong with well-fed hungers.

She pulled Meg close with a new determination. She let her hand linger on Meg's smooth back, tracing her fingers down her spine and, in a moment of courage nearly unbelievable even to her, past the elastic waistband of her pajama bottoms. She let her fingers play with the fine down at the base of Meg's spine, then slip over her tightly rounded buttocks. She was so transported with happiness that she nearly didn't hear Meg's small murmurs of encouragement, or heard them but at first couldn't place their source. "Don't stop, angel," she made out at last, and Grace's heart leapt and pounded, a spreading heat claiming her thighs and groin. She circled her hand around to Meg's flat, cool stomach, past the tangle of soft hair, and found her, just as she herself was, warm and wet and open.

"Touch me like this," Meg breathed into Grace's ear, trembling suddenly. She reached down and began to guide Grace's fingertips with her own hand.

But Grace had already found the place and, fired by instinct and energy, traced a slow, sure pattern. Meg muffled her moans against Grace's collarbone. Only briefly was Grace aware enough of her surroundings to worry that they might actually wake Mrs. Heinz. After a certain point, everything faded but the feel of Meg, the folds of her against her fingertips. Meg arched and angled herself urgently, and kept up a low murmur of exclamations as she held onto Grace with what seemed all her might. Then her whole body went rigid for a long, suspended moment, and she clutched Grace as if she were falling from a great height. She shook hard, and then lay pressed against Grace's breasts as if no place else on earth had ever mattered and nothing would ever come between them. For Grace, her eyes hot with tears, inhaling the scent of her lover's body, its sweet and pungent perfume, nothing ever would.

* * * * *

185

"This material is almost totally unacceptable, Grace," Sister Mary Alice said from behind the desk in the classroom where they were having a private *Voices* meeting. Grace had turned over her prose and poetry selections for the magazine by last week's deadline. She was confident that what she had pulled out from the submissions was the very best of what she had read. Sister's pronouncement made her queasy.

"I'm not sure what you mean," Grace said. She began fiddling with the silver necklace Meg had given her for Valentine's Day, the only other piece of jewelry she ever wore aside from Meg's watch.

Sister fixed on her a searching stare. "I almost don't know how to respond to that, Grace. Because I feel you're too bright not to have a very clear idea of what I mean, especially in light of our last conversation about the purpose of *Voices* and the example we want to set. And yet if you do understand, as I feel you must, I have no choice but to believe this is an act of pure defiance."

Grace's cheeks were burning. Defiant wasn't the word she might have chosen, but she saw now that perhaps she had been overly daring. She had tossed aside all the prose and poetry she had earmarked as falling into the "beauty of the grass growing" category. What remained was only the most powerful, exhilarating stuff. In these, Grace saw reflected many of her own preoccupations, and other ideas just as bold — meditations on suicide, utopian worlds, androgyny, fights with parents, insecurity and alienation.

"Don't you have anything to say for yourself?" Sister asked.

Grace's neck was hot. She felt as if someone had a hand at her throat. An angry outburst would not do, she warned herself. But no one submitted anything from Psalms, Grace thought sarcastically.

"I tried to make a judgment, Sister," Grace began, "based on the quality of the work. And what I've given you was the best-quality writing."

Sister folded her hands neatly in front of her. "What I tried to explain to you over these last few meetings, Grace, is that there are other considerations, such as theme, that should be just as important — even more important — to the editor of this magazine."

"Theme *was* important to me, Sister," Grace said, feeling a new recklessness spur her on. "The stuff I chose was the most sincere, the most honest and relevant and meaningful to the students who would be reading it —"

"This is a Catholic institution, might I remind you, Grace Molino. You may find support and encouragement for such secular opinions in other circles in which you travel, but as a student here at Immaculate Blessing, I would have thought you'd have found such material base, crude, offensive and ungodly. Frankly, I don't know how you read half of it without blanching. The other half should have sent you straight to the confessional for even having laid eyes on it."

Grace was dumbstruck. She struggled to regain her equilibrium. "But these are all things Catholic students are writing and feeling, Sister —"

"And I have said prayers for each and every one of them, Grace, yourself included. But that has nothing to do with whether or not they have a place in *Voices,* and any girl who is the editor of this magazine would know that they don't."

This last was a knife in Grace's heart. All she could do was shift awkwardly in her seat.

"I'm willing to give you a second chance, Grace. You are to go through the rest of the material that you rejected and come up with a radically different set of selections. Feel free also to specifically approach any honors English student and ask if she'd write something for us, perhaps even suggesting possible subjects. I want the new material in five weeks, or I'll have to find a new editor of *Voices.*"

Grace nodded, but she was nowhere near consent. At the moment, however, she was too stunned by Sister's icy anger to react. She hadn't seen herself as being on the vanguard of heresy and dissension, but the way Sister had characterized it, she might as well have been leading a revolution. Yet none of the poems and stories and essays she had chosen had remotely shocked her. Rather, they had sparked recognition, and she didn't think she would be alone.

Grace stared down at the desktop. Sister Mary Alice was asking her to paint a smiley face over all their pain, to ignore all glimmers of doubt, of dissent, of individuality, to refuse to tell the truth. She was asking her not only to stand in as the sanctioned messenger of this sanitized view, but to believe it in her heart. But believing that would have meant turning her back on Meg long ago, turning her back on her own happiness. And Grace had no intention of doing that. But by the time she decided to tell Sister Mary Alice she'd have to think it over, the nun had already left the room, taking the objectionable submissions with her.

"There she is," Grace said, her voice taut with excitement. She and Meg were leaning against the cold concrete wall outside the courtyard after their last class. Linda Amato, her legs crossed at the ankles, was leaning against the driver's side of the same white car as last time. One long arm was stretched across the roof, and her hand kept time to the music floating out from the car radio. Occasionally, someone sports-minded, for whom Linda's basketball victories were a high point of Immaculate Blessing lore, would stop to greet her loudly, slap a shoulder, tousle her hair. Grace watched the affectionate exchanges jealously.

"I want to go over and ask if she remembers me," Grace said.

"What are you going to say? Get to see your girlfriend in the convent much?"

Grace shot Meg a disapproving look, as if she had just cursed in church, but then they both burst out laughing. "Well, I think she's got someone new, anyway," Grace said.

"And who's Joan the novitiate got, I wonder?"

"Yeah, I don't know." The subject of Joan deeply distressed Grace. She could only imagine how it made Linda feel — Linda, who stood here now, both proud and casual, straightforward and mysterious, beloved and outcast.

"Let's see if she spots me and then maybe she'll

come over and say something first," Grace said, straining for nonchalance as she inched her way down the wall till they were directly opposite Linda and her car, not more than twenty feet away.

"How about I give her a little hint, like if I lean over and kiss you on the lips?" Meg smirked.

"Very funny."

"What are you going to do if she does come over?"

Grace panicked. She hadn't really thought it through. All she knew was that Linda could tell her things, Linda had the key pieces of a puzzle that she was missing. "I don't know exactly. I guess I'll have to play it by ear. Aren't you curious, though? Don't you want to know if they went through what we're going through? If there are lots of other students here in the same kind of relationships? If there's someplace they all go?"

Meg was shaking her head. "I don't know." She struck a match hard and let it sizzle against the end of her cigarette. She took a drag and exhaled slowly. "I don't know if I want to know all that. I just know I love you. And that's enough for me. Why isn't it enough for you?"

Grace looked into Meg's eyes and all her distraction evaporated. "It's everything to me, Meg," she said sternly. "That's exactly why I feel like I have to find out more." Grace was about to pursue the subject further when she spotted the senior with long, blonde hair headed toward the car. She wore a tweed coat and high-heeled black boots. "That's her," Grace whispered.

Grace couldn't hear the words Linda and the senior exchanged in greeting, but she was sure they were intimate. A slow, admiring smile crept up Linda's face, making her seem at once more womanly yet more handsome. The blonde headed confidently for the passenger side, swung open the door, and tossed her purse onto the front seat. Linda yanked her door open and, as she ducked inside, her glance fell squarely on Grace. Grace froze, unable to look away. She couldn't tell if Linda recognized her but there was no mistaking the conspiratorial, merry wink Linda gave her before she pulled away.

Going to church every Sunday was one of the things Father Frank had counted in Grace and Meg's favor during his sessions with them, and that was one of the reasons Grace kept going, though she was increasingly tempted just to sleep late and start her homework. But she worried that he would quiz them about a reading and she wouldn't have an answer, and that would hurt her case and make him take that much longer to recommend to her mother that she and Meg be allowed to see each other again.

Grace went to Mass alone. Her brother didn't go anymore, out of pure apathy, and her parents were hardly in any position to lecture him, since they didn't go either. Her mother wore the moral badge of wronged outcast about her own falling away from the church, and her father didn't feel strongly enough about it to go without her.

Grace settled into a small pew off to the side under a stained-glass window. Despite the inevitable boredom of most of the Mass, Grace still felt a certain dogged hopefulness at the start of every service. Maybe it all came down to the sensual appeal — the sweet smell of burning candles, the plush velvet and starched white cotton of the altar vestments, the ghostly hum of the organ. She always imagined she would hear some searing words of wisdom, feel some life-altering sense of peace before she blinked her way back out into the sunlight. Not only had that never happened, but the reverse was usually true — that a boring priest gave a dull or tyrannical sermon, putting her in a worse mood than she'd been in to start with.

While she waited for Mass to begin, she flipped through the weekly bulletin. She read the back first — it always had curious little ads from local businesses, or announcements about community activities. The front page always ran some inspirational essay, not necessarily related to the religious season, and Grace rarely read it. This week, however, the subject caught her eye. It was about the difference between venial and mortal sins — venial being forgivable infractions such as lying and cursing, mortal being the ones that banished the sinner irrevocably from eternal afterlife with God.

Grace's eye was drawn immediately to the list of ten mortal sins. Certainly there were more, the article cautioned, but these were ten of the most serious. After murder, adultery, thievery and others, "homosexual acts" was listed as number eight. Grace stared at the words in their blue ink for a long while, unable to sort through what she was feeling. After all, homosexuals were not a group she felt she owed any allegiance to. She didn't even know any. She had nothing in common with people who wanted to have sex with every member of their own sex, regardless of considerations like love. And she and Meg were just that: she and Meg.

All through Mass Grace was unable to shake the image of the words *homosexual acts,* in blue ink, from her mind. It began to dawn on her that it did not say "homosexuality," or "homosexuals" in general. "Homosexual acts" threw out a much wider net. It could apply to a happily married man and woman who had once kissed another man or woman on the lips. That would fall under homosexual acts. And if that fell under homosexual acts, then surely what she and Meg were doing must also be included.

When it was time to receive Communion, Grace remained kneeling in her pew. Her cheeks were hot and she imagined that everyone knew she must be guilty of one of the ten mortal sins listed on the front of the bulletin. Because if she wasn't, then she would be up there receiving Communion like everyone else.

And yet, Grace didn't feel sinful, let alone mortally so. Today she was in church, praying the same prayers, singing the same hymns she had been praying and singing all her life, and suddenly the church had decided she was irretrievably sinful. As sinful as a murderer. Here she was today the same girl she had been all along, the one who had won a Knights of Columbus scholarship, the one who was Sister Mary Alice's pet, the one who was held up as a role model as one of Immaculate Blessing's best students. And now, none of that mattered. It was all canceled out.

Grace got up and left the church before the final

blessing. Out in the cold March sunlight, she felt no peace, only a certain bitter wisdom. She didn't want to stay in a place where she wasn't welcome, but just then, she would have liked to have had a word with whoever had made up the guest list.

— 11 —

The college directory was open on the bed between Grace and Meg as the late afternoon sun came through the blinds in stripes across their bodies. They lay on their stomachs with their feet up, their legs crossing each other's at the ankle.

"Here we go," said Grace. "The University of New Mexico is cheap. Maybe we could swing that, if we both got jobs at night."

"New Mexico? Are you sure that's even a state?" Meg dragged the thick book closer to her, and Grace buried her face in Meg's hair as Meg scanned other names on the page. "New Jersey. Now that's a little more familiar."

"Our parents can't exactly afford Princeton."

"You could probably get a scholarship. But there's no way I'd be able to go."

"Then forget it," Grace said, parting Meg's hair so she could kiss the back of her neck. She slid her hand underneath her and cupped her breast, gently pinching her nipple.

"You know I can't concentrate when you do that."

"Exactly." Grace had already lost interest in the book, except for the hypnotic crinkle the thin pages made as Meg methodically flipped them. The sun in her eyes, the warmth of the bed, and Meg's scent, had all conspired to mesmerize Grace. For her, time was divided into two categories: being with Meg, and waiting to be with Meg. Everything else she had ever felt or imagined paled hopelessly beside her.

"Does it ever scare you?" Meg whispered, though no one else was in the house. She reached down idly and let her hand roam over Grace's thighs.

"Does what ever scare me?"

"The way we feel about each other. I mean, how other people feel about the way we feel about each other."

Grace ran her finger along the line of Meg's jaw. "The only thing that scares me is what might have happened to me if I'd never found you."

"You'd be going to the Sacred Soldier's senior prom, for one thing."

"And wondering why I felt like a complete outsider looking in."

Meg shifted uneasily. "And now we're just plain outsiders."

Grace studied Meg's face. "What is it? Has someone said something to upset you? Are you letting Father Frank get to you?"

Meg reached for her pack of cigarettes on the floor. "Sometimes I just wonder how come, if it really is so right, everybody else is so dead set against us."

"As long as we believe it's right, I don't care anymore what anybody else thinks."

"Then why didn't you tell Glen the truth when you broke up with him?" Meg asked, slicing a match hard across the matchbook.

Grace rolled back and leaned against the cool wall. "Is that what's bothering you?"

"It's just a question," she said, running her hand through her hair.

Grace watched the sun glance off Meg's hair. "It really wasn't any of his business. And it wouldn't have helped anything. Besides, I didn't exactly go out of my way to lie. I was just vague."

"I guess I just get sick of, you know, not being able to lay claim to you in front of everybody. In front of our parents. At school. On the street. This room," she said, looking around her flinchingly, as if she were suspicious the walls would literally close in on them, "is the only safe place we have."

"I love this room. I love *you*. It's going to take some time to make the room bigger. We have to be patient." Grace closed the small gap between them on the bed and squeezed Meg full up against her.

"Sometimes I wish," Meg said, searching her face

with an intensity that frightened Grace, "that I could be a man for you. Then we wouldn't have any of these problems."

"No, never. Don't you see? I wouldn't be here if you were a man." Grace's own words surprised her. She hadn't really thought about it that way before, that she might be with Meg for any other reason beyond the fact that Meg was Meg.

"Wouldn't I be the same person if I were a man, except that then I could marry you, have a baby with you?"

"I don't know. I'm not sure you would be."

"I could have one of those operations —"

"Don't be crazy," Grace said, her voice breaking. "I don't ever want you to be somebody else. I love you the way a woman loves another woman. That's what we have, that's what we are."

Meg looked like she was on the brink of tears. She kissed Grace hard, anxious, Grace suspected, to get to the place where their passion, which was beyond reason or logic, took over. In the small room, on the sun-drenched bed, their bodies pressed up against each other, that didn't take very long.

"How about this one?" Anne said, yanking a royal blue taffeta cocktail dress off the rack and smoothing it against her in front of the mirror.

Grace sighed and stood behind her to scrutinize the effect. "I don't know, Anne. How can you tell how anything looks on a hanger? These things take on a life of their own once you slip them over your head."

Anne sighed impatiently. "Grace, it's not every day you go to your first Sacred Soldier's senior prom. Of *course* I'm going to try it on. I'll try on a thousand if I have to."

"Well, great, then we've only got two hundred and fifty more to go because this is the third department store you've dragged me through."

"Well, I know how it works. Most of the guys, like turkeys, wait till a few weeks before the prom to ask a girl and then, like a horde of locusts, all of Immaculate Blessing descends on Queens all at once and overnight there's not a decent dress or gown left in sight."

"Don't gloat. Just because Rick asked you light-years in advance."

Anne smiled smugly. She had told Grace the story at least five times, going back to flesh out details she might have overlooked in earlier versions. How they had checked into the Turnpike Motor Lodge, ordered room service, and then dove into bed. By the time the busboy had arrived with their club sandwiches, she was no longer a virgin. Anne adopted a world-weary tone during these retellings, and Grace suspected she was keeping her elation in check only because she was afraid of appearing to have changed too much with one dramatic adult gesture that seemed so far out of Grace's own reach. To Grace, Anne seemed the same, only more so. She was finally acting on the turbulent instincts that had always made her seem somewhat larger than life.

"I wish you were coming to the prom," Anne said, suddenly meditative. "If you gave Glen any encouragement at all, I think he still would ask you."

"*Anne,*" Grace said, barely containing her anger.

199

Anne yanked some dresses sharply along the rack. "You know, a hundred girls would be dropping dead if Glen was pining after them the way he's pining after you."

"Maybe I don't want what a hundred other girls want. Or a thousand or a million. Their wanting it can't make me want it. And believe me, I've tried."

"Maybe you haven't tried hard enough." Anne took an aimless swipe at the rack of glittering, glossy gowns. "Maybe you expect too much. I mean, what do you think? That you and Glen are going to get along like you and me? That he'll always, you know," Anne said, her voice tight with exasperation, "be able to tell you exactly how he feels, or know exactly how you feel, the way you and I, or any best girlfriends, can? That he'll see things we way we do, or won't ever do or say something typically stupid, like guys do? I mean, grow up. It's not always going to be like a pajama party with the girls when you're with a guy."

A cacophony of impassioned rebuttals swirled in Grace's head, but she was stunned silent. Anne was embarrassed by her, she could tell. "Are you through?" she managed finally, and turned away from the racks of sequins and spaghetti straps and chiffon dolman sleeves.

"Wait," Anne said, her hand firmly on Grace's arm. "I just miss you, that's all. I just wish. . . ." She looked down at the floor.

Grace took a few deep breaths before she had the nerve to speak. "I know," she said. "Me too."

* * * * *

200

"So," Father Frank said, leaning back into his chair and folding his arms across his chest. He had grown visibly more comfortable during their recent visits as Meg and Grace continued to assure him that the physical element of their friendship had become less important. But as he grew more at ease, Grace became more agitated. The truth was the exact opposite, and there seemed something profoundly reckless about so systematically deceiving a priest.

"Today I thought we'd talk a little bit about marriage," Father Frank said, oddly cheerful about his subject, Grace thought, since it was something forbidden to him, too. "Do you think you'd like to be married one day? Let's start with you, Grace."

Grace folded and unfolded her hands while steadfastly avoiding Father Frank's inquisitive stare. The truth crouched somewhere in the corner of her mind and she suddenly didn't trust herself to say the right thing. What she wanted to tell him was that she thought of marriage all the time, and if being married meant being with the person you loved most in all the world, then how dare anyone tell her she wasn't allowed to marry Meg?

"I do," Meg said, interrupting her thoughts. "I want to be married."

Father Frank looked away from Grace reluctantly. "And what do you imagine that life being like?"

Meg glanced at the ceiling as a sly smile crept up her face. "Oh, I see myself in my own house, where my parents can't tell me what to do, and I see a baby in a bassinet in the living room, and I'm in the kitchen heating up a bottle and the sun's coming in the window. And just then the phone rings, and it's my husband —" Meg said, addressing Grace directly now — "calling from work just to say he loves me."

"Uh huh, uh huh," Father Frank said, rubbing his jaw. "And you, Grace?"

Her heart raced, as if she were perched at the top of a roller coaster before it nose-dived down a steep incline. "I don't think it's a good idea," she said finally, looking up to see Meg blanch, "to fantasize about marriage unless you've got somebody specifically in mind you think you'd be able to do it with." She paused but Father Frank made no move to speak. Inching forward in his chair, he seemed genuinely interested. "I think it makes people impatient and unrealistic," Grace added.

Father Frank's eyebrows rose markedly. "Do you think your parents have a good marriage, Grace?"

"Yes."

"And what do you mean when you say that?"

I didn't say it, you did, Grace thought irritably. "Just that they belong together," she said, carefully keeping her tone polite. "Just that they chose to be together and nobody kept them apart and they're still happy about it."

Father Frank nodded solemnly and Grace saw Meg, out of the corner of her eye, fidgeting nervously. "I want to say a few things about marriage that I tell couples who come to see me for pre-canaan counseling," Father Frank said, folding his hands into the shape of a steeple. "Being married means literally becoming one," he said, "and that means spiritually, emotionally and physically. Now I know that these days, more and more young people take lightly the notion of becoming one physically before marriage. They think that love — and sometimes baser notions than that — is enough to justify a physical union." His eyes darted anxiously from Grace to Meg. "But divorce is forbidden in the Church for a reason, girls, and that's because any union that God makes, mere mortals do not have the right to abandon. And that's why when God makes a union in His Church, the man and woman are to come to it pure and worthy, and to do anything else is to make a mockery of God's divine plan." Father Frank paused and leaned back meaningfully. "Do you understand?" he asked, looking hopefully at Grace.

Grace nodded and smiled wanly but she had been only half listening. She was thinking instead about what Father Frank would say if she asked him how exactly he had become privy to the details of God's divine plan.

"Being a wife is one of the highest callings a Christian woman can answer," Father Frank said. "Likewise, bearing children."

Meg practically beamed in her chair. "I come from a long line of mothers."

"I'm sure you do," Father Frank said, laughing.

Grace bit her lip, happy despite herself. This was what she meant by a good marriage: just plain feeling great when the person you loved was near.

At eight o'clock, when Meg's front door bell rang, Grace's heart stood still. She listened at the top of the stairs, just outside Meg's bedroom, while Meg went down to see who was at the door. Mr. and

Mrs. Heinz were visiting relatives in Staten Island, and no one was expected tonight. Grace hurriedly tucked her blouse back into her jeans.

"Oh, what a surprise!" Meg was saying downstairs as she yanked open the front door. Next Grace heard the murmur of a male voice from outside. Then Meg's voice again: "Nothing. A girlfriend of mine is over, that's all."

The door shut and the male voice advanced further into the house. The blood drained from Grace's face. "I just got off work," the voice — which Grace guessed belonged to a boy of about eighteen or nineteen — said. "I figured I'd cruise by and see if anyone was around."

"And here I am," Meg said. "Grace!" she called up the stairs. "Come on down and say hello to someone." Then both voices retreated further into the house toward the kitchen.

Grace went back into Meg's room and sat on the bed, her stomach flip-flopping wildly. This couldn't be happening. Who the hell *was* this guy? And why in God's name had Meg invited him in on a rare night when they had the house all to themselves for hours on end? Grace hugged herself hard and tried to control her trembling. She should have known it was all too good to be true. Reality was asserting itself. Here she was, sitting on the bed that was still warm from their bodies, in the room where the air was still heavy with all their promises to each other, and a mere staircase away, Meg was sitting in the kitchen with a boy-man Grace had never heard of, making pleasant small talk.

Anger propelled Grace to her feet. Why hadn't

Meg told her anything about this guy, whoever the hell he was? Then again, maybe it was a good sign that she hadn't mentioned him. Maybe that meant he really wasn't important. In fact, maybe Meg was down there right now, desperate to be rescued from him.

Grace hovered at the top of the stairs. She could hear only the drone of the two voices from the kitchen, and an occasional mutual laugh. Grace's mood blackened again. After all, Meg had sounded genuinely pleased to see him in her doorway, had invited him in so readily — and on a night they had both so looked forward to.

Grace checked her face in the bathroom mirror and decided to brush on a little of Meg's blush. She stood back and tried to decide if she was pretty. Meg thought so, and Glen had always seemed to think so. She liked her dark hair — when it was freshly washed and brushed, anyway. She thought perhaps her chin was too pointy, and that it would have been nice to have blue eyes. Her introspection was interrupted when she heard a burst of male laughter float up the stairs.

Grace's stomach squeezed like a fist when she saw Meg at the kitchen table, her legs crossed, her chin resting cozily in the palm of one hand. The boy was possibly older than Grace had suspected. The beginnings of a beard darkened his jawline, and underneath his blue plaid shirt, his chest and arms seemed massive. Light blue eyes looked up at her from underneath a shock of black hair.

"Grace, this is Danny," Meg said, smiling. Grace tried to cram as much disapproval as possible into her glance at Meg. She sank into a chair and nodded at him across the table. She thought he looked as disappointed to have company as she was.

"Danny's a friend of my cousin's across the street," Meg said. "We met a few times over there. He just got off his shift at the Hess station on Hillside — you know the one? — and thought he'd stop by."

"Oh," Grace said, barely swallowing her fury, "you work at the station after school?"

Danny considered Grace warily. "No. I just work there, period. I dropped out. Can't make any money there." He laughed, and Meg joined him. "So, uh, you want to go out somewhere tonight?" he asked Meg. "Go down to Smitty's and get a few beers? Or we could go into Middle Village. There's a new band playing at one of the rock clubs."

Meg sat up straight and looked over at Grace.

"You guys go if you want," Grace said quickly. "I'll just call a car service back to my house."

"Absolutely not," Meg said. "You know, Danny, maybe we could plan it for another night. Grace is helping me study for a chemistry exam. I have a strong D average right about now."

"Then you're doing better than I ever was." He flashed a smile and he and Meg laughed again.

Jealousy whipped around in Grace's gut like Slice-O-Matic on overdrive. Meg looked up at him as he rose from the table to his full height somewhere over six feet, her eyes full of the promise of intimacy. It was a look Grace could not mistake. He leaned down, took her by the elbow, and kissed her on the cheek.

"I'll give you a call," he said, and then was out

the front door. Grace watched Meg wave at him from the front window as he mounted a motorcycle and roared off.

Grace walked into the living room, lit only by a small lamp, and was waiting when Meg turned around. She wished she could stop trembling. "Why did you tell him you had a D average?" she asked finally. "You know you're right on the brink of getting a B."

Meg looked puzzled, and then laughed. "I never would have guessed that would be the first thing you'd ask me." She came over and reached for Grace's hand, but Grace backed away.

"What were you expecting me to ask first — who the hell is this guy? How well do you know him that he has your number and kissed you and drops over with plans for beer dates? Why haven't you mentioned him to me before?"

"The way you're behaving right now is exactly why I didn't mention him to you."

"Are you saying I have no right to behave this way? After the things you said?"

"I'm saying you have no cause. There's nothing between us."

"Danny obviously doesn't think so. And I can see why, from the way you were coming on to him." Suddenly exhausted, Grace sank to the couch.

"Coming on to him? You've got to be kidding. I just told him I'd rather study chemistry with a girlfriend than see him tonight and then I practically kicked him out! For most guys that means he won't be able to get it up for days."

"What would you know about what makes him get it up?" Grace shouted, on her feet again.

"Nothing!" Meg shouted back. "I go over to my cousin's a couple of times a week, you know that. A few times, he was there. He's a friend of hers. She gave him my number. This was the first time he was ever in my house."

"Why'd you tell him you'd have to *plan* another night to get together?"

"I was just being polite, for God's sake."

"Don't lie to me," Grace said, back on the couch. "What makes you think you can lie to me?" She hugged a throw pillow against her and, though she hated herself for losing control, began to cry.

Meg sat down next to her and pried the pillow free. "Come here," she whispered into her hair, and Grace reluctantly allowed herself to be surrounded by Meg's arms. "Sometimes I just don't know all the rules. I could never love anyone the way I love you, want anyone the way I want you. But I don't know what to do with the part of me that still turns to mush when I see a guy like Danny."

Grace clung to Meg in the dusk of the living room, half hoping if she held on tight enough she could stop her from slipping away. Though it was largely incomprehensible, Grace knew, in a place where there were no words or explanations, that somehow the moments when Meg was totally, completely hers had already passed, passed without calling attention to themselves, passed without cautioning her to savor them. Grace had given Glen up willingly, because she could, and Meg's nature was just a wholly different thing. How could it be that they had arrived at loving each other so fiercely from such completely different directions? And what did that mean about where they were headed?

Meg was covering Grace's face with little kisses, brushing away her tears as she went. "Come upstairs," she whispered urgently. "I want to make love to you."

Grace got uncertainly to her feet and took Meg's hand. Already she had compromised, she knew, but she was powerless to say no.

− 12 −

Grace slid into a seat in the empty classroom and prepared to wait. She was ten minutes early for her meeting with Sister Mary Alice and she couldn't remember dreading anything as much as this. Before she had a chance to again turn over in her mind the dilemma that had kept her awake nearly all last night, she heard the crisp click of Sister Mary Alice's pumps coming down the tiled hallway.

"Hello, Grace," the nun said cheerily. "I've been

looking forward to this meeting," she said, wheeling the chair away from the desk at the front of the room. "Please, bring a chair up here next to me. This is where the real fun of planning the magazine begins."

Grace dutifully dragged a chair to the front of the room and watched Sister open up a portfolio and take out large cardboard posters marked up with blue ink to show a place for a table of contents, an editor's page, a staff box. Grace had to hold her breath to quell her excitement.

"Then there's the matter of the actual material," Sister said. "Have you got your new set of recommendations?"

Grace looked down at the much-handled folder she'd been clutching. Then she looked up at Sister Mary Alice's expectant face. As always, her auburn hair attractively framed her face. Her necklace with its delicate gold crucifix rested at her throat, and her brown dress was notable only for its plainness.

"Um, I have the submissions that I originally rejected," Grace said. "The ten or so at the top are the least amateurish, and I managed to get three other girls to write short nature essays." Grace put the folder at the edge of the desk and took a deep breath. "But I have something else to say, Sister," Grace said, staring into her lap.

"Yes?"

"I can't be the editor of *Voices* if you print these submissions and not the ones I selected first." She sucked in her breath sharply. "To me, *Voices* always meant the voice of all the students, and I think that rejecting those whose ideas we don't agree with is censorship." Grace looked up at the nun's frowning face. "And I can't be a part of that."

The room vibrated with silence and Grace feared she would hyperventilate from the combined effort of holding her breath and sweating. She didn't dare look up again until Sister spoke.

"Frankly I'm stunned by your irresponsibility, Grace," Sister Mary Alice said finally. "To be a quitter in the first place, and at the eleventh hour no less. And to pretend that you feel betrayed by rules that were clearly stated from the very start."

"Maybe the rules weren't so clear to me, Sister. I thought you said I had a choice to act according to my conscience. Now you're saying that what you really meant was that I had no choice but to act according to yours." Grace's palms were so clammy she wouldn't have trusted herself to touch anything for fear that she would stain it. She didn't know exactly where she was getting her nerve, except that she felt as though she were somehow fighting for more than just the integrity of *Voices.*

"What you're doing is extremely inadvisable, Grace, and, I think, uncharacteristically cowardly. There's no point in pandering to people's worst instincts. Literature should be uplifting and redeeming, inspirational and wise. It shouldn't be just a reflection of people's warts and nightmares, without any attempt to teach or put life's purpose into perspective."

"Maybe what I had to choose from wasn't so great, Sister, because none of us are professionals. But I'd rather see us print something rough and honest than polished and faked." Grace felt suddenly lightheaded with conviction. "I mean, we can't just hold up a circus mirror to reality and see only what we want to see."

Sister Mary Alice blinked several times. Then she stuffed the big boards back into the portfolio, snagging them on the corners as she unevenly forced them in. "I give you until the end of the week, Grace, to reconsider. You're throwing away a real growth experience for what I can only identify as adolescent stubbornness. There's a time and a place to say and think and do different things, and you've hopelessly scrambled the equation. I'm deeply disappointed in you, but I do hope you'll come to your senses."

Sister Mary Alice finished gathering up all her material and stiffly retreated from the room.

Grace headed straight for the locker room and walked between row after row of olive-colored lockers. Meg's locker was just a few down from her own, and she slid to the floor midway between the two of them. Meg had a dentist appointment near her mother's job, and Mrs. Heinz was picking her up afterwards to drive her home. It was endlessly frustrating to Grace whenever Meg wasn't a bus trip or a phone call away. She took out a notebook and began to write her a letter. She told her all of what she remembered of Sister Mary Alice's accusations and made herself sound more brave and eloquent than she had actually been. After twenty minutes, she had exhausted her righteousness and got up. She and Meg had given each other their locker combinations, and she opened Meg's locker with ease.

Grace looked over the familiar items with a tingle of pleasure. Someday she'd be able to open Meg's dresser drawers in the apartment they would share. There was the class schedule Meg had taped to her door, on which the breaks they shared in common were colored in red. A gray and black sweater hung in the back. Grace pressed it to her face, inhaling Meg's scent. On the floor was a plastic bag in which Meg stored all of Grace's accumulated letters. Grace left this new one on top so that Meg would see it first thing tomorrow morning.

Just as she started to close the locker door, a large, unfamiliar manila envelope in the corner caught her eye. She picked it up, guilt making her cheeks hot, and pulled out a fistful of letters addressed to Meg in a hand she didn't recognize. The postmarks showed they were mailed from Queens, the earliest one a month ago, in March. She took the most recent one — from just last week — out of its envelope and sat back on the floor again, anxiety clawing at her throat.

"Darling Meg," the letter began. "Our talk last nite was one of the best we ever had. You are jus so beautifull it makes me crazy. I hope my plans dont scare you but I'm going to make you my wife. Definatley. I've never loved anyone so much ever and the looks on your face show you feel the same way, to. Your kisses are like rose petals and I'm going to make you bloom. I cant hardly wait to have my arms around you again. I love you, Danny."

Tiny colored balls of light danced in front of

Grace's eyes and her stomach churned like the Grand Rapids. She leaned her head back against the cool locker door and forced herself to breathe evenly until the nausea passed. She rifled through the rest of the letters with unsteady hands. The other letters were more of the same, talk of marriage and escape from Meg's parents, passionate kisses recalled, references to meetings that clearly outnumbered the few casual run-ins Meg had told her had taken place at her cousin's house.

Grace was stoic with shock. If Meg were here now, she felt she could walk past her with a mere nod and consider the whole affair over and done with. The worst thing that could have possibly happened was happening, and it was with considerable surprise that Grace realized her heart was still pumping and her lungs forcing air in and out. With acute self-conscious amazement, she got up and replaced the large envelope. She hesitated for a moment, wondering if she should make an effort to reorder the letters the way she found them, and felt another bolt of nausea. Having secrets from each other was an alien experience. But obviously not as alien to Meg.

After dinner, Grace finished her homework with monomaniacal precision. Then she holed up in her room for the rest of the night, dedicating herself to staring blankly at the wall. This was the time she would usually talk to Meg. Because Meg couldn't call her in case Mrs. Molino should pick up the phone, Meg's signal was to ring the phone twice and hang up. That way, Grace knew to call her back. Tonight the phone rang their signal three times in a half hour and yet Grace forced herself to ignore it. Some part of her was relishing her pain, finding it cathartic. Another part of her, she knew, merely wanted to make Meg suffer. But when the phone rang a fourth time, it kept ringing. Grace picked it up.

"What the hell is going on with you two?" Anne asked.

"Well, hello to you too," Grace said.

"Look," Anne barreled on, "Meg called me to say you aren't answering her signal to call her back. So, of course, being rational, I ask her why she just can't call you herself to ask why you aren't calling her, and then she tells me her mother's got some kind of chastity belt on the phone because she runs the bills up so the agreement is that you'll call her. So she's convinced something is wrong or that you're not home because why else would you ignore her signals —"

"Maybe I don't want to talk to her," Grace said, frightened because she could feel the edges of hysteria threatening to break through her rigid self-control.

"Well, would you call her yourself to tell her that — because she's acting like God knows what kind of crazy woman, raging about how she hopes it's not something with your mother like the last time, and of course, being rational, I ask her what the hell she's talking about, but nobody wants to give me a straight answer. Except you, Molino. You're going to tell me what's going on."

A warm glow burned inside Grace. Anne's concern always took a belligerent form — the more she bullied, the more you knew she cared. Grace realized all at once how much she had let her love for Meg cut her off from everyone else. "I can't tell you, Anne. I can't even tell her. Just tell her you got my mother on the phone and she told you I was out. With Glen."

"With Glen," Anne repeated. "You know, you've gone out with Glen more in your fantasies than you ever did in reality."

Grace started to laugh, and once she did, she found it hard to stop.

"Hey, it wasn't that funny," Anne interrupted.

"It's funnier than you know. Sorry you got caught in the middle."

"Yeah," Anne said, clearly not amused, and then hung up.

All night, long after her grandmother had come to bed and begun her muted snoring, Grace lay awake, terrified to sleep and have the night pass quickly into tomorrow, when she would have to know what to say to Meg. She faded in and out of a strange, hazy stupor, sometimes forgetting the source of her grief, and then remembering it all over again with a jolt. With the night pressing in all around her, she realized she had been kidding herself. Without Meg, she was only technically alive. The most vital parts of her were dead.

Grace headed up the hill from the subway to Immaculate Blessing's courtyard. It was a mild April morning, and gentle gusts of wind tickled her nose and lifted her hair off her shoulders. The sun was just starting to burn through the early clouds and show glimpses of turquoise sky. It was the kind of morning that normally would have set Grace's blood racing with possibilities and plans. But this morning, she was queasy. Danny's letters were a shadow over her happiness, and with the knowledge of Meg's betrayal, Grace felt as though part of her guts had been carved out. She couldn't bear to have her worst fears confirmed, that it was over, that Meg's love had its limits. And yet, she couldn't quite believe that everything that had come between them was merely exchangeable.

Grace had timed her arrival so that she would just make homeroom; she wanted to avoid everyone hanging out by the wall in the spare minutes before the bell rang. She didn't have the heart for cheery banter. It was an effort even to speak above a whisper. So when she spotted a lone figure leaning against the wall, moving a cigarette from her mouth to her side, Grace's heart pounded painfully. When, a few yards off, she was certain it was Meg, her legs grew leaden and, to her great frustration, her vision blurred with tears.

"You can avoid my phone calls," Meg said, taking a deep drag as Grace neared, "but I knew it'd be harder in person."

Grace came to a full stop several feet from where Meg stood, and still the breeze carried the disarming traces of her perfume. Grace rested her books on the concrete ledge, nervous sweat coating her upper lip. "So," she said, "have you set a date yet, and am I at least the maid of honor?"

Meg did not look surprised. She took another drag, pointed her chin at the sky, and blew the smoke high over her head. "I finally figured it out last night — that it must have been that you found Danny's letters."

"You wanted me to find them, didn't you?" Grace started to tremble.

Meg shrugged and folded her arms across her plaid jacket. "Not really. I mean, I didn't know how to tell you myself. I feel better now that you know."

Grace spread her palm out on the cool concrete ledge for support. Her stomach bucked and she was afraid she might really get sick. "So you're not denying it then?"

"How can I deny it when you found the letters?"

"Exactly how much of it aren't you denying?"

Meg dropped the cigarette at her feet and ground it out under her heel, not taking her eyes off Grace. "You don't really think I feel the same way about him as he does about me, do you? I mean, you don't think I'm going to marry him?" She reached out for Grace's arm, but Grace jerked away. "Angel, you don't really think — my God, you do." Meg was directly in front of her now, her hands on her shoulders. "I haven't done a thing to encourage him. I mean, I told him there's someone else."

Grace squirmed away. "Don't lie to me anymore," she said, her voice breaking. "I read the letters, remember? I know you met him other times besides at your cousin's house." She squinted as the sun began to burn through more brightly.

"Just once or twice, to be polite. He bought me a burger one night. You know I'm always happy for one less meal than necessary with my parents. And I went for a ride on his bike once —"

"Why didn't you ever tell me? I have a right to

know." Grace turned away. She was crying freely now, and was clumsy with anger.

"Because it didn't mean anything, and because I was afraid," Meg said, reaching out for her again, her voice shaking. "I can't make the feelings go away."

Grace whirled around. "Which feelings? The ones you have for him, or the ones you have for me?"

Meg took a few steps back. "Both."

The double bell for the beginning of classes sounded, its shrill cry jangling Grace's nerves. They had missed homeroom, and now were officially late. Grace had never been late before during her entire three years at Immaculate Blessing. She picked up her books. "We have to go."

"Don't. Come home with me. I need —" Meg started, and then broke off in a sob. A sweet breeze cooled Grace's face, and she glanced up at the classroom windows where students were beginning chemistry lab or a discussion of World War II. She looked at Meg's face, rosy with tears, and wondered if she dared put her arms around her out here in the open.

"Let's go," Grace said decisively.

Grace was feverish by the time they arrived at Meg's. They had never been alone in the house at this time of day, and the mellow morning sun through the windows made the place look strangely new. Grace kept glancing around to make sure all the familiar items were in their place — the albums by the record player, Mrs. Heinz's sewing machine on the dining room table. She couldn't shake an odd, lightheaded feeling that maybe she was dreaming. Her head cleared as soon as Meg firmly took her hand and they ascended the stairs to her room.

Meg closed the door, more out of habit than necessity now, and covered Grace's face with quick, light kisses. Grace pulled her close, and they fell to the bed, banging their teeth during frantic kisses, hopelessly wrinkling their school skirts and blouses and tangling their bras and pantyhose as they struggled out of them. When Meg started to tease down Grace's underwear, Grace grabbed them back, her stomach coiled in self-conscious fear. So much of their groping had been done under clothes that Grace had gotten used to the corduroy burns and zipper bites. But Meg was unwavering. She pulled her own and Grace's underwear completely off, dropping them, rolled cigarette-thin, to the floor.

They had never been fully naked in front of each other before, and Grace struggled to muffle a grateful sob. Meg, so breathtakingly beautiful and womanly, knelt over her, pinning Grace's hands down on the bed, her breasts brushing against Grace's own as she bore into her neck with electrifying kisses. Grace whimpered, embarrassed but helpless with excitement, her eyes shut tight against the blaze of the morning sun. But the more they kissed, the more the few boundaries left between them fell away, so that finally, no shred of shame or shyness remained. Grace opened her eyes and watched her lover keenly, drank in the lines of her, her every sacred move.

Meg's warm mouth traveled down to Grace's breasts, her tongue tracing dizzying circles around each nipple till both were painfully taut. She released Grace's wrists, and left a trail of kisses over her rib cage and stomach, and then her thighs. Then Grace felt her legs being pushed wide apart as a white heat raced through her body, spreading out from the place where Meg's tongue was dancing and daring her, making the room float over her head, making her toes curl and her stomach go to mush. She felt nudged by wave after wave of pleasure, like a raft being carried recklessly out to deeper waters. Through it all, one thought and one thought only made itself coherent in Grace's mind: this is Meg touching me this way, loving me this way, Meg, Meg, Meg. . . . Then a powerful tremor shook her hard, and she caught Meg's head in the grip of her thighs. Grace's breathing slowly clattered back to normal, and she clapped her palm to her own dewy chest as if she could somehow calm her hammering heart.

"Nutcracker," Meg said hoarsely into Grace's ear, one leg thrown across Grace's hips. Grace recognized the tangy-sweet scent on Meg's cheeks as her own, and her face went scarlet. "You nearly crushed my skull there at the end."

Grace laughed giddily, half from triumph, half from fear. She ran her fingertips slowly over Meg's full breasts, watching the nipples wrinkle and stiffen, then down Meg's hips and round the curve of her buttocks to her inner thigh. Then she crouched low and tasted her, parting the wet and velvet folds with her tongue tentatively, delicately, then gradually more purposefully. Grace felt Meg begin to shiver, and her own heart swelled to nearly bursting. The whole world, even the specter of Danny's letters, was blotted out. What other love beside their own could be so powerful, now or ever? She drank in the details of this moment, tried to memorize how they were, lying naked in bed, the house empty, Meg beneath her, hungry for her touch. Because as happy as she was, Grace couldn't shake the feeling that this might be their last safe day together.

Anne and Grace sat at a cafeteria table that was littered with the remains of their late lunch. They were at a table by a window that overlooked the courtyard lawn where clusters of seniors, the only ones privileged to be out there, lounged on benches or blankets. "Next year, that's us," Anne said, her feet up on an empty orange chair.

"Yeah, it's hard to believe. I mean, I've been waiting for this what feels like forever. And now that it's almost here, I feel sort of like an impostor."

"Sex is like that."

"Do tell, oh seer," Grace said, smirking and kicking away the chair supporting Anne's feet.

"Hey!" Anne said, retrieving the chair with exaggerated irritation. "I don't know. I guess a part of me thought I was going to be somebody else after I —" She lowered her voice, "— started sleeping with Rick. And like, I was just the same old Anne, only I had slept with Rick."

Grace gave Anne a long, sarcastic stare. "Thanks for sharing that."

"No, come on, I'm serious. It's like, how can I explain it?" Anne dropped her head back and let her arms dangle. "I mean, I guess I thought I'd feel older, more sophisticated, wiser. I don't know *why* I thought I'd feel that way." She looked out the window distractedly. "I don't think I expected Rick

223

to be any different. Maybe just a little less frantic. Which he is." She leaned her chin in her hand. "I don't know. You tell me how you feel when you've been there."

A swell of frustration lodged in Grace's throat. She couldn't tell her that she already knew, that making love to the person she loved *had* changed her, had made her come through to the other side a different person, with a different knowledge of the world and herself. But she said nothing, only kept staring hard out the window.

"Hey," Anne said, pressing closer to the window. "Isn't that the senior we saw meeting Linda Amato after school that day?"

Grace leaned forward to see her, sitting cross-legged on a blanket with three other seniors. Her long, dark blonde hair hung regally down her back as she turned her face toward the sun. Grace scraped her chair closer to the window. She wasn't sure how she knew, but she was suddenly sure that this senior was Linda's lover, and that the three other girls on the blanket, sunshine reflecting off their white blazers, had no idea. How did she live with her secret? Were there many more like her right here in school? Was there any way she could get to know them? And she had to, Grace realized all at once, because she was one of them.

"We could probably find her picture in the yearbook and find out what her name is," Anne said idly.

"That's a great idea," Grace said, shaking Anne by the shoulder. "A great idea."

"Oh yeah?" Anne said, turning to her. "And then what are you going to do about it?"

Grace shrugged. "I haven't the foggiest idea." But she knew she'd think of something.

Meg sat with her feet up on the living room table. It was a gesture that drove Mrs. Heinz to hysterical shrieking, and that only seemed to inspire Meg to do it more. She did it when her mother wasn't home also, but it didn't seem to hold the same pleasure for her without her mother's objection.

Grace flipped through the stack of albums piled by the stereo, and put on the old Carole King album they both loved.

"Oh, not that," Meg said, reaching for her cigarettes. "Put on something more upbeat. That one's so sad." She struck a match several times before it lit.

Grace reluctantly lifted the needle off the record, a lump building in her throat. "This is your favorite."

"It still is. Just not right now." She dropped her head back and closed her eyes, inhaling deeply.

Grace put on a Peter Frampton album. "Did you see Danny last night?" she asked, settling on the couch. They had arrived at an uneasy agreement: the subject of Danny could be brought up only if Grace initiated it. And she did so regretfully every time, because the subject always made Meg agitated and restless. Still, Grace had to know what was going on.

"He was at my cousin's, if that's what you mean."

"Bearing letters?"

Meg shrugged.

"Did you read mine this morning?" They had long

225

been in the habit of exchanging letters after homeroom. Grace was painfully aware that these days she was writing more than she was receiving.

"Uh huh." Meg contemplated the tip of her cigarette. "I've been thinking. Maybe I won't go to college. Maybe I'll get a job and earn some money first."

"Jesus H. Christ!" Grace exploded, her cheeks burning. "Is this Danny's sage wisdom? And after all, why shouldn't you listen to his advice? Look how well he's done. He's practically management-trainee material over there at the gas pumps."

"You know, lay off him already, Grace. Don't you think I have a mind of my goddamn own? I'm capable of original thought. And just because college is right for you doesn't mean you have to ram it down my throat." Meg stabbed out her cigarette and folded her arms tightly across her chest.

"Oh God," Grace said, rubbing her pounding temples. "I'm sorry. I just — I guess I was counting on our getting away somewhere together. I wish we were a year older. We'd be leaving soon. We —" She broke off, hugging herself and rocking. She missed Meg, missed her even while she was sitting right next to her on the couch.

"I know," Meg said, reaching out. "I still want that, too."

For a long moment, they clung to each other, and Grace held her breath, afraid that the slightest motion would frighten Meg off. Still, being close to her, smelling the warmth of her scalp, the particular sweetness of her skin, Grace felt deeply stirred. She pressed her lips to Meg's throat. Then she heard it — a small gurgle, then a giggle, then a full-blown laugh.

226

It was like the unexpected sour note struck in a song that spoils the entire melody.

"I'm sorry," Meg said. "I'm ticklish."

Grace leaned away. "Yeah," she said, getting up to turn the album over. "I feel kind of funny myself."

When Father Frank opened the door to his office, his pale face looked even more drawn than usual, and his chest, under his black vestments, looked sunken. He did not smile as he ushered Grace into the room and made his standard offer of a glass of water. Grace decided to accept it in order to buy herself time. As Father Frank padded away down the hall, she sat down heavily in her chair.

Grace alone had been invited to this meeting; a note had been delivered to her during her last class of the day. Sister Clara had handed it over with the solicitous smile the nuns reserved for dealings with priests. During her walk over to the rectory, Grace racked her brain to think of some way to contact Meg, but she was no doubt on the bus home. Grace was sure this meeting had something to do with her mother's decision about them, and since she was invited alone, it couldn't be good.

Father Frank came quietly back into the room with the pitcher and glasses. He closed the door and fussed an inordinately long time over the water before he settled down. When he finally did, he looked exhausted. Dark circles ringed his eyes. He looked gray all over.

"Grace," he said in a hushed tone that frightened her. "I have failed you." He closed his eyes and, folding his hands in prayer, rested his forehead heavily against his fingertips.

"What do you mean, Father?" Grace asked hoarsely.

"I have failed you, I have failed your mother, and I have failed Meg," he said, giving her the most sorrowful look she could remember seeing on a priest since the last wake she attended. "But I have also failed this school, the community, and ultimately, our Father in heaven."

Grace gripped the arms of her chair, totally at a loss. "I don't understand."

"This is going to be painful, Grace," Father Frank said, leaning forward in his seat.

Grace felt as if a ton of steel were resting on her chest. Could her mother somehow have found more letters, overheard some phone conversation, had them followed by a detective, spoken to Mrs. Heinz? "Tell me," she said, when she got her breath.

"Meg came to see me yesterday."

"Meg?" Grace asked dumbly. "You mean, my mother didn't call this meeting?"

Father Frank shook his head slowly. "And I've struggled greatly over whether or not I should tell your mother about this, even though Meg agreed to talk to me only on the condition that I tell no one about this but you."

"So what is it, already?" Grace laughed nervously.

Father Frank sighed deeply and leaned back. "Well, to begin with, she told me the truth about the real extent of your physical relationship."

Grace went rigid with fear. Why would Meg want to destroy all the progress they'd made?

"Grace," he said, shaking his head, "this is where I must ask your forgiveness, for not being able to see that you and Meg were too frightened to tell the truth, so that I could truly help you. Instead, I didn't question hard enough, or look more deeply into both your souls. I could have saved you sooner from sinning so gravely."

Save it, Father, were the words that sprang to Grace's mind, but she managed to contain her impatience. "Is that all Meg came to tell you?"

"No." Father Frank leaned over and roughly closed his hand over Grace's. "She told me that she wants your relationship to end. She has fallen in love with a boy who wants to marry her and raise a family. And she doesn't know how to tell you."

Though she struggled to control herself, hot tears welled in her eyes. "I don't believe you," she said. "It's not true. It's a setup." She searched the priest's face and saw only his sincerity. Terror stabbed at her heart.

"I'm sorry, Grace."

"*Sorry!*" she exploded, jumping to her feet. "What do you know about it? It's what you and my mother wanted all along. Everyone drove her to this. She's terrified. You've made us pariahs. No wonder she's running away from me."

"Grace!" Father Frank grabbed her forcefully by the shoulders. "Calm yourself!"

Grace struggled in his grasp and broke free. "Calm myself! You're the one who told us love is worth fighting for."

"This isn't true love, Grace —"

"What the hell would you know about it, Father?"

Father Frank staggered back a few steps, reaching behind him for his chair. He had a little color back in his cheeks at least, Grace noticed.

"Grace, I'm prepared to take your confession right here and now." He closed his eyes and blessed himself.

Goosebumps sprang up along Grace's arms and neck. "No thank you, Father. Forgiveness isn't what I had in mind right now." She flung the door open wide and heard the echo of her own feet as she ran breathlessly down the hallway. Though she couldn't have explained why, she felt as though she were running for her life.

– 13 –

Grace sat on the edge of Anne's bed, tugging at a cuticle. Anne was on the floor, impatiently spinning the radio tuner. She stopped when she heard the jazzy beat of "Hijack." "God, remember this from sophomore year?"

Grace did. It was one of the first songs she and Meg had danced to at Sacred Soldiers, back in the heady days when their love was first unfolding. Now it had been a full three weeks since she and Meg had spoken at all. During the free periods that they used to spend in the auditorium or cafeteria, passing notes back and forth, rhapsodizing about what they would do and say once they were alone together later, Grace now worked in the library or in resource centers, struggling to concentrate. Her phone didn't ring at night. Even the meetings with Sister Mary Alice, and with Father Frank, had stopped. Loneliness pressed in from all sides.

Now that they weren't arranging their schedules around each other, it was surprisingly easy to move through Immaculate Blessing's four floors without once even catching a glimpse of Meg. It hardly mattered though. Every hallway and threshold, every classroom and lab, held some richly textured memory that ripped away her carefully cultivated callouses and exposed the raw flesh below.

This Thursday, though, Grace had passed Meg in the hall. Panic and hope collided painfully in her chest when Grace spotted her, and from a few paces off, she was even able to imagine a reconciliation — Meg giving her one of her stealthy smiles and saying what an idiot she had been, that it was all behind them now, and of course they would be together again, and always. But as Grace slowed her pace, Meg had kept on going, smiling mournfully in her direction. Grace had ducked into a bathroom, barricaded herself in a stall, and sobbed silently till her ribs ached. She would have thought that after crying herself to sleep every night, there would be no tears left during the day, but she was wrong.

"All right, enough of this crap," Anne announced. "I'm not blind. What's eating your gut? You don't leave this room alive unless you spill it."

Grace grudgingly laughed. She looked out the window at the baby-blue sky of the early May day.

This should have been a joyous time for her, for her and Meg — bicycle rides, picnics, and soon, trips to the beach. She thought of Meg stretched out on a beach towel, tanned and glistening, next to a lunch basket they would have prepared together.

"Grace? Are you with us?"

Grace looked up. Her heart was beating fast in her throat. "I can't tell you," she said finally. "You wouldn't want to know me anymore."

Anne flounced down on the bed next to her. "Grace, if you keep up the long-suffering silence, pretty soon I'm not going to know you, anyway." She ruffled Grace's hair. "Besides, there's nothing you could tell me that would change the fact that you're my best friend. Even if you told me you killed someone," Anne said, her voice growing robust, "I'd testify for you in court. I'd say there must be some mistake."

"What if there was no mistake? What if the terrible thing was true?"

"Why don't you show me the body and find out?"

Grace got up to pace. Fear made her throat dry and her stomach unreliable. Telling Anne loomed before her as the hardest thing she ever had to do, harder in some ways than not seeing Meg. It would mean saying she was both serious and not sorry. "It's important. No kidding around."

Anne sat up straight and put on her most somber face.

"Meg and I," Grace said, her voice quavering, "are — I mean, we were, anyway — lovers." Grace shivered. "Since the fall. But she left me."

An odd look passed over Anne's face, as if she

233

had just taken a swallow of a meal and someone told her it was cat meat. Worse, her own cat. "Okay," she said slowly. "Now a lot of things make sense."

"That's exactly how I felt when I realized what I was feeling for Meg," Grace said hopefully. Through tears, she told Anne the whole story in one long breath — about Glen, about her mother, Father Frank, Danny, even their plans to live together during college, and after.

When Grace was finished, Anne sighed heavily, cracking her knuckles vengefully. "I'd be lying if I said it didn't make me feel a little sad." Tears made her eyes shine. "But I don't really know why. Does it make you unhappy?"

"Not loving her," Grace said. "Just how hard it is for everybody else to let me."

"Why do you think it is? I mean, maybe you haven't met the right guy yet?"

Grace shrugged. "Maybe you haven't met the right woman."

The two girls burst out laughing, and Grace felt the tension in her shoulders ease.

"So," Anne said, "what are you going to do about it?"

"Nothing — I don't need anyone's blessings," Grace blurted, knowing it was a lie, that that was part of what she wanted more than anything, though she had no idea who could give it to her.

"No, I mean about Meg. Breaking your heart and tossing the pieces to the wind. Are you going to let her get away with that? The little chicken-shit. The little two-timing, yellow-bellied worm."

"There's nothing I can do. She's made her choice.

How can you make someone love you again?" Grace curled up on the bed, hugging a pillow.

"You fight for her. You go and grab her by the collar and say, You are making a *big* mistake, sweetheart!" Anne was on her feet, swinging her fist in the air, totally absorbed.

"No, this is a little different," Grace said, sitting up. She was profoundly touched by Anne's swift and sincere acceptance, but it was premature, undigested. There were so many details Grace had had time to think through that hadn't yet even dawned on Anne. "Danny's got everything on his side — he can marry her, have children with her, live openly in the world with her. All I have to offer is my love."

Anne planted her hands on her hips and frowned down at Grace. "And if she can't see which side the scale comes down on," she said, hugging Grace hard, "then she doesn't deserve you."

In the strength of Anne's embrace, Grace tried hard to believe she was right.

Nighttime was the worst. During the day she had quickly grown a hard shell of hostility in order to be able to walk down the halls, past the auditorium or into the cafeteria without succumbing to paralyzing despair. Sometimes, after a particularly intense class, she would experience a tantalizing moment of transcendence, of falling through a time warp. She'd look up and expect to see Meg waiting outside the classroom door, or she'd pack up her books anticipating meeting her by the bus stop. But then she'd shake it off, feel all the air get sucked from the room. Her head would pound and her stomach would buck, and she could feel her now familiar scowl return.

Still, the days were nothing compared with the night, when there was no escape from memory and its special tortures of total recall. There was no sleep for her, and when there was, her dreams were drenched with Meg, or Meg impostors — animals or strangers that had her mannerisms or voice, or knew hers and Meg's secrets. There was no balm but to plot and to hope. Danny would leave her, she would leave Danny, Danny would be killed or banished by Mrs. Heinz. The promise of their reunion was what kept Grace sane, and she believed with every fiber of her soul that there would be one. Love just didn't evaporate. The part of Meg that had loved her must love her still, Grace was convinced, and it would return to dominance.

In the meantime, her world had stopped. Her vision of the future had receded and stopped at final exams. After that, she'd be out of school and there wouldn't be even the bittersweet comfort that they were occupying the same building. There would be no chance run-ins, no spying Meg across the courtyard, with her sweater draped over one arm, a cigarette between her fingers. There would be no connection between them but promises made and broken.

By morning, she'd be hoarse from dry sobs (having to muffle them because her grandmother was just across the room), her eyes swollen, her lips chapped. She told her mother, who eyed her in the morning the way a warden might an untrustworthy prisoner, that she had developed bad allergies. She told everyone else very little. She knew a rumor had started that she had begun to regret her breakup with Glen, and she did nothing to correct it.

Harder than anything was resisting. The phone sat on her dresser, silent and mocking. Meg was only seven numbers away, and if only she could talk to her, she could think of the thing to say that would bring back her love. Sometimes she found herself in front of the dresser, her head on the phone, rehearsing speeches in her mind, losing track of how long she'd been there.

What stopped her from calling was scalding humiliation. She reminded herself that Meg had wanted to end it, that Meg had sent Father Frank as her messenger, that Meg surely would have known the abyss of pain she was sending her down into alone with the priest in that overheated interrogation room. The betrayal was at least twofold: handing her over to their enemies, leaving her for an unequal rival.

And then she'd remember, too, that not once had her phone rung, not once had a letter of explanation or remorse turned up in her locker. Sometimes Grace imagined that there were two sets of Meg and Grace, one of which went on, still in love, in some parallel time zone, out of their reach. Who that meant they were now, in reality, she wasn't sure. Just outlines, perhaps, like the cicada shells of August, tan, fragile husks split open down their backs, out of which the beautiful monster escaped and flew away.

* * * * *

"It's perfectly simple," Anne said, pulling off her jacket as they sat down at the far end of a cafeteria table just before the lunch rush. "If you want to make contact, you've only got a few weeks left to act. Then Adele will have graduated, and there's no telling if Linda will ever be back here."

Adele Fitzgerald, Grace had discovered by looking her up in the yearbook, was the senior with the long blonde hair who slipped into Linda's waiting car. Grace knew Anne was right, but a stabbing headache was distracting her from "The Plan," as she and Anne had come to call it — the plan to make contact with Linda Amato.

"Tell me again what you had in mind," Grace said, massaging her temple and pushing away her trigonometry textbook.

"Jeez, pay attention." Anne tipped her chair forward eagerly. "We write the note," she said, glancing around anxiously, "which says something like, 'About the play you and Joan Sweeny rehearsed last year. We'd like to come to the premiere. We think we know the lines by heart.' " Anne grinned. "Not bad, huh?"

"Yeah, so, then what?"

"Then we say that the next Friday she comes to school — because you know she always comes on Fridays — we'll both be wearing red blouses and waiting by the courtyard wall. That's how she'll know who to make contact with."

"And how do you propose we get this letter to her in the first place?"

"Piece of cake. We follow Adele one day to see where her locker is. When she leaves, we slip the note in through the vents. The envelope will be addressed to Linda, of course."

"You're going to get us killed. Or arrested." Despite herself, Grace yielded to a shiver of excitement. She had no idea what she'd say to Linda and Adele if they ever came face to face, but the prospect seemed so remote, she wasn't worried. She did feel sure that they were kindred spirits, though, and even this bizarre, tenuous connection to them gave her hope. "But let's do it."

Anne whipped open a notebook and uncapped a black felt-tip pen. "Dear Linda," she recited as she wrote.

"You're really doing it?"

"Goddamn it, Grace!" Anne slapped the pen down on the tabletop. Two sophomores at the other end gave them a quizzical look, and then respectfully retreated. "You think I'm fooling around here? You've been like the living dead. Linda got over Joan," she said, lowering her voice, "and found someone new. Now you're going to have to do the same thing, and she's going to help you."

Someone new. The words bounced off the inside of Grace's skull. Someone aside from Meg? It was impossible. She would never love anyone aside from Meg. Neither man nor woman. She wasn't heterosexual, or homosexual, or even bisexual. She was Meg-sexual.

"There," Anne said, sliding the note over to Grace. "Seem okay?"

Grace scanned it. It read as promised. "I don't know. It's risky."

Anne stared at her long and hard. "Old friend, in

case you haven't noticed, you are *way* out on a limb already."

Grace smiled reluctantly. She reached out and squeezed Anne's shoulder. "I'll think of some way to repay you." Her voice broke, and she looked away, ferociously embarrassed.

"Yeah. You can name your firstborn after me." For a moment, they were both stunned silent, and then they exploded in laughter. A gaggle of freshmen coming in for lunch steered carefully around them.

Grace pulled her locker open, and the flimsy tin door shook like a dog in the cold. She dumped her trig books onto the locker's floor and pulled her history text down. It was one of the last classes before finals, and the material they were covering now would be crucial on the test. Everyone had grown still and serious with concentration, momentarily soothed by the warm breeze and its promise of imminent freedom.

As Grace slammed the locker door shut, she found herself face to face with Meg. Their lockers were still just a few doors apart, although Grace had thought often of moving to avoid just this moment. Now that it was upon her, she understood why she hadn't. Her back went damp with fear but her heart, listening for strains of hope only it could hear, danced.

"Hi," Meg said, smiling. It was a smile Grace knew well — intimate, mischievous, shy — but no longer trusted.

"Hi," Grace croaked in return, her throat tight. All

her hours of rehearsed approaches — studied nonchalance, irresistible seductiveness — were futile. She was helplessly sincere before Meg, and all she could muster was grief and anger. She didn't trust herself to speak further.

"I, uh, wrote you about a million letters and then tore them all up," Meg said, glancing around to make sure no one was within earshot. "None of them made any sense."

"I wish you had let me be the judge of that. I would have appreciated the effort."

"God, you sound so cold."

Grace shut her eyes against tears. "Just what were you expecting?"

"I can't take it," Meg said, kicking her locker. "Seeing how much I'm hurting you." She covered her mouth for a moment. "I — I do love you, Grace. That's never changed."

"Don't," Grace said, stopping to get her breath. "I've got a class to go to. It's important." She tried to back away but the room was reeling.

"It's just, my whole life is screwed up," Meg was saying. "Danny wants me to marry him and I'm too young. My mother doesn't have the money for school next year, and they might have tried to swing some I.O.U.s if I wasn't pushing a couple of D's. And you're the best person I've ever known but I just can't, I just can't —"

"Yeah, I know," Grace said, a sudden fury giving her back her wind. "It really cracks me, I have to tell you, how we busted our horns because we thought everybody else was trying to keep us apart. I mean, you name it, we blamed them. My mother, Glen, the school, the church, hey, what the hell —

241

the state and the federal government, while we're at it! But you know, nobody had the power to keep us apart but you and me."

"Don't," Meg said, crying now. "This hurts me, too."

They were just a few feet apart. If only that were all the distance between them, Grace thought. Desire, like an undertow, pulled her a few steps closer.

"All I ever wanted," Grace whispered, "was to be with you always."

But Meg wouldn't meet her eyes. Grace shook her head and, crying, ran.

They were at the courtyard wall early. Red was not a color Grace was prone to wearing, tending toward quieter shades, so all day she had felt hotly conspicuous. She had skulked around the halls, terrified of running into Adele, and although Anne assured her other juniors and seniors who were also allowed to wear other than uniform white blouses were in red that day, too, Grace would not be consoled.

"What if she doesn't show up?" Grace asked. "You're sure you put the note in the right locker?"

"She will and I did, goddamn it," Anne said. "Do yourself a favor — don't ever get pregnant. You couldn't live through nine months of suspense."

"I'm touched by your concern. But I don't think I'll have to worry about it."

"Don't mention it. And you never know."

Grace combed her hair again, and adjusted her

skirt. She was deeply grateful for Anne's support but she was too emotionally exhausted to show it.

Suddenly, Anne's hand was like a clamp on Grace's arm. "She's coming."

The white car turned the corner. Terror made Grace tingle from head to toe. "Good God, what if we're dead wrong? What if none of it's true, about her and Joan and Adele? What if she kicks the living daylights out of us for accusing her?"

"That's the beauty of the note, Grace. We didn't spell a thing out. If she gets coy on us, we just say we were being friendly, admired her basketball game or something."

But Grace watched Anne's face as the white car slowed to the curb and saw that she was worried, too. The car stopped further down the block than usual, and for several long minutes, no one made a move to get out. Grace began to wonder if it was a different white car when Linda, in a black sweat suit, emerged from the driver's side.

"This is it, we're dead meat," Grace said. She watched Linda, her hands deep in her pockets, come strolling toward them.

"Shut up and smile," Anne warned.

Linda stopped a few feet away from them as Grace summoned all her willpower not to bolt. "Yeah," Linda said, coming closer so that Grace could see the spray of freckles across the bridge of her nose, "I recognize you two. Still spying on me, huh?"

"Well, no, we weren't spying —" Grace started.

Linda laughed. "You're right. Nothing anyone couldn't see in broad daylight, right? But the thing is, not everyone sees what's in front of them. Usually people see only what they're looking for." Linda was eyeing both of them, her left foot jutting forward. From a distance, it might have looked like a challenging pose, and in fact, Grace saw the few students who were bounding down the courtyard stairs glancing curiously in their direction. But Grace suddenly felt completely at ease.

"Come on, step into my office," Linda said, leading the way back to her car. Grace shot Anne a hopeful look, but Anne seemed noncommittal. They piled into the back seat as Linda got behind the wheel and stabbed the key into the ignition. The radio came on and Olivia Newton John's lovelorn voice filled the car.

"Aren't we waiting for Adele?" Grace asked.

Linda smiled into the rearview mirror. "No. I'm the whole welcoming committee." She pulled away from the curb, driving with her right arm across the top of the passenger seat, tapping her hand in time to the music. All the windows were rolled down and Anne's hair was swirling wildly around her face. Grace was happier than she'd been in weeks. If only Meg were around to share it.

"So," Linda shouted over the wind and the music, "whose idea was it to wear red shirts? Shouldn't it have been lavender?"

Anne shot Grace a puzzled look. "Well, neither of us have anything purple."

"Uh huh." Linda smiled a slow, amused smile. "Newer in these parts than I thought," she said, more to herself than to them.

"Where are we going?" Anne asked.

"Right over here," Linda said, turning the car

down a side street. She stopped next to a small park. In the distance, two teams of teenaged boys were kicking a soccer ball back and forth. Linda turned off the car. "So, it's poker time," Linda said, swiveling to face them, stretching her legs out leisurely across the front seat. "Who shows their hand first?"

"Well, we —" Anne and Grace started simultaneously.

"No, let me," Grace told Anne. "You've done enough for me already." Grace looked at Linda sternly. "My friend Anne really isn't — I mean, she's not involved to the same degree. She did this because she's my friend but I'm really the one who needs to talk to you."

"Fine," Linda said. "Talk." She gave Anne a quick but thorough look.

"Anne, you can go back, really, I'll be okay," Grace said.

"No way. This was my idea," Anne protested.

"I'll be fine," Grace said, with more confidence than she felt. "I mean it. It'll be better this way."

"Okay," Anne said reluctantly. "But I'm going to call you," she said, looking at her watch, "in exactly two hours. If you're not home, I'm calling the police. She gave Linda a warning glance.

Grace blushed. "Just go, already." She leaned forward and watched silently as Anne headed back down the street toward Immaculate Blessing. A flutter of anxiety rose in her throat. The car seemed unbearably small with just the two of them in it. Suddenly Linda was laughing, a robust, contagious sound, her head thrown back, the sun painting gold in her hair.

"What's so funny?" Grace demanded.

"Ohhh," Linda said, wiping her eye with the back of her hand, "it's all just so cloak and dagger. Let's just say it. You figured out about me and Joan, and now you figured out about me and Adele. Am I right?"

"Uh, well, yeah, if by 'figured out' you mean —"

"Are you in love with your friend, there?" Linda asked, gesturing at Anne's retreating back.

"Anne?" Now it was Grace's turn to laugh. "No, not with Anne."

"Another girl, then?"

Grace nodded, unable to meet her eye. "This whole year. She just left me. Probably to get married."

"Jesus, I'm sorry." Linda squeezed Grace's arm briefly.

The small gesture of kindness seemed to open some dam in Grace. She began to cry, but here her grief felt legitimate, dignified.

"She was your first?" Linda asked quietly.

Grace nodded. "Was Joan yours?"

"Well, not the very first, but definitely the most important. Everybody has one of those. You spend the rest of your life trying to figure out why it went wrong and why everyone else falls short."

"Do you ever talk to her?"

Linda looked out the car window, across the playing field. "I sent a few letters. No word."

"Maybe she never got them. Maybe the nuns screen the letters and didn't give them to her."

"Yeah, I thought of that. But I did what you did in your note to me — spoke in code. There wouldn't have been much that didn't sound perfectly innocent — to anyone but Joan, that is." Linda turned the

246

ignition key a notch so the radio came back on. "But you didn't go through all this trouble to hear my soap opera. You did a brave thing, by the way, you and your just-friend, Anne. Do you know anyone else who's gay — besides me, I mean."

Gay — the word only dimly had meaning to Grace. Lesbian, with its faintly antiseptic tone, was the only description she had ever heard. This new word, the way Linda used it, had an edge of arrogance, and Grace liked it. "No, no one else."

"Well, we'll just have to bring you out, then. There's a bar, not far from here, just before the city line. You'll find a lot of over-educated Catholic girls there. That is, the ones who didn't go into the convent. Guilt is the great unifier."

Grace laughed, though she was slightly stunned by Linda's irreverence, not just toward Immaculate Blessing and the church, but toward her own heartbreak. "Is that where you met Adele?"

"Yes, as a matter of fact. It was her first time there. And tonight, if you want, can be yours."

"Are you serious?"

"Absolutely. We'll pick you up at nine. And for now, I'll drive you home, but do me a favor? Come up front. I don't want to feel like a chauffeur."

Grace gave Linda directions to her house, using Sacred Soldiers as a landmark. Inside her head, a jumble of questions fought for prominence. Finally, she settled on one. "Did you meet Joan at this place, too?"

"Ha! Joan in a gay bar? She'd have been tarred and feathered first. Joan is what we call a closet case, Grace. I met her at school. It was the usual thing. We were drawn to each other like magnets. I knew

247

we were falling in love. She didn't. But I never pushed. She kissed me first."

Grace watched Linda's profile as she spoke. Talking about Joan seemed to rob her of some of her usual energy and animation. There was a definite boyish air about her, but it was fresh-scrubbed, earnest, even sensual. And her hair, softly curled and blonde, and long-lashed green eyes, confounded the impression. When she smiled, she was downright pretty. It was the topspin of androgyny, though, that made her seem powerful, mysterious, unpredictable.

"Anyway, when she started talking about the convent, I thought I would lose my mind. You know," Linda said, glancing over, "I was serious that night you heard us. I swear to God I thought about turning her in so they wouldn't let her enter. But then, I knew that would only make her more desperate. I still hope sometimes that she won't make it, that eventually she'll leave the convent and we'll get back together."

The tree-lined streets passed by slowly, bathed in May sunlight.

"I pray all the time that Meg won't get married. I mean, I *know* she'll come back to me."

"Let me give you a tip, Grace," Linda said. "Women like Joan and your girlfriend, they'll do anything to pass as straight. They'd rather be miserable, as long as they pass. You have to remember you can't reason with that. You can't talk someone into courage."

A new terror struck at Grace's heart. "But how do you know that isn't what they really are — straight, I mean?" Grace was working hard to keep up with the new terminology.

"How do you know? There's a simple test, Grace. Just remember the way she loved you."

Grace bit her bottom lip hard. Remembering was the easy part. It was forgetting that was impossible.

– 14 –

Mrs. Molino, arms folded, waited on the porch while Grace went out to the white car. Adele, her long blonde hair like a shawl down her back, smiled when Grace leaned down to the passenger window. Linda made hurried introductions. "Ready?" she asked.

"Um, well, there's one little thing," Grace said. "My mother said she wants you to introduce yourself." Grace wished the sidewalk would open beneath her feet and swallow her up. "You know, with the car and everything," she trailed off miserably.

Linda shot Adele a tense look and then laughed. "What should I say? Don't worry, Mrs. Molino, I'll take good care of your daughter at the gay bar? None of those mean, ugly dykes for your little girl?"

"Linda," Adele said, lightly touching her arm. "Give her a break. This is tough stuff."

"I'm sorry," Linda said. "Just my inappropriate sense of humor kicking in." She got out of the car, wearing jeans and a leather vest over a denim shirt. "Adele says I have what she calls R.A.P. — residual authority problems. Where'd you tell her we were going?"

"A party at your house," Grace mumbled, leading her to her door, which her mother was holding open.

"Mrs. Molino?" Linda said as she took the front steps two at a time. "Pleased to meet you at long last."

Mrs. Molino took Linda in with one sweeping glance and Grace saw that her mother wasn't completely pleased. But she did force a pleasant social smile. "Grace is embarrassed at my wanting to meet you, Linda, but I don't let her get into a car with anybody I don't know. There's just too much that goes on today, with drinking and drugs, boys and reckless driving. And you girls are older than Grace, so I want you to know I'm serious about her twelve-thirty curfew."

Grace thought it would be just fine if she died right then.

"Twelve-thirty! Well, then we better be on our way," Linda said, studying her watch with exaggerated surprise. "Don't worry, Mrs. M. I'll keep Grace out of the punch bowl." Then she flashed her most Immaculate Blessing-worthy smile. Grace waved to her mother from the car, slightly stunned that it looked like she would get away with this.

"How'd you do?" Adele asked once they were down the block.

"Had her eating out of the palm of my hand," Linda said. "Right, Grace?"

"I'm really sorry about that," Grace said, her forehead damp.

"No problem. How'd you say we knew each other?"

"Oh, I said you were friends with the last editor-in-chief of *Voices*, that you used to come to some meetings and stuff." As soon as the words were out, Grace regretted them.

"Ah, the pervasive influence of Joan Sweeny," Adele said, blessing herself. "Or should I say the perverted influence?"

Grace settled into the back seat and gripped the armrest. Suddenly she wished she were at home in the safety of her own room. What if the bar were raided? She'd heard of things like that. Would they run her picture in the paper? That would mean she'd have to leave school, her father might have to quit his job, they might all have to move to another state under an assumed name.

Adele swiveled around. "Hey," she said, "don't be nervous. You're going to have a good time. How can I describe it? It's sort of like a Sacred Soldier's dance except that everybody moves well." Adele and Linda burst out laughing.

As they got closer to the city line, the houses got bigger and more sprawling. Grace recognized that the front yards were landscaped. The shrubbery professionally trimmed, not clipped with hedge cutters by someone's father. Discreet little lanterns glowed at the end of long driveways. And the darkness was more complete, blanketing everything in cozy secrecy. Before Grace knew it, Linda was pulling the car into a pebbled parking lot alongside a low white building. When she opened the car door, Grace could hear the beat of loud music, almost feel it throbbing in her rib cage. She saw the awning with the name "Oasis" written across it in script.

"Come on, we're not going to abandon you," Linda said, taking Grace by the arm. When she pushed open the front door, the air was heavy with the scent of cigarette smoke and beer.

"For three," Linda shouted over the music, handing the bearded man at the door some bills. She leaned over to whisper something else in his ear. When he looked right at her and grinned, Grace felt her face go scaldingly hot.

As they turned the corner, Grace waited for her eyes to adjust to the darkness. There was sawdust beneath her feet and a long mahogany bar stretched into the back. Men and women were pressed close to it on stools and on foot, laughing and talking. It looked like any other bar in New York, Grace imagined, except that on closer inspection, it was the men who were arm-in-arm, the women who were holding hands or swaying together at the edge of the crowded dance floor.

"What are you drinking, Grace?" Linda leaned close to shout. "My treat."

"I don't know, I don't usually —"

"Get her a spritzer," Adele said. "Her mother might give her a breathalyzer or something."

Linda laughed loudly, wrapped her arm around Adele's waist and kissed her full on the lips. A few single women glanced shyly away, turning their attention instead to the dance floor. Grace felt her face steaming with embarrassment. Never in her wildest imaginings did she ever think she'd see so many couples like herself and Meg. Maybe if Meg could see this and know that they weren't random freaks of nature, she'd have the courage to come back.

"Come on, we can still get a table," Linda said, handing Grace her drink. She led the way past a pool table and up a short flight of stairs to a tiny table in the corner with three wobbly wrought-iron chairs. Linda pulled a fourth up and put her feet on it. She held up her bottle of beer. "Cheers," she said, tapping the bottle's dark neck to Grace's glass. "Happy coming out!"

Grace forced a smile. Her stomach was in knots. Did loving Meg mean she belonged in a place like this? Did she have anything in common with these people? Some of the men were slickly handsome, but walked like women. Some of the women had blunt haircuts and leaned against doorways like Humphrey Bogart.

"Feeling a little culture shock?" Adele asked.

"Yeah, I guess so."

"It's natural. Don't forget, you get the whole population in one little room each night. We don't have enough bars so that you can divide up different classes or tastes. In a way, we're better for it. We socialize with a broader range of people. In a lot of straight bars, if you don't have the right kind of sneakers on or the right color tie, you're exiled for the night."

The music roared on, punctuated by the crashing of pool balls. Gradually, the darkness, the music's steady beat, the fizzy drink, and Linda and Adele's reassuring smiles conspired to help Grace relax. A stream of women, some of whom Grace recognized from graduating classes of Immaculate Blessing, came over to greet Linda and Adele loudly. Grace started keeping a mental list of their affiliations: basketball team, choir members, yearbook staff, Honor Society officers.

Grace leaned over the round table. "I can't believe how many people from school are here."

"Believe it," Linda said. "When I first came out, I thought saying 'Catholic lesbian' was redundant."

Grace shook her head. "I really wish Meg were here to see this. She wouldn't get over it."

"Come on," Adele said, "no reminiscing allowed. Let's dance." She stood up and took Grace's hand as casually as if they had known each other all their lives.

Grace was acutely aware of the slight pressure of Adele's cool palm, of her fingers entwined proprietarily through her own. Every nerve ending in her body sprang to attention. When Adele led them to the center of the dance floor, their shoulders brushing against other couples', Grace reluctantly released her hand. Suddenly Adele was just another swaying body in the crowd, and Grace shuffled awkwardly till she found her rhythm. She stared hard at the floor, trying to ignore the dizzying pattern of spinning lights, the few shirtless men dancing pressed up against their partners' backs, the women couples all around them hooting and laughing and gyrating with abandon. But most of all, she tried to avoid Adele's eyes. She was sure Adele thought her utterly boorish and absurd. She didn't know how she could ever face her again in the halls at school.

"Let's try this," Adele said, suddenly at her side. She put one arm around Grace's waist and took her other hand, moving them around the floor in a careful pattern. "This is great," she said. "Linda never lets me lead."

Grace laughed, and felt herself really relax for the first time all night. Adele was a confident dancer, and Grace loosened up under her subtle direction. Adele's body was warming with their efforts, and Grace could smell her perfume rising up from her neck.

"You're very pretty, Grace," Adele said, her mouth by Grace's ear. "It's your girlfriend's loss, totally. There are lots of women here who want you. I can tell."

Grace lost her footing briefly, and tried not to bolt. Though joy swept through her like a bonfire, she didn't trust her reactions. Happiness here, in this place, at this moment, was its own special terror. Grace felt herself moving further and further away from not only Meg and their safe, solitary room, but from every idea of adult life her parents and the nuns had ever envisioned for her. She stepped out of Adele's embrace.

"Tired you out, huh? Let's go back." Adele walked ahead of her but at the edge of the dance floor, she stopped suddenly. "Thanks for the dance," she said, leaning her lithe body close and pressing her mouth lightly against Grace's. Her lips were parted almost imperceptibly, but the damage was immediately done.

At their table the rest of the night, Grace sat in mortal, self-conscious guilt and longing. Linda seemed blissfully undisturbed, pointing out various couples and giving Grace and Adele the background on each romance. When she announced at twelve-fifteen that it was time to go, Grace at first thought she was joking.

"Linda, why don't you go ahead," Adele said. "I'll hold down the table and wait for you."

Grace gave Adele a tight good-bye smile. "I'll meet you out front," she announced, as Linda was giving Adele a long kiss.

Outside, the night air felt as cool as rain on her skin, and carried with it the scent of unknown blossoms, as sweet as the powdery recesses of her grandmother's dresser drawers. Grace imagined that a faint vibration of Adele's kiss lingered on her lips.

Glancing down the block, Grace spotted a man walking a small dog. They stopped under a streetlight, and Grace watched as the dog nosed the new grass leisurely. The bald back of the man's head shone in the light. For a moment, man and dog were both so still they looked like an old snapshot, yellowed with age. When they started walking again, Grace saw that the man planned to pass directly in front of the bar. When he did, he looked up at the awning, hitching up his too-big pants in the back. The puppy wriggled over to Grace's feet, squirming with indiscriminate glee.

"Hey," the old man said, his voice gravelly in the relative quiet, "a young girl like you ought to stay away from here. This place," he said, his face

pinched with disgust, "is full of queers and dykes."
Then he tugged the dog's leash and continued his
slow shuffle down the block into the darkness. Linda
came bounding out the door seconds later.

"What's with you? You look like you just got
flashed or something."

Grace told her what had just happened and, to
her horror, Linda threw back her head in laughter.
"Well, you just faced your first moral dilemma, Grace,
one that the nuns of Immaculate Blessing would
appreciate. How many times did Peter deny Christ?"
She unlocked the car doors. "You passed up your
first chance to educate one of the masses, Grace. On
the other hand," she said, pebbles grinding under the
car's wheels as she pulled out of the parking lot,
"you can revel in the security of knowing that you
'pass,' in the time-honored tradition of light-skinned
slaves who escaped to the northern land of
opportunity."

She slowed for a light. "The kind of prejudice and
discrimination you'll face as a gay person, Grace, is
totally different from the kind any other minority
faces. People can insult you to your face because
your difference doesn't show. That's either a blessing
or a curse. You'll have to decide which."

Grace sat self-consciously still in the passenger
seat. A half moon shone directly overhead. She felt
humbled by the hint of many experiences Linda must
have lived through — experiences, Grace thought
with apprehension, that could not be explained, only
felt.

"Such a glum look! Let's talk about the juicy stuff.
So, you like Adele, huh?"

258

Grace folded her arms. "She's very, yes — nice," Grace stammered.

Linda was laughing again. "It's okay, you can admit you have a crush on her. Adele doesn't consider any meeting a success unless the woman goes away a little starry-eyed. She's a complete and compulsive flirt. Nothing personal, you understand." Linda frowned for a moment. "Still, I know we won't last because of it. She's too busy seeing how many women she can enthrall."

Grace watched as the sleeping houses passed them by. "Maybe you just tell yourself that because you're still waiting for Joan."

"Whoa, a direct hit." Linda slapped the steering wheel and mouthed the sounds of an explosion. She looked over with — Grace could tell — a notch more respect than before.

"It doesn't take a sage or anything," Grace said. "People are just always surprised when someone actually pays attention to what they say."

Linda nodded solemnly, driving slowly down the nearly deserted road. "About your girlfriend," she said. "I have a funny feeling she left you because she loved you more than she wanted to, not less. That's rotten consolation, I know. But you must have scared the shit out of her." Linda shook her head. "It's a shock when you find out that you break up and part ways just like everybody else, just like all the straight people you ever knew. Because when you love a woman for the first time, you feel like you've really hit on the secret of the universe, like you're removed from all the rules, like you're breathing some kind of goddamned rarified air. Because, I mean, who would go so far out of their way to find love if they weren't freaking *chosen* or something?"

Grace smiled. She felt contented as a cat on a radiator. She imagined herself and Linda at eighty, great friends sitting around a fireplace, reviewing their past romances. But maybe that was wishful thinking. Linda pulled the car to the curb in front of Grace's house. "Exactly twelve-thirty," she announced, holding up her watch for inspection.

Grace saw the light on in her parent's bedroom, shining like a lighthouse in a harbor.

"Next time," Linda said, "I'll take you into Manhattan. That's the real initiation. This was just kid stuff."

"Okay," Grace said, certain that Linda could never know how grateful she was. "I'm ready." When she closed the car door behind her, she knew it would be a long time before she fell asleep.

A few of the publications of
THE NAIAD PRESS, INC.
P.O. Box 10543 • Tallahassee, Florida 32302
Phone (904) 539-5965
Mail orders welcome. Please include 15% postage.

MURDER BY TRADITION by Katherine V. Forrest. 288 pp.
A Kate Delafield Mystery. 4th in a series.   ISBN 0-941483-89-4 $18.95

BENEDICTION by Diane Salvatore. 272 pp. Striking,
contemporary romantic novel.   ISBN 0-941483-90-8   9.95

CALLING RAIN by Karen Marie Christa Minns. 240 pp.
Spellbinding, erotic love story   ISBN 0-941483-87-8   9.95

BLACK IRIS by Jeane Harris. 192 pp. Caroline's hidden past . . .
ISBN 0-941483-68-1   8.95

TOUCHWOOD by Karin Kallmaker. 240 pp. Loving, May/
December romance.   ISBN 0-941483-76-2   8.95

BAYOU CITY SECRETS by Deborah Powell. 224 pp. A Hollis
Carpenter mystery. First in a series.   ISBN 0-941483-91-6   8.95

COP OUT by Claire McNab. 208 pp. 4th Det. Insp. Carol Ashton
mystery.   ISBN 0-941483-84-3   8.95

LODESTAR by Phyllis Horn. 224 pp. Romantic, fast-moving
adventure.   ISBN 0-941483-83-5   8.95

THE BEVERLY MALIBU by Katherine V. Forrest. 288 pp. A
Kate Delafield Mystery. 3rd in a series. (HC)   ISBN 0-941483-47-9   16.95
                                    Paperback   ISBN 0-941483-48-7   9.95

THAT OLD STUDEBAKER by Lee Lynch. 272 pp. Andy's affair
with Regina and her attachment to her beloved car.
ISBN 0-941483-82-7   9.95

PASSION'S LEGACY by Lori Paige. 224 pp. Sarah is swept into
the arms of Augusta Pym in this delightful historical romance.
ISBN 0-941483-81-9   8.95

THE PROVIDENCE FILE by Amanda Kyle Williams. 256 pp.
Second espionage thriller featuring lesbian agent Madison McGuire
ISBN 0-941483-92-4   8.95

I LEFT MY HEART by Jaye Maiman. 320 pp. A Robin Miller
Mystery. First in a series.   ISBN 0-941483-72-X   9.95

THE PRICE OF SALT by Patricia Highsmith (writing as Claire
Morgan). 288 pp. Classic lesbian novel, first issued in 1952 . . .
acknowledged by its author under her own, very famous, name.
ISBN 1-56280-003-5   8.95

SIDE BY SIDE by Isabel Miller. 256 pp. From beloved author of
Patience and Sarah.   ISBN 0-941483-77-0   8.95

SOUTHBOUND by Sheila Ortiz Taylor. 240 pp. Hilarious sequel
to *Faultline.*   ISBN 0-941483-78-9   8.95

STAYING POWER: LONG TERM LESBIAN COUPLES
by Susan E. Johnson. 352 pp. Joys of coupledom.
                                          ISBN 0-941-483-75-4   12.95

SLICK by Camarin Grae. 304 pp. Exotic, erotic adventure.
                                          ISBN 0-941483-74-6   9.95

NINTH LIFE by Lauren Wright Douglas. 256 pp. A Caitlin
Reece mystery. 2nd in a series.   ISBN 0-941483-50-9   8.95

PLAYERS by Robbi Sommers. 192 pp. Sizzling, erotic novel.
                                          ISBN 0-941483-73-8   8.95

MURDER AT RED ROOK RANCH by Dorothy Tell. 224 pp.
First Poppy Dillworth adventure.   ISBN 0-941483-80-0   8.95

LESBIAN SURVIVAL MANUAL by Rhonda Dicksion.
112 pp. Cartoons!   ISBN 0-941483-71-1   8.95

A ROOM FULL OF WOMEN by Elisabeth Nonas. 256 pp.
Contemporary Lesbian lives.   ISBN 0-941483-69-X   8.95

MURDER IS RELATIVE by Karen Saum. 256 pp. The first
Brigid Donovan mystery.   ISBN 0-941483-70-3   8.95

PRIORITIES by Lynda Lyons 288 pp. Science fiction with
a twist.   ISBN 0-941483-66-5   8.95

THEME FOR DIVERSE INSTRUMENTS by Jane Rule. 208
pp. Powerful romantic lesbian stories.   ISBN 0-941483-63-0   8.95

LESBIAN QUERIES by Hertz & Ertman. 112 pp. The questions
you were too embarrassed to ask.   ISBN 0-941483-67-3   8.95

CLUB 12 by Amanda Kyle Williams. 288 pp. Espionage thriller
featuring a lesbian agent!   ISBN 0-941483-64-9   8.95

DEATH DOWN UNDER by Claire McNab. 240 pp. 3rd Det.
Insp. Carol Ashton mystery.   ISBN 0-941483-39-8   8.95

MONTANA FEATHERS by Penny Hayes. 256 pp. Vivian and
Elizabeth find love in frontier Montana. ISBN 0-941483-61-4   8.95

CHESAPEAKE PROJECT by Phyllis Horn. 304 pp. Jessie &
Meredith in perilous adventure.   ISBN 0-941483-58-4   8.95

LIFESTYLES by Jackie Calhoun. 224 pp. Contemporary Lesbian
lives and loves.   ISBN 0-941483-57-6   8.95

VIRAGO by Karen Marie Christa Minns. 208 pp. Darsen has
chosen Ginny.   ISBN 0-941483-56-8   8.95

WILDERNESS TREK by Dorothy Tell. 192 pp. Six women on vacation learning "new" skills. ISBN 0-941483-60-6   8.95

MURDER BY THE BOOK by Pat Welch. 256 pp. A Helen Black Mystery. First in a series. ISBN 0-941483-59-2   8.95

BERRIGAN by Vicki P. McConnell. 176 pp. Youthful Lesbian — romantic, idealistic Berrigan. ISBN 0-941483-55-X   8.95

LESBIANS IN GERMANY by Lillian Faderman & B. Eriksson. 128 pp. Fiction, poetry, essays. ISBN 0-941483-62-2   8.95

THERE'S SOMETHING I'VE BEEN MEANING TO TELL YOU Ed. by Loralee MacPike. 288 pp. Gay men and lesbians coming out to their children. ISBN 0-941483-44-4   9.95
ISBN 0-941483-54-1   16.95

LIFTING BELLY by Gertrude Stein. Ed. by Rebecca Mark. 104 pp. Erotic poetry. ISBN 0-941483-51-7   8.95
ISBN 0-941483-53-3   14.95

ROSE PENSKI by Roz Perry. 192 pp. Adult lovers in a long-term relationship. ISBN 0-941483-37-1   8.95

AFTER THE FIRE by Jane Rule. 256 pp. Warm, human novel by this incomparable author. ISBN 0-941483-45-2   8.95

SUE SLATE, PRIVATE EYE by Lee Lynch. 176 pp. The gay folk of Peacock Alley are *all cats*. ISBN 0-941483-52-5   8.95

CHRIS by Randy Salem. 224 pp. Golden oldie. Handsome Chris and her adventures. ISBN 0-941483-42-8   8.95

THREE WOMEN by March Hastings. 232 pp. Golden oldie. A triangle among wealthy sophisticates. ISBN 0-941483-43-6   8.95

RICE AND BEANS by Valeria Taylor. 232 pp. Love and romance on poverty row. ISBN 0-941483-41-X   8.95

PLEASURES by Robbi Sommers. 204 pp. Unprecedented eroticism. ISBN 0-941483-49-5   8.95

EDGEWISE by Camarin Grae. 372 pp. Spellbinding adventure. ISBN 0-941483-19-3   9.95

FATAL REUNION by Claire McNab. 224 pp. 2nd Det. Inspec. Carol Ashton mystery. ISBN 0-941483-40-1   8.95

KEEP TO ME STRANGER by Sarah Aldridge. 372 pp. Romance set in a department store dynasty. ISBN 0-941483-38-X   9.95

HEARTSCAPE by Sue Gambill. 204 pp. American lesbian in Portugal. ISBN 0-941483-33-9   8.95

IN THE BLOOD by Lauren Wright Douglas. 252 pp. Lesbian science fiction adventure fantasy ISBN 0-941483-22-3   8.95

THE BEE'S KISS by Shirley Verel. 216 pp. Delicate, delicious
romance.   ISBN 0-941483-36-3   8.95

RAGING MOTHER MOUNTAIN by Pat Emmerson. 264 pp.
Furosa Firechild's adventures in Wonderland. ISBN 0-941483-35-5   8.95

IN EVERY PORT by Karin Kallmaker. 228 pp. Jessica's sexy,
adventuresome travels.   ISBN 0-941483-37-7   8.95

OF LOVE AND GLORY by Evelyn Kennedy. 192 pp. Exciting
WWII romance.   ISBN 0-941483-32-0   8.95

CLICKING STONES by Nancy Tyler Glenn. 288 pp. Love
transcending time.   ISBN 0-941483-31-2   9.95

SURVIVING SISTERS by Gail Pass. 252 pp. Powerful love
story.   ISBN 0-941483-16-9   8.95

SOUTH OF THE LINE by Catherine Ennis. 216 pp. Civil War
adventure.   ISBN 0-941483-29-0   8.95

WOMAN PLUS WOMAN by Dolores Klaich. 300 pp. Supurb
Lesbian overview.   ISBN 0-941483-28-2   9.95

SLOW DANCING AT MISS POLLY'S by Sheila Ortiz Taylor.
96 pp. Lesbian Poetry   ISBN 0-941483-30-4   7.95

DOUBLE DAUGHTER by Vicki P. McConnell. 216 pp. A Nyla
Wade Mystery, third in the series.   ISBN 0-941483-26-6   8.95

HEAVY GILT by Delores Klaich. 192 pp. Lesbian detective/
disappearing homophobes/upper class gay society.

                                            ISBN 0-941483-25-8   8.95

THE FINER GRAIN by Denise Ohio. 216 pp. Brilliant young
college lesbian novel.   ISBN 0-941483-11-8   8.95

THE AMAZON TRAIL by Lee Lynch. 216 pp. Life, travel & lore
of famous lesbian author.   ISBN 0-941483-27-4   8.95

HIGH CONTRAST by Jessie Lattimore. 264 pp. Women of the
Crystal Palace.   ISBN 0-941483-17-7   8.95

OCTOBER OBSESSION by Meredith More. Josie's rich, secret
Lesbian life.   ISBN 0-941483-18-5   8.95

LESBIAN CROSSROADS by Ruth Baetz. 276 pp. Contemporary
Lesbian lives.   ISBN 0-941483-21-5   9.95

BEFORE STONEWALL: THE MAKING OF A GAY AND
LESBIAN COMMUNITY by Andrea Weiss & Greta Schiller.
96 pp., 25 illus.   ISBN 0-941483-20-7   7.95

WE WALK THE BACK OF THE TIGER by Patricia A. Murphy.
192 pp. Romantic Lesbian novel/beginning women's movement.
                                            ISBN 0-941483-13-4   8.95

SUNDAY'S CHILD by Joyce Bright. 216 pp. Lesbian athletics, at last the novel about sports. ISBN 0-941483-12-6   8.95

OSTEN'S BAY by Zenobia N. Vole. 204 pp. Sizzling adventure romance set on Bonaire. ISBN 0-941483-15-0   8.95

LESSONS IN MURDER by Claire McNab. 216 pp. 1st Det. Inspec. Carol Ashton mystery — erotic tension!. ISBN 0-941483-14-2   8.95

YELLOWTHROAT by Penny Hayes. 240 pp. Margarita, bandit, kidnaps Julia. ISBN 0-941483-10-X   8.95

SAPPHISTRY: THE BOOK OF LESBIAN SEXUALITY by Pat Califia. 3d edition, revised. 208 pp. ISBN 0-941483-24-X   8.95

CHERISHED LOVE by Evelyn Kennedy. 192 pp. Erotic Lesbian love story. ISBN 0-941483-08-8   8.95

LAST SEPTEMBER by Helen R. Hull. 208 pp. Six stories & a glorious novella. ISBN 0-941483-09-6   8.95

THE SECRET IN THE BIRD by Camarin Grae. 312 pp. Striking, psychological suspense novel. ISBN 0-941483-05-3   8.95

TO THE LIGHTNING by Catherine Ennis. 208 pp. Romantic Lesbian 'Robinson Crusoe' adventure. ISBN 0-941483-06-1   8.95

THE OTHER SIDE OF VENUS by Shirley Verel. 224 pp. Luminous, romantic love story. ISBN 0-941483-07-X   8.95

DREAMS AND SWORDS by Katherine V. Forrest. 192 pp. Romantic, erotic, imaginative stories. ISBN 0-941483-03-7   8.95

MEMORY BOARD by Jane Rule. 336 pp. Memorable novel about an aging Lesbian couple. ISBN 0-941483-02-9   9.95

THE ALWAYS ANONYMOUS BEAST by Lauren Wright Douglas. 224 pp. A Caitlin Reece mystery. First in a series. ISBN 0-941483-04-5   8.95

SEARCHING FOR SPRING by Patricia A. Murphy. 224 pp. Novel about the recovery of love. ISBN 0-941483-00-2   8.95

DUSTY'S QUEEN OF HEARTS DINER by Lee Lynch. 240 pp. Romantic blue-collar novel. ISBN 0-941483-01-0   8.95

PARENTS MATTER by Ann Muller. 240 pp. Parents' relationships with Lesbian daughters and gay sons. ISBN 0-930044-91-6   9.95

THE PEARLS by Shelley Smith. 176 pp. Passion and fun in the Caribbean sun. ISBN 0-930044-93-2   7.95

MAGDALENA by Sarah Aldridge. 352 pp. Epic Lesbian novel set on three continents. ISBN 0-930044-99-1   8.95

THE BLACK AND WHITE OF IT by Ann Allen Shockley. 144 pp. Short stories. ISBN 0-930044-96-7   7.95

SAY JESUS AND COME TO ME by Ann Allen Shockley. 288
pp. Contemporary romance.   ISBN 0-930044-98-3   8.95

LOVING HER by Ann Allen Shockley. 192 pp. Romantic love
story.   ISBN 0-930044-97-5   7.95

MURDER AT THE NIGHTWOOD BAR by Katherine V.
Forrest. 240 pp. A Kate Delafield mystery. Second in a series.
                                              ISBN 0-930044-92-4   8.95

ZOE'S BOOK by Gail Pass. 224 pp. Passionate, obsessive love
story.   ISBN 0-930044-95-9   7.95

WINGED DANCER by Camarin Grae. 228 pp. Erotic Lesbian
adventure story.   ISBN 0-930044-88-6   8.95

PAZ by Camarin Grae. 336 pp. Romantic Lesbian adventurer
with the power to change the world.   ISBN 0-930044-89-4   8.95

SOUL SNATCHER by Camarin Grae. 224 pp. A puzzle, an
adventure, a mystery — Lesbian romance.   ISBN 0-930044-90-8   8.95

THE LOVE OF GOOD WOMEN by Isabel Miller. 224 pp.
Long-awaited new novel by the author of the beloved *Patience
and Sarah*.   ISBN 0-930044-81-9   8.95

THE HOUSE AT PELHAM FALLS by Brenda Weathers. 240
pp. Suspenseful Lesbian ghost story.   ISBN 0-930044-79-7   7.95

HOME IN YOUR HANDS by Lee Lynch. 240 pp. More stories
from the author of *Old Dyke Tales*.   ISBN 0-930044-80-0   7.95

EACH HAND A MAP by Anita Skeen. 112 pp. Real-life poems
that touch us all.   ISBN 0-930044-82-7   6.95

SURPLUS by Sylvia Stevenson. 342 pp. A classic early Lesbian
novel.   ISBN 0-930044-78-9   7.95

PEMBROKE PARK by Michelle Martin. 256 pp. Derring-do
and daring romance in Regency England.   ISBN 0-930044-77-0   7.95

THE LONG TRAIL by Penny Hayes. 248 pp. Vivid adventures
of two women in love in the old west.   ISBN 0-930044-76-2   8.95

HORIZON OF THE HEART by Shelley Smith. 192 pp. Hot
romance in summertime New England.   ISBN 0-930044-75-4   7.95

AN EMERGENCE OF GREEN by Katherine V. Forrest. 288
pp. Powerful novel of sexual discovery.   ISBN 0-930044-69-X   9.95

These are just a few of the many Naiad Press titles — we are the oldest and
largest lesbian/feminist publishing company in the world. Please request a
complete catalog. We offer personal service; we encourage and welcome direct
mail orders from individuals who have limited access to bookstores carrying
our publications.